SUN GATE

Bohemian Grove Trilogy

BY

T.M. WILLIAMS

For: My husband

The whispers spiraled. "We will lose her," they said.

"We already did," he informed them.

"You must love her," they responded.

"I always have," he thought.

"We must take you," they decided.

"I'm ready," he relented.

PROLOGUE

𒁹 𒀭 𒂍𒀭 𒂍𒁹 ‑𒈨 𒀸 𒅇 𒂖 ‑𒈨 𒂍𒁹 ‑𒉺 𒂍𒁹

CARTER STARED AT THE DARK crimson *blood that now covered her palms. The reality was gone. Kneeling on the floor, she stared at his body, which lay motionless and cold—gazing in disbelief as his vacant eyes stared forever into the distance, at nothing, forever.*

"You killed him," John whispered.

She jumped at the sound of his voice. When she turned to him, the skin on his face grayed and scales formed at his hairline. She pushed back from him in fear. What was happening?

"You killed Jack," he said again. "You're killing all of us," he said louder, his brows coming together in clear anguish.

"I don't understand," she whispered to herself—and she didn't.

"That's the problem, you stupid child; you will never understand," Jibril hissed at her as she screamed, seeing the reptilian slits in place of his pupils. Where had he come from? This nightmare was forever. Yet it was as real as it was unreal.

Carter bolted upright, dripping in sweat as the nightmare's lingering effects paralyzed her. "Jack," she whispered out loud.

She had switched on the lamp on her nightstand and peered into the light when an object at the corner of her eye caught her attention. She looked down to see the lava bracelet that her best friend had given her had finally fallen off. Carter twisted the beads between her fingers, remembering when Julie had given her the bracelet, in another lifetime.

"Julie," she whispered to herself.

She twisted the beads between her fingers mindlessly, thinking of her best friend. The beads felt unusually warm beneath her fingertips and sent an ominous chill up her spine.

CHAPTER 1

ᛄᛣ ᚳᛣ ᛄᛡ ᛬ᚲᛥ ᛬ᛅ ᛣᚳ ᚳᛡᛤ ᛄᛡ ᚳ ᛬ᛅ ᚳᛡ

H ER MIND CONTINUED TO LINGER on the memories of her night-mare as John urged her to keep reading.

"In the beginning God created the heaven and the earth," Carter read the passage again, this time focusing on what she was doing.

"Change 'God' to 'the Gods.'" John crossed his arms in front of him and leaned against her dresser, watching her carefully, concerned by her lack of concentration.

"In the beginning the *Gods*," she said, stressing the last word dramatically, "created the heaven and the earth." She paused, tilting her head as she thought. *The Gods created the heaven and the earth*—the words echoed in her mind.

Still, she seemed distracted. "Are you okay?" he asked.

Carter bobbed her head. "I'm fine, just didn't sleep well."

John frowned. "I'll give you time with that," he said, and left her alone to read.

1

She realized an uneasy feeling creeping in the pit of her stomach as she read the passage again, although the Bible sitting on her lap seemed benign. She smoothed her palms against her pant leg, blowing out a breath as she tried to steady her rapidly beating heart. Was she having an anxiety attack?

Holding the book to her chest, she walked over to the one small window in her room and stared out at the endless rooftops that stretched for miles, barely seeing the mountaintops in the distance as she squinted through the haze. Her Anunnaki blood made her vision exceptional, yet not exceptional enough. She had learned a lot about her ancestry in the few months they had been in Peru and even more about her astounding gifts, which had only begun to develop. Things she didn't realize had always been there: exceptional eyesight and hearing, keen sense of smell. How would she have known? It wasn't as if she had anything to compare it to.

The weather had been in the comfortable sixties since their arrival, and now that the end of December was approaching, the weather began to warm. Stan, one of the men in her protection detail, and now her friend, explained to her what to expect when they landed. A reverse in weather due to the equator was just one of many things she had to look forward too.

Her protection detail consisted of her father, John, and his subordinates: Stan, Paulo, Anthony, and Rafe. Jack and William were also a part of their odd group. They were on the search for Jibril, and their last lead had brought them to Peru. Part of the reason they were searching for Jibril was that he was head of the Vaticates, which also meant he was in charge of the raids that had been taking the lives of Anunnakis around the world, as well as the most recent raid on Bohemian Grove, which took the life of her longtime friend Carl. Carter's heart still ached every time she thought of him, and she was still ridden with guilt.

The other aspect was that the Vaticates were dead set on putting an end to Carter's mission to communicate with the Anunnaki, meaning that Carter was their primary target. She still didn't know whether she wanted to communicate with the Anunnaki and figure out exactly what was going on. She still struggled to accept the fact that she was alien. After all, she looked like everyone else. It wasn't until recently when working with William did she discover that she had more than just human tendencies. It was more than her exceptional five senses. It was that she had very strong sixth and seventh senses—as did all Anunnaki, though they mostly adapted to using their human senses to better blend in. It was something she had no challenge doing, as she was still feeling quite human.

They had been in Peru for months and had gotten nowhere. They had even ventured into the jungle, something Carter still hadn't forgiven the team for. Sure, they had warned her it would be humid, but she had no idea *how* humid. The jungle reminded her of the steam room at her gym, something she had tried only one time. How was it humanly possible that any place on earth could be so relentlessly uncomfortable and unforgiving?

Just the memories and flashbacks of that day were enough to make Carter feel sick again. Besides the humidity—no, not the humidity, the wretched steam room of a jungle—was the abundance of exotic and strange-looking bugs and spiders of all shapes, sizes, and colors. For days after the trek, Carter kept imagining giant bugs infesting her room, waking up in the middle of the night nearly scratching herself to death.

She got used to sleeping with the light on, but that did little to comfort her, especially when she woke up in the middle of the night with a red, seemingly harmless spider sitting on the pillow next to her. There was a beat, Carter remembered, when she made eye contact with the spider. Despite John's protesting and waving her off as if she were crazy, she knew what she saw: thousands of spider-eye reflections staring back at her on top of a mound of red spider fur. Of course, she did exactly what she should not have done: she tried to sweep it away with her right hand while frantically screaming and jumping around like a rabid dog.

The spider bit her.

Her screams drew everyone. Jack and William both came running into the room at the same time, crashing into each other like two wolves going in for the last game. If it weren't for her complete terror, she might have found the situation comical. William ended up killing the spider, which apparently never left the pillow. She found out before the trip to the jungle in Peru that *all* spiders in Peru were poisonous. *Great.* So of course, this prompted swift action from Jack and William, who for the first time in months paid any real attention to her. It didn't help that no one knew what kind of spider it was, and it especially did not help when the bite on her hand grew a tail the next day—yes, a *tail.*

Every time she looked down at her hand, she wanted to throw up. The red bull's-eye mark on her hand had a whitish, semiopaque, semi-hard, taillike growth coming out of it, and Jack made jokes about giving birth to a real alien. His jokes stopped when John threatened to find a spider from the alley and plant it in his room to see how he felt about it. No one could figure out whether John was serious or not, and no one questioned him.

After numerous doctor visits and antibiotics, the bite finally began to heal. Carter looked down at the seahorse-shaped scar left on her hand and absent-mindedly rubbed it. She hated the scar because it reminded her of that night, reminder her of Carl, of Bohemian Grove, of everything spiraling out of control. Just one more thing added to the list of things that were wrong in her life.

✧   ✧   ✧

SHE FROWNED AT HER REFLECTION in the window. She gave up trying to see the mountain that gave her some reprieve and decided she hated South America. Now looking at the Bible on her bed, she decided she really hated Jibril.

She sat on the bed and picked up the Bible, reading through it and changing "God" to "the Gods" again.

So the Gods created man in their own image, in the image of the Gods created they them; male and female created they them.

She ran her fingers over the words. *Male and female created they them.*

"Sounds like Yoda," Carter whispered to herself in frustration.

Carter flipped through to the next page and scanned over the words that caught her attention about the slaying of Abel.

And Adam knew Eve his wife, and she conceived, and bare Cain, and said I have gotten a man from the LORD—Behold, thou hast driven me out this day from the face of the earth; and from the face shall I be hid; and I shall be a fugitive and a vagabond in the earth; and it shall come to pass, that every one that findeth me shall slay me.

Carter stared down at the book so lost in her own thoughts that she didn't even notice William walk into the room.

"A lot of good info in there," William said, gesturing at the Bible in her hands.

She shrugged, unwilling to admit her real feelings to him. To say the last few months with William and Jack had been awkward was an understatement.

"Did your dad give that to you?"

☆ ☆ ☆

CARTER SQUIRMED AT THE QUESTION. The idea of John being her dad still remained foreign to her. She was having a hard time wrapping her mind around it, more so than any other aspect of her life that she had recently discovered.

Jack had become a hermit since they landed in Peru, and Carter often wondered why he did not just return home to the States. It was clear that he was miserable. She had made endless attempts to talk to him, but he was always too busy. William hadn't been exactly welcoming to her either. He figured out quickly what had happened between her and Jack while he was "dead," and though she tried explaining everything, he still gave her a deaf ear. She was getting the silent treatment from both ends, and she had grown tired of it. She looked up at William again, suddenly remembering his presence in the room.

"Did you need something?" she asked coldly, not in the mood to be polite. It was clear that her demeanor threw him off as he ran his fingers through his shaggy hair. She wasn't use to seeing him without his composure, and it almost made her feel sorry for him. She resented both him and Jack.

"Carter, I thought we could talk," he said, finally making eye contact with her. His gaze lingered long enough to warm her. She forgot what feelings he stirred in her, and it sent her head whirling. She was glad that she was sitting on the bed and angry at herself for letting her feelings get in the way of her logic. William took her lack of response as an invitation and sat next to her on the bed. He took in a deep breath and exhaled shakily. He really was nervous, and this made Carter more curious than before. She traced invisible patterns on her pant leg to distract her from William's sudden proximity.

"William, what is it?" Her voice had changed, and he recognized it as well. He turned to face her and was about to reach out for her hand without thinking but then quickly retracted it. When had things gotten so awkward between them?

"I guess I just didn't expect you to recover from my *death* so quickly." He paused, the word floating in the air, leaving behind a bad taste. "But I've been unfair. We had never made any commitment to each other, and well, we have never been on a date. Or, well, we were about to be when I got shot." He frowned as he spoke, stumbling over his own words.

Carter sighed inwardly and wanted to reach out to hold his hand and comfort him, but she also wanted to hear what he had to say, what she secretly hoped he would say. She had wished since they arrived in Peru that he would reach out to her again. He had become like a drug to her, and having him so close without being able to reach out had become torturous.

"Which is why I want to talk to you," he continued, interrupting her thoughts. "That day—that was reckless. I got cocky and let my feelings for you blind my common sense. It's not going to happen again." She blinked at him, unsure of what he was saying. "Carter, you belong with Jack," he said, looking down at the floor.

"What day?" she asked.

"When…when I took you to Santa Barbara. I should never have done that."

"So you regret that?" She hated how mousey her voice sounded.

He pressed his lips together and clenched his jaw.

"Say it to my face, Will." She felt her face flush, her heart ache. She didn't think she was capable of feeling anger and hurt at the same time. "Say it to my *face*, Will." She knew he didn't mean it and that he wanted to be with her. It wasn't until he took away that possibility that she knew how she really felt for him.

He looked into her eyes, the intensity of his gaze catching her off guard. He searched, and for a fleeting moment, she saw the old William—the William who left her breathless and him without restraint. She knew she saw it. Her heart ached in his presence, but it ached more without him.

"Carter, I don't want to be with you," he simply said, without a hint of emotion on his face. "It was fun, there was chemistry, but you're..." his breath caught. "We'll get each other killed. I know what happened in that cabin that Jibril had you in. Jack got you out. When we were together, I almost got you killed in the process." Carter just stared at William, blinking at him, not knowing how to respond. She searched his eyes for some truth, but they were just empty reflections.

"Well then, thanks for the update," she said, desperately trying to contain the crack in her voice and hide the emotion. Anger boiled to the surface, and she felt her face flush red hot under his stare. She saw the pity in his eyes, and she wanted none of it. How dare he. How dare he leave her vulnerable like this. She watched his back as he walked out of the room, shutting the door behind him. As she stood there for what seemed like eternity, the sudden realization came to her: she had fallen in love with William. She knew her feelings were real because as she stared at the closed door, she felt nothing but a void inside of her. No tears came, no ache in her heart, just an empty feeling that could be fixed only by him.

✫　　✫　　✫

AN ABRUPT KNOCK ON THE door startled her out of her reverie.

When she opened the door, she was surprised to see Jack. The dark shadow that fell across his face and the sorrow that hung there were almost too much for her to bear.

"What?" Her tone came out sharper then she intended, and she instantly regretted it when she saw the pain it caused him. Before she could apologize, though, he reclaimed his normal, everything-is- okay self.

"We have a lead."

"Again?" She worked hard to soften her tone this time, but it was a struggle. She could tell by his expression that he was exasperated by the dead-end leads as well.

He nodded at her slowly. "This is my last expedition with you. I'm heading back to the States on Thursday."

This hurt her more than she expected. She had known it was coming and so had prepared for this, but she was still put off by his announcement. She couldn't possibly love both Jack and William, could she? Yet neither of them wanted anything to do with her now. She didn't blame them. In fact, hadn't she made a promise to herself to not let anyone get close to her, for destruction and pain followed her? This reminder to herself set her back on her feet.

"Of course, Jack. You've been more than generous with what you've already done. I'm sure your family misses you." Her voice was so lacking in emotion that it caught her by surprise. She didn't even recognize herself anymore. Yet her heart ached in an all-too-familiar way.

"We're meeting downstairs in five minutes. It's just somewhere here in town; you shouldn't need to change or anything." Carter just nodded at him. He turned to go.

"Jack, wait."

He turned around and looked at her; the haunted look that she had always known him to have had returned. She had done that.

"Yeah?" No, she had done more to him. He wasn't only haunted anymore, but he had aged. Lines had formed around his eyes, and his cheeks had become hollow.

"Nothing, sorry. Thank you again for everything."

He forced a thin-lipped smile at her before he turned and walked down the hall. She watched him go. Then she turned around and with a sigh grabbed the Bible off the bed and stuck it in her satchel that she had started bringing along on their expeditions. She had started keeping notes of random things they would find, thinking it might be of use some day. In truth, it just made her feel as if she were doing something productive.

She stopped in the doorway before heading out. A sudden feeling of dread had overcome her and almost knocked the wind out of her. The panic she had felt earlier was returning with a vengeance. She had never had a feeling like that before. She was realizing how much William walking away from her was affecting her. So this was what love felt like? Yet she didn't think that was really it. It was almost a foreboding feeling.

When she reached the bottom of the stairs, she saw John waiting for her. She smiled at him, realizing that he was still there for her and grateful for that. Soon, Jack and William would both be gone, and she would have to carry on. Her personal life would have to wait; there were bigger things to be done anyway.

"Jack and Sergio went ahead of us. They're going to check out the area, and we'll go in and see what's going on." Sergio was their Peruvian guide whom Jack had become close too since their arrival. Their friendship was a surprising one. Sergio was a happy-go-lucky sort of guy. Carter never understood how they connected so much, considering that Jack seemed to spend so much of his time brooding. She could see why Jack liked Sergio, though. It was hard not to, and she liked that Jack took to him. It was the only time she ever saw him laugh anymore. They would spend hours playing cards, ignoring the world around them like long-lost brothers.

"Where's Will?" she asked reluctantly, hoping not to give anything away.

"He's at the embassy getting his final paperwork completed."

Carter couldn't tell whether John knew what had happened or not; he rarely gave anything away. She liked this quality in him, even though it was mostly inconvenient for her.

On cue, William walked back in through the front door. He looked up at Carter, and she saw regret flash in his eyes.

CHAPTER 2

𒐂𒐊 𒐊 𒐊𒐊𒐂𒐊 𒐊𒐊 ⊢𒐁𒐁 𒐀𒐀 𒐊𒐂 𒐂𒐊 𒐁𒐁⊢ 𒐊𒐊 𒐊 ⊢𒐊𒐂 𒐁𒐊𒐊

›

CARTER NEVER ASKED WHERE THEY were going. She didn't expect this expedition to be any different from any other. The building they arrived at looked ordinary—too . Jibril's team had already been hiding out, and John's team didn't realize how close to the threat they were. Too close.

So everything changed in that moment—drastically. It was different from Bohemian Grove, somehow more surreal. Maybe it was because it was completely unexpected, catching all of them off guard. Most likely it was because she didn't think she would lose someone she had only recently gained in her life, someone she thought was invincible.

John drove, Jack sat in the front seat, and Carter sat in the back, mindlessly watching the buildings pass behind the window. William was in the car following them with Stan and Sergio. Paulo, Anthony, and Rafe were already staking out the building, having arrived before them. Carter was already bored. That was how she remembered the last moments before his death: boredom.

Each and every lead they had gotten since their arrival in Peru had been a dead end. She knew Jibril was playing games with them, always one step ahead. They all knew. Yet there was nothing they could do except continue to try to find Jibril and his crew. The soft hum of the engine was so hypnotic that Carter didn't even realize they had come to a stop. It was so hypnotic that she didn't even recognize the popping sound in the distance.

Although John and Jack hesitated only for a split second, it still felt like slow motion. John turned to Carter, yelling at her to duck as he drew his gun. She understood him and felt as if she had moved as soon as he yelled at her. Yet for some reason she couldn't move fast enough. In reality, everything probably happened in less than five seconds, but those five seconds might as well have been five years for all the good their speed did.

Carter heard the next pop and the shattering of glass almost at the same time. Did that mean they were close to whoever was shooting at them? She felt completely exposed, especially since she still had no idea what was happening. She vaguely realized that John and Jack were both yelling. At least she thought she heard them both. Because later, looking back, it might have just been her mind playing tricks on her—a coping mechanism of some sort, her mind lying to her, telling her that both John and Jack were both still alive.

The back door opened, and Carter screamed. She felt herself being dragged out but could not grip anything as her hands desperately slid over the leather seats. She kicked whoever was grasping at her until she heard William's voice.

"Carter, it's me—let's move!"

She turned to see William behind her, ducking down behind the open door. He was not watching her; he was peering over the window of the car door. She backed out of the seat when she noticed blood smeared over the tan leather. Was that hers? Glass shattered, exploding over her in a million fragments. She heard cursing and realized it was her own voice.

William looked tragically pale, his face etched in fear. He peered through the gap in the seats toward the front.

The blood.

The blood on the back seat was not hers. The blood on the back seat was from the front seat. The reality hit her. She felt her heart lodge in her throat as she fought back a scream and lunged out of the back seat.

"William?" Her voice was barely audible, a question. Did he know who was hurt? He continued to stare at the front while the popping of gunshots continued.

Stan suddenly appeared crouching next to William. She had never imagined she would see Stan look so stunned as he did at that moment. He was just as pale as William, his eyes wide, his hands shaking.

Seconds. Only seconds had passed.

"I've got you guys covered. Move behind that building and take this."

Stan handed William a gun as William locked his hand around Carter's. He pulled her with him the six feet to the brick building and dodged out of sight and into safety.

"Are you OK?" he asked.

Carter spun around to see Jack. He was breathing heavily and watching her in wide-eyed fear. The shock on his face was clear, and she wondered if that was what she looked like as well. Jack stood there, covered in John's blood.

CHAPTER 3

ꗸꗸꗸꗸꗸꗸꗸꗸꗸꗸꗸꗸꗸꗸꗸꗸꗸ

S HE STOOD FROZEN, STARING AT Jack, who stared back in stunned silence. The popping of gunshots finally stopped. Carter felt as if her body were moving a second ahead of her mind and her mind were constantly racing to catch up, not quite understanding and grasping what was happening. Now, now that time had caught up, she was afraid to ask the questions. It was safer to stand in silence—ignorant to reality.

Jack ran his hands through his hair in frustration as William began kicking the brick wall angrily. She felt as if she should stop him but couldn't bring herself to react.

She turned back finally to look at their car. Rafe and Paulo stood at the driver's side; the grim looks on their faces nauseated Carter. The sound of sirens in the distance seemed as if it were coming through water. Carter, Jack, and William stood as a trio by the brick wall, watching in a daze as their friends tended to John's body still in the front seat, frozen in time.

"He never even knew what hit him, never even saw it coming," Jack whispered.

William crouched down, his head falling between his shoulders in a slump and his arms over his knees—as if he had fallen from grace. Carter slid to the floor numbly and sat with her legs folded underneath her. She watched with blurry eyes as a dozen emergency service vehicles surrounded them in a whir of activity. Police officers spoke to them in broken English, but Carter could not hear their words.

Carter sat between William and Jack. Her mind failed to process anything that was happening. The floor beneath her swayed. She felt entirely different than she had when Carl died or when she thought she lost William. When they lifted John's body out of the car and onto the gurney, Carter watched. She felt she owed it to him. She watched William walk over to the car and stand behind the medical examiner. They wouldn't let him by. Carter sighed.

John's body was covered in a sheet, but she saw the tips of his fingers under the edge of the white sheet. It made her realize how she had been robbed of him from her life. Not just then, but as a little girl. She had never gotten to hold those fingers, her father's fingers. Never felt his comfort growing up. Yet somehow, his presence in the last months had changed everything for her. He had become more of a father to her than she could have ever hoped for.

Jack reached out and rubbed Carter's back gently. It was a small gesture, but considering how little Jack had spoken to her since they arrived in Peru, it was comforting.

William returned, his eyes glazed in sorrow.Carter watched Stan as he nodded at whatever the police were saying to him. He approached them slowly with his head down and his body stiff, as if he literally carried the world on his shoulders.

"They're going to take us in for questioning." Stan crouched down and spoke softly to the three of them. "It's standard. The questioning won't go any further, and it's just for official reasons."

"What should we say?" Jack asked.

"The truth," Stan replied. He had aged years in just a matter of an hour. Standing up, he brushed himself off and went to speak to one of the police officers who stood nearby.

"So I take it the police here will just cover our tracks?" Jack asked, a strain audible in his voice.

Carter ran her hands through her tangled hair. When she looked down, she saw blood caked into the creases of her palm. Wiping her hands against her jeans, she stood up and turned to Jack.

"I don't know, Jack. I assume so." Tears welled up in her eyes, and she turned around and walked up to the police officer. Carter gave their bloody car, now being towed, a wide berth. She was standing in front of Stan and the police officer when Rafe approached them.

"I'm ready whenever you are." She did not trust herself to speak louder than a whisper.

"I'll ride with her," Rafe said. He smiled gently at Carter.

Rafe slid into the backseat with Carter without saying another word. Carter watched ahead through the glass partition and wondered when the moment would come that she would break. The emotions she could not feel frustrated her. Rafe leaned forward and ran his fingers through his shaggy hair. She had lost her father, friend, and protector today, and Rafe had lost his friend and boss.

"We should have protected him, Carter. I'm sorry." Rafe turned to look at Carter, and his eyes were swollen and bloodshot. He was in command right after Stan. While Stan's detail was to specifically protect Carter, Rafe's was to oversee all general security and help Stan. He would take this as a failure on his part more than anyone else. Her heart ached for him.

"Rafe, no one is blaming you. I'm not blaming you." She reached out and took his hand in hers, squeezing it. "I don't think anyone expected th—"

"It was my *job* to expect it."

She didn't know what to say. She still couldn't process anything, and her mind swirled with random, discombobulated thoughts.

"I'm sorry, Carter. I'm sorry." His voice cracked. She watched the muscles in his jaw clench as he struggled to maintain composure.

"I don't blame you, Rafe, and I know my father wouldn't have."

He nodded solemnly. She held his hand the entire car ride to the police station.

CHAPTER 4

𒈾 𒁹 𒐊 𒈾 𒁕𒈫 𒀸 𒑊 𒐊 𒁹 𒁕𒈫 𒐊

T HE QUESTIONING WAS BRIEF, JUST as Stan had promised. Most of her answers were that she didn't know or hadn't seen. It was the truth, but sometimes it didn't sound like it. She needed to pay attention to her surroundings more, she realized.

When she stepped into the lobby of the police station, William and Jack were both sitting there as far away from each other as they could possibly be in the tiny space. She ignored them and walked out of the police station. The sun kissed the tops of the mountains, turning the sky a burnt orange. Carter felt tightness in her chest and began to panic. She took a deep breath, or at least tried. Suddenly the air was taken from her, and she felt as if she were drowning.

"Carter? Carter? You okay?"

Carter vaguely heard Rafe's voice behind her, and he clutched her shoulders, holding her upright.

"Carter? We should get you to a hospital. Can you breathe?"

She managed a nod.

"I…" what was happening to her? "I just saw the sunset and just thought of John, my dad, and he didn't get this sunset. I just started to panic—"

Carter gasped for air in between sobs.

"What's wrong with her? Carter?" William asked from behind her.

This was too much. She needed an escape. Rafe must have sensed this or just knew. Maybe he needed an escape too.

"She's okay I'll take her home," Rafe said.

"Maybe I should take her home," William said.

Carter cringed. She didn't want to be around William or Jack.

"No, I'll take her." The finality in Rafe's voice startled her. The authority he carried reminded her of John.

Rafe wrapped his arm around Carter's shoulders and supported his weight as they walked away from the station.

"It's okay, let them go. She'll be okay with Rafe," Stan said.

Great, she had an audience.

"It's eighteen blocks back. Do you want to walk? We can catch a cab," Rafe said.

"No, let's walk."

About halfway home, they stopped and sat in the grass of a park. Carter's gasping sobs had subsided, and the numbness had returned. She pulled at the blades of grass mindlessly, and the tears flowed freely now. She kept wiping at her face.

"We killed three of Jibril's men?" Carter asked.

Rafe nodded. "Yes."

"I don't understand," Carter whispered. "They're really just trying to wipe out the Anunnaki? There's no other reason? What have we done to them?"

"The Vaticates are a lot more than just faith. It's power, money. A lot of people at the top don't want to lose that, Carter. Today, it was a lot more than just us losing John. He was an integral part of keeping the Anunnaki safe and protecting them. He was also a key part in helping you uncover the key to talking with the Anunnaki, and now that's gone. You'll never know how sorry I am for that. I failed."

It was the most she had ever heard Rafe say. Something tickled Carter's mind, a thought she couldn't quite catch hold of. "You would think that if the Anunnaki wanted us to contact them, they would make it easier for us to do so."

Rafe nodded. "It's been over three thousand years since they have been here. We believe they can't interfere with us until we figure it out. Leaving clues in our DNA was the only way they could."

"Why can't they interfere?"

"We believe it's because of an order kept by other species not to interfere with beings on planets until they are ready," Rafe said.

"Why does that sound familiar?" Carter asked, but before Rafe could answer, they heard rustling in the leaves of a bush just six feet from them. Carter looked around nervously, noticing how dark it had become.

Rafe went to draw his gun but cursed instead. "They took my gun at the station."

They both slowly stood.

"Carter," whispered the air.

Carter, startled, turned to Rafe, but he just kept staring ahead at the bush. "Did you hear that?" she asked.

"There's something in the bush," he said.

That didn't answer her question. "Did you hear someone whisper my name?"

"Carter," came the whisper again.

"That—did you hear that?" Carter pleaded with her eyes.

"No, I didn't hear—"

An ear-splitting shriek like nothing Carter had ever heard before came from the bush. It sounded like part bird and part human, and most of all, it sounded pissed.

"I heard that!" Rafe grabbed Carter's arm and yanked her, running full speed out of the park. She managed to look over her shoulder out of morbid curiosity. Standing in the bush was the same man she had seen back at the anthropological center in Bohemian Grove—still tall, still covered in graying scales, and still with the same empty, hollow eyes. Except this time, he was looking straight at her.

"Carter," whispered the air again, *"run."*

His mouth never moved, and she knew the whispers weren't coming from him. They were there because of him, but to protect her. She didn't know how she knew that, but she did. Carter stumbled over her own footing, and Rafe caught her. When she looked back, the reptilian man had vanished. A shiver ran up her spine as she realized that she may not be able to see him, but he was still there. He was always there.

They ran the entire way back, and Carter never stopped feeling as if they were being followed. They burst through the front doors to a startled Jack, Paulo, and Stan. She noticed both Paulo and Stan reaching for their guns, and as they saw Carter and Rafe, their hands stopped abruptly, hovering over their hips.

Stan stood quickly. "What happened?" He looked out the kitchen window, assuming the threat was directly behind them.

Carter looked to Rafe. What *did* happen? He returned the same confused look.

"What? What's going on?" Jack was now standing.

"Where's William?" Carter asked.

Paulo answered. "Upstairs in his room. He—"

Carter bolted out of the kitchen and up the stairs, taking the steps two at a time. She felt all four men on her heels as she threw the door open to William's room.

"William, I—"

She tripped over herself as she saw William sitting on his bed next to a beautiful woman with caramel-colored skin and ebony eyes and hair. They held hands and were leaning into each other. She looked as if she had been crying.

"Carter, I uh...Carter, this is Amara. Amara, this is Car—" he stopped, noticing the audience behind Carter. "Something happened."

What?"

Carter couldn't speak. Seeing William on his bed with another woman stole the words from her. She fell against the frame of the door, bracing herself. She couldn't handle any more that day.

"I, um—sorry, I didn't mean to..." Carter stumbled over her words as she willed herself to find her footing again—anything to leave the room.

"Carter?" Rafe looked at her curiously, and seeing him snapped her back into the moment. She suddenly realized why she needed to speak to William.

"William," said, avoiding looking at the dark beauty on the bed. "Who was that man we saw at the anthropological center in Bohemian Grove?"

William paled. "I don't know what you're talking about," he answered too quickly, shifting in his seat.

She didn't need to feel his energy to know he was lying. She narrowed her eyes at him as she felt blood rush to her face. Suddenly, the anguish of losing John, of fearing for her life, of being in South America, of going on a wild goose chase for Jibril, and just seeing some alien being brought everything crashing down on her. Her breathing became heavy, and her hands clenched and unclenched. She had acquiesced to her role from the beginning, and the results were unfair. It seemed the more she complied, the worse off they were.

Carter struggled to gain exposure; anger boiled inside her, and she didn't recognize her own emotions. She had been kidnapped from her home, thrown into a new life with no time to adjust, lost people she loved, put her friends and family in danger, and flown around the world only to be bitten by a furry red spider that still gave her nightmares. And now—now she was being lied to by someone who had supposedly once cared about her, which was apparently a lie as well. It was her fault for not having delineated boundaries, but she was tired of the games.

She was just as surprised as everyone else when she walked up to William and slapped him across the face. Her hand stung. She didn't think she had it in her to do anything like that, and William sat stunned.

"Don't—you dare—lie—to—me," she hissed through clenched teeth. She still struggled to get her anger under control. Who had she become? She didn't know anymore.

Everyone stood motionless until Carter stepped back out of the room slowly.

"Carter, what did you see?" Stan asked, the concern on his face clear. Yet he was ignoring the elephant in the room.

"I saw a man, a very *tall* man, covered in scales. He wasn't human. Who was he? And why is he here? And no more lies!" Her words came out in a near growl. Yet Stan remained indifferent and aloof, watching her carefully as if she were a specimen.

Stan grimaced. "Let's go downstairs and sit down. I'll explain it all to you there."

CHAPTER 5

𒌋𒁹 𒀝 𒌋𒀝 𒌋𒁹 𒊩𒈪 𒃻 𒅗 𒀀𒍅 𒐏𒈨 𒌋𒁹 𒀝 𒊬𒅗 𒀝𒁹

H E HELD A CHAIR OUT for her at the kitchen table. But she didn't sit, so he took the seat instead. Jack and Paulo joined him at the table, and Rafe took watch outside. This time he had a gun. Carter leaned against the kitchen counter with her arms crossed in front of her.

"What you saw was an Anunnaki," Stan said with a matter-of-fact tone.

"Come again?"

Stan rubbed at his eyes; it had been a long day. "We don't know much about them, but we know they're Anunnaki. We know that when we were altered by DNA when the Anunnaki first came here, we weren't the only ones altered. Not all of the alterations were a success, and what you saw tonight was one of them. We're of the same descent. They are human mixed with reptilian blood. That's why they have scales."

Carter just stared at Stan. "Is this some sort of joke?"

"And they're hostile," Paulo said.

"No shit," Carter said. "They tried to kill us at the anthropological center."

"They work for the Vaticates," Paulo said, and Stan gave him a dirty look.

"Next you're going to tell us they have magical powers," Jack said, clearly as irritated as Carter felt.

"They do," Paulo said.

"Paulo, do you mind?" Stan growled the words at him, and Paulo shrugged.

"What? They asked."

Stan shook his head. "This is a lot to take in, especially after today. Are you sure you want to talk about this now? Maybe tomo—"

"No, now," Jack said, and Carter nodded in agreement. Except now she chose to sit down before her legs gave out on her. Carter thought she saw what seemed like empathy in Paulo's eyes.

"Why do they work for the Vaticates? I thought the Vaticates wanted to wipe out all the Anunnaki?" Carter asked.

"Because these Anunnaki, the reptilians, are not exactly welcomed by the Anunnaki that created us."

"I don't understand," Jack said.

"That makes two of us," Carter said.

"We don't really know ourselves. We just know that they aren't supposed to still be here."

Carter shivered. She turned to Jack, realization dawning on her. "That first night at my house in Santa Barbara? The knocking on my door? That must have been them."

"I thought that was John," Jack said.

"No, that wasn't us," Stan replied. "We had a feeling that it was either the Vaticates or the Reptilians."

"Or both," Carter said.

"Both?" Stan asked. "What makes you say that?"

"There were two men, humans, there. I saw them through the peep-hole. However, there were other things that happened that night that were definitely not normal. That must be why."

"That changes a lot of things," Stan said.

"Yeah, we're in a lot of trouble now," Paulo said, but remaining aloof.

"Paulo…" Stan glared.

"Wait, why does that change things?" Carter asked.

Just then William came walking through the kitchen with his guest. Carter tensed in her seat, her back becoming rigid as she distracted herself with the pattern of the kitchen table. Everyone sat in silence as William stepped outside with the woman. A knot formed in Carter's throat that she couldn't swallow.

Carter could feel the tension rolling off of William and knew he could feel her pain. For the first time, she hated the connection they had.

"Ya know," Stan said, standing up, "I'm really tired. It's been a long day, and I would like some time to myself. I'm going to retire for the night. Carter, we can finish this conversation over breakfast." He left before waiting for an answer, and Carter sighed.

She could hear William's muffled conversation through the kitchen door, and she cringed. She knew Stan was just excusing himself to help her. "Yes, that would be great. I'm tired too." She followed Stan to the foot of the stairs. "Stan?"

He turned to face her, smiling warmly.

"Thank you."

He nodded in response.

She walked slowly back up the stairs and to her room. She looked around, and it seemed so desolate now. The last time John was in this room, he had given her the Bible to read. Now it sat on her table where she had last left it, when he was still alive. She had barely closed the door behind her when there was a soft knock. With resolve she walked back to open it.

CHAPTER 6

𒂉 𒀸 𒂖𒀸 𒂉𒀸 ~𒁹𒁹 𒀹𒀹 𒁹𒂓 𒂖𒀸 𒀹𒁹~ 𒂉𒀸 ~𒁹𒂓 𒀸𒂉𒀸

"CARTER, I KNOW YOU ARE tired. I just wanted to check in on you before I went to bed."

She watched Jack standing in the frame of the doorway, and her heart ached. Jack, somehow, continued to be there for her regardless of what she put him through. She stepped aside, inviting him in.

He walked in and to the desk, looking briefly to the Bible sitting near other books.

"You've been reading a lot."

"John has been—" Carter rubbed her hands over her face. "John *was* supplying me with books. He was helping me with my research."

Jack picked up a book with a plain orange cover and a large X on the front. He read the inside jacket, and it mentioned something about a tenth planet.

When he turned around, Carter was sitting on her bed, staring at her feet.

"You never leave your hair down anymore," Jack said without thinking. The second he said it he regretted it. He frowned.

Carter responded with a chuckle. He was surprised to get a laugh out of her.

"I didn't think you noticed things like that."

He sat down next to her and ran his hands through his hair, which had become shaggy in the last few months. Carter watched his fluid movements, and everything seemed to move slowly, as if she were purposely watching every moment in her life. She suddenly felt the shortness of life. This was the way it would be, she realized. Always fighting a cause that would be marked with blood. Blood of the people she loved, blood of the people she hated. She watched Jack and felt as if she had already lost him in so many ways. Their time was running out, she knew.

She felt the tears roll over her cheeks. She wiped at her face, but they relentlessly fell. Jack took her hand in his and lifted her chin, wiping the tears for her. He kissed her cheek and felt the salty tears on his lips. When he pulled away, she watched him and felt the heat well up in her, the heat she had tried to ignore. His sudden shift in mood with her was disorienting. Didn't death usually have a weird effect on people in that sense? They suddenly felt time ticking and acted irrationally? Carter didn't know what to make of it.

She shook her head no, no against the feelings she couldn't fight anymore. Her connection with William was more than chemical, it was an alien connection that seeped into parts of her mind she could not control. Yet what she had with Jack was love, a love without any outside interference that she had no control over.

She didn't know what she wanted anymore. She thought of William and the woman who had sat on his bed, intimately leaning into him.

Carter realized that what she wanted probably didn't even matter anymore. William had made his choice.

"Carter." Jack's tone was pleading, his eyes searching, and still she shook her head no. "You can't deny this," he said.

Her head jerked up to meet his eyes head on. Why was he doing this now? After all this time? It wasn't fair. Fresh tears flowed, and now it wasn't for loss anymore. Her heart drummed in her ears, and her eyes fell on his lips. She didn't care what happened yesterday, what happened today or tomorrow; she just wanted this with Jack, she realized. She wanted what she'd been denied for so long. Tomorrow was promised to no one, and the reality of that bore down her like the rushing water of a flood.

Without thinking, without listening to the chaos in her mind but rather to the joy in her heart, she closed the distance between them and pressed her lips against his. Suddenly, her body reacted without her understanding as she found herself hungrily climbing on top of him, resting in his lap. He pulled her against his body tighter, and she felt the heat and built-up tension between them pulsating fervently, relentlessly.

Jack lifted her in an effortless scoop and slid her underneath him on the bed as their kisses grew impassioned and more desperate with each breath. He whispered her name between kisses as if he couldn't believe she was there. She felt her skin flush with heat as his hands skirted underneath the hem of her shirt, his rough hands gracing the soft, warm skin underneath her waistband. The more he kissed her, the more he touched her, the more she wanted. She wrapped her legs around his waist, arching her back against his touch instinctively.

Somewhere in the far reaches of her mind, she heard the knocking, but she ignored it. She felt Jack hesitate as he listened to the soft rapping on the door. He hovered over her, listening intently, and the heat lingered on her skin.

"Ignore it," Carter whispered, and she kissed him again on the lips. He reciprocated eagerly.

"Carter? Are you there?" William said through the door.

Carter felt her heart falter, and she tried to ignore it. Jack looked into her eyes, searching, and she knew he saw the war waging in her thoughts. He brushed the hair from her forehead gently.

"Carter? I feel your energy. I know you're awake."

Jack narrowed his eyes at her and what he decided, she didn't know. But in an instant, she saw regret pass through his eyes, and it felt as if an ice storm had suddenly entered the room. Like that, he was distant again.

He got up quickly and began buttoning his shirt back up. When had she done that? Without looking back to her, he opened the door as he fastened the last button.

"She's with me," Jack said through the door, annoyed. Carter raised her eyebrows at him curiously.

She was so startled and confused by the events of the last moments that it didn't register in her mind that she should pull herself together. William stepped into the room and upon seeing her raised his eyebrows curiously. She looked down to see her black bra peaking out from her shirt. Carter fumbled with her shirt and tried to stand up but was so tangled in the sheets on her bed that she nearly tripped over herself in the process. By the time she stood to meet Jack's bemused expression, she had turned ten shades of a deep scarlet.

"Just find me tomorrow, Carter. We need to talk," William finally said.

Carter heard William pull away from the door, and she felt his pain. She sat up in bed and saw Jack's annoyed expression.

She took a deep breath, reigning in her emotions. She knew Jack cared for her deeply and knew he was protective of her. She glanced out the window, and seeing the rooftops of the homes in Peru reminded her how far from home she really was, in more ways than one. She also painfully remembered that she would wake up in the morning and not see John. "Jack—"

"Carter, don't. I know what you're going to say: this is bad timing or some BS, but it's never going to be a good time, not with everything that's going on."

He was right. It would never be a good time. "Jack, you should go."

He watched her for a moment, and she thought he would protest. But he didn't. She watched him leave the room and close the door behind him. The tears flowed freely then. She spent the rest of the evening into the morning crying into her pillow. She had now lost two people in her life, and she couldn't justify their deaths for the greater good. John believed in protecting Carter and what they were doing, but for what?

.

CHAPTER 7

𒁹 𒀸 𒂊𒀸 𒂊𒁹 𒀠𒅀 𒀹 𒉺 𒂗 𒂊𒀸 𒐊𒅀 𒂊𒁹 𒀸 𒀠𒂗 𒂊𒁹

CARTER AVOIDED BREAKFAST THE NEXT morning and stayed in her room, hoping to avoid contact with anyone. That idea was short lived, though, when there was a knock on her door. She reluctantly let Stan in.

"It was John's wish to be cremated," Stan said. She watched as he rocked back and forth from foot to foot. "We're going to have a memorial for him here and thought you would like to help us plan. I know John would've liked that."

Carter nodded. "Sure, of course."

"We'll be meeting downstairs in about an hour."

After Stan left her room, she decided that would give her enough time to check on something she had been thinking about. She grabbed her messenger bag and slung it over her shoulder.

Sometime during the night, she had realized that there would come a point when she would need to go out on her own if she was going to figure out what was going on. She knew her idea to seek out Jibril was crazy, but that was exactly why she needed to do it. Neither side would ever expect it, and she knew, somehow, that surprising Jibril and confronting him solo would be the element she needed to gain his trust. If they were going to work things out as Anunnaki and Vaticate, she needed his trust and needed to understand why they were so adamant about keeping the Anunnaki at bay. Her mother seemed to agree with Jibril to a certain point, which meant there was something she didn't know and wasn't being told. He also seemed to trust her mother and had had plenty of opportunity to kill Carter already, but hadn't. She knew she would be safe enough and wouldn't risk losing anyone else.

After all, there were always two sides to a story, weren't there?

She ran down the stairs and out of the kitchen so quickly that she didn't even say hello to Rafe and Stan, who were still sitting around the breakfast table. She hopped on Rafe's bicycle, which was leaning against the frame of the house, and rode the fourteen blocks back to the park where they had been the night before. She didn't think she would find anything, but something pulled at her and told her she needed to check to make sure.

The park felt so benign that she began to second-guess what she had experienced there just the day before. Carter walked across the park to where she and Rafe had sat less than twenty-four hours before. She sat on the same rock, looking around half expectantly. She rubbed at her eyes, desperately trying to wipe away the fogginess she suddenly felt. When her vision became more blurred, she froze in her seat, afraid to move. The weight of her messenger bag felt heavy on her shoulder. She couldn't move even if she wanted to, as her legs and arms had become like cement when the pressure in the air bore down on her chest.

Her breath was heavy in her chest as she waited—for what she didn't know. A dark shadow cast rapidly across the grass, stopping just before her feet on the ground, lifting up and taking form in front of her, hovering over her quivering body. She felt the darkness of the entity creeping into the edges of her mind, and she remembered the night in their hotel room in Northern California when she first encountered the terrifying darkness.

"You are the one to sssssssssssseek us," the whisper hissed in her mind.

Carter clawed at her head, feeling the whisper like a bad scratch as the darkness crept into all corners of her mind, stealing her thoughts and stealing her breath. The battle raged in her mind as the whispers fought the darkness until the darkness won.

✻   ✻   ✻

IT WASN'T UNTIL SHE FOUND herself lying in the grass gasping for air that she realized that she had been unconscious. She found herself sitting near a pond she hadn't even known existed and felt the dampness under her palms and her jeans soaked from the edges of the water. Carter wondered how long she had been lying there and sat up, gathering her thoughts and struggling to understand what had just happened.

When she looked around to try to understand her surroundings, she spotted Rafe's bike across the street near the park. Vague memories tickled her mind as if she were trying to remember something but couldn't.

The entire ride back to the home, she felt as if she were forgetting something important, and it left her despondent. When she stepped into the living room to the gloomy faces waiting for her, all was completely forgotten.

CHAPTER 8

𒂍 𒀸 𒆠 𒂍 𒉿 𒍢 𒂍 𒀸 𒅕 𒂍 𒀸 𒊏 𒂍

CARTER RAN HER FINGERTIPS OVER the delicate paper mindlessly as she thought about her father and the day she first saw him in her kitchen. Even then, there was something familiar about him, and she never felt threatened. Instinct? She wondered. She thought of his sparkling eyes and his aloof demeanor, always silently looking out for her, and she realized that he was like that because he had been watching over her, her entire life.

"Penny for your thoughts?" Stan asked as he took her hand in his, walking her to the shoreline.

"So there's no life after death?" Carter asked. "It's times like these that I envy those with faith in heaven."

Stan smiled sadly. "Carter, we are not saying that there is no life after death. We are just saying that the stories that belong to religion really belong to our ancestors, and even our ancestors aren't the highest form of life. There's more to this life than what we see and what we understand."

She had never thought of that, and as the water and sand tickled her toes, she also realized there was so much she had never gotten to know about her father, this being one of them. They lit the candles, and she watched the flames flicker as they placed them in the lanterns. Carter could see why this had appealed so much to John. When she watched the lantern glow from within, she knew how much it represented her father in so many ways.

"The lanterns?" she asked.

"He was in Thailand at the Lantern Festival. Talked about it for years after. Whenever we lost one of our people, he would light a lantern for him or her and say that maybe the lights could be seen or felt from the heavens. The heavens, of course, being the energy that consumes us when we pass."

The tear that fell was swept up by the breeze as if it had come to wipe it away.

She crouched down on the pebbled shoreline and watched as the lanterns floated upward, dotting the magenta sky with spots of light. The soft breeze continued to drift around them, cooling her skin against the humid and dank air. She closed her eyes and listened to the sounds of the water, the whispers of her friends, and the silence around them. When she opened her eyes, she saw she was surrounded by them. Stan, Jack, William, Rafe, and Paulo formed a semicircle around her, and they all stared off as the sun sent its last light over the water, turning the sky from a magenta to a deep purple and then night blue. An hour passed before anyone spoke, and she knew in her heart that these people were more than just anyone she worked with or barely knew. They were friends on a deeper level. More than even family.

✵ ✵ ✵

MOST HAD A NEWFOUND MOTIVE to find Jibril now—something to channel their grief into. Carter wished she shared in their sentiment.

Carter spent her days training with William on her telepathy and Rafe and Stan on physical defensive and offensive moves. She even spent some time working with Paulo on strategy. They didn't think she would ever actually need it, but it gave everyone something to focus on.

One afternoon in March, she decided to go into John's room—a place no one had touched since his death. She slowly opened the door, and even though it had been months since he had died, she could still smell him in the room. She stood there for a moment breathing him in, her eyes closed. She could almost feel him there with her. There was a book on the nightstand, and she walked over to look at it. It was open face down, where John had apparently left off reading it. Her heart ached at the thought.

Lost Land in the Desert—by Dr. G. Paul Griffin

She sat on his bed and held the book to her heart. She then folded the page where he had left off and closed the book. Curling into a fetal position on his bed, she hugged his book against her. His scent was everywhere. For the first time since his death, she felt something besides pain and numbness. She felt longing. This felt different from when she had thought William had died, or even when Carl died. He had been a part of her life before all this in a different way, and she knew he had cared for her. She realized, as well, that it felt as if she had lost her mother all over again, and in a way, she had.

She knew in her heart that John had wanted to protect her as well as help her figure things out. The proof was cradled in her arms now, and she wondered if he had been searching for answers in this book.

The tears flowed freely, spilling over onto his sheets. She felt someone stroking her hair away from her face, wiping her tears that wouldn't stop, and she wasn't sure who it was. Jack maybe? Eventually her tears stopped, and the exhaustion overcame her. For the first time since Bohemian Grove, she had a dreamless sleep.

When she woke in the morning, she felt better but knew it would be a long road before she felt normal again—or as close to normal as she could possibly ever get. She wasn't ready to face anyone yet, so she decided that she should at least distract herself. She found her satchel sitting on the nightstand in her room and pulled out the Bible that she had started reading that fateful day, placing it gently next to John's book.

CHAPTER 9

𒂖 𒀸 𒆠 𒂖 𒉺 𒅀 𒍝 𒊩 𒆠 𒄭 𒂖 𒀸 𒉿 𒆠

S HE LOST TRACK OF HOW many times she read *Lost Land in the Desert*. She would go downstairs to grab leftover meals after she knew everyone was already in bed for the night and bring the food back to her room. The book spoke of a Native American tribe in New Mexico called the Zuni and their ability to communicate with the gods through fire. She read it over and over expecting some answer to pop out at her. Yet nothing came. She continued to read anyway.

She was somewhere in the beginning of the book again one afternoon when there was a knock on the door downstairs. She waited a moment, listening to the house, and when no one went to open the door, she dragged herself downstairs to see who it was. A familiar, dark-skinned beauty stood on the stoop staring at her with red-rimmed and puffy eyes. She had been crying, and Carter callously wondered why she should care.

"Amara," Carter said coldly.

She nodded in response. "Carter, I wanted to speak to you."

Carter sighed. William had tried on several occasions to explain to Carter who Amara was, but she had refused to listen. It didn't matter, she decided. Carter stepped out and closed the door behind her.

"I wanted to tell you that there's nothing going on between me and William."

"Um, okay?" Carter looked around, looking for an excuse to get out of the conversation.

"That day when you walked in on us, we weren't doing anything. There wasn't anything going on."

"Okay, thank you, Amara. But I'm not sure why you're telling me. William and I aren't—"

"Well, you should be."

"I'm sorry?"

"You and William, you belong together. I can see your auras. There is a lot of passion there, and you are meant to be together. Since that day, I've spoken to him a few times, and he's told me that there's nothing going on with you guys."

"He was right, but I don't see how any of this is your business."

"I'm a friend of his. Well, my husband was."

"Was?" Carter got a sick feeling in her stomach as she suddenly realized who Amara was. She could kick herself for being so stupid and cold.

"My husband, Sergio, was killed in a car accident the morning that John was killed. He worked for your father, and he was there to clear the area, and—well, I think that's why everyone was taken by surprise, because he wasn't." Amara took a deep, shaky breath before continuing. "I was with William that night because I was so upset, and he knew Sergio."

Carter sat down on the front steps of the porch, suddenly nauseated. Amara joined her.

"Amara, I don't know what to say. I'm really sorry."

Amara nodded again. "It's okay, but there's more. That's not the only reason I came by. There was something I wanted to show you. Something that…" Amara stopped, clearly struggling to say her late husband's name. "Something that Sergio and John were talking about the night before." Carter reached out and held Amara's hand and squeezed it lightly. It was the first time that Carter had wanted to reach out to anyone since John's death. *A sister in grief,* she thought. No, it was more than that, she realized. She just wanted to help *someone,* to feel useful for once.

"Let me just grab my shoes." She left Amara standing in the doorway while she ran up the stairs and grabbed her satchel and shoes. When Carter stepped outside, she noticed Amara was standing between two bicycles. Carter took one and followed Amara, who was already riding down the street. They rode in silence, which Carter was thankful for. There was much she wanted to know about this beautiful woman, but she was not ready to strike up conversation yet—not after her weeks of silence. She didn't know who Amara was or where she was going. Carter was beginning to feel nervous and was about to say something when they finally came to a stop at the outskirts of the city. She looked up to find herself looking at a small, humble home. It was modest and old but taken care of with pride. A meager vegetable garden framed the right side of the home. This home suddenly made her feel guilty about her house back in Santa Barbara. She had never taken pride in anything before, not even her clothing designs. She frowned as she looked around the tiny house, ashamed of how she had judged Amara before and ashamed of living lavishly with no qualms.

"Are you well?" Amara asked, concern etched in her features.

"This home is beautiful," Carter whispered as tears filled her eyes. She turned to Amara, who watched her with raised eyebrows and eyes filled with curiosity. "Sorry, I just—this is your home, isn't it?"

Amara's eyes filled with tears in return. "This *was* our home. Sergio's family's home. It was he who loved this place. He said love begins at home, and it is not how much we do, but how much love we put in that action. I feel that I love this home now, that he is still here with me," she said carefully.

Carter managed a soft smile for her new friend.

When they stepped inside, the home appeared even smaller.

Leading her to the kitchen table where piles of documents and photos were sprawled out, Carter recognized John's handwriting on one of the maps. She ran her fingers over the rough penmanship—there was so much she didn't know about him. She looked out the kitchen window and watched the palms sway in the wind. It reminded her of that fateful day they left Bohemian Grove, when she felt as if the trees were singing a song of sorrow for her. With a shuddering sigh, she sat down at the kitchen table, and Amara joined her. Carter's heart felt heavy in her chest, and her throat pained as she fought back tears.

"You loved him," Amara said. It wasn't a question.

"I did."

"He loved you too," she said, surprising Carter. "When he spoke your name, it was filled with love, but it also hurt. He loved you, Carter, very much. But for your kind? That is not always so easy."

Who was this strange woman who enraptured her emotions? Unable to find her voice, Carter simply stared down at the map. "What were they doing anyway?" she asked, trying to understand the scribble.

"I do not know exactly. But they were very excited about what they found here." Amara pointed down to an area of the map that Carter had grown to recognize easily.

"We've been there a few times already and found nothing."

"No, there is something they were talking about the night before, something called the Sun Gate?" Amara said, excitement stemming in her voice. It was clear that she was hoping that this would mean something to Carter, but she had never heard of the Sun Gate before. Carter just shook her head in response.

"I'm sorry, Amara. I don't know what the Sun Gate is."

Amara let out a long, shaky sigh. "What do we do?"

Carter wasn't sure there was anything they could do. She thought for a moment. "Well, we could go there. Maybe knowing something is there will change things." Carter didn't believe they would find anything different that they hadn't found before, but it was something to do. And she wasn't sure whether she could read the Bible or John's book one more time anyway.

Amara nodded enthusiastically, and this alone brought relief to Carter. Yes, they would go to Machu Picchu again and search. What was the worst that could happen? "Are you free tomorrow?" she continued. "We can go at first light."

CHAPTER 10

𒐖𒐊 𒀳 𒐊𒐊 𒌋𒐊 𒑱 𒐊𒐊 𒑱𒐊 𒌋𒐊 𒐊𒐊 𒌋𒐊

THE FIRST TIME CARTER MADE the trek up Machu Picchu, she thought she was the most out-of-shape person on earth—especially when their seventy-two-year-old guide seemed to put no effort into the hike. By the time she made it to the top of the mountain, she was too exhausted to make note of the breathtaking view. They set up camp and spent the night at the top. Carter was the first one to wake in the morning, and when she stepped out of her tent, she staggered. She felt as if she had stepped onto a different planet. The fog had settled around the ruins, making it look as if they were floating, like a castle in the sky.

"Is this real?" Jack's voice came out as a whisper behind her. It was the first time he had spoken to her since they had arrived in Peru. She remembered turning to look at him and being just as awestruck by his face as by the ruins around her. The wondering expression made him look like a curious child.

"It's a dream," Carter said, and half chuckled at her lame comment.

Jack just nodded at her instead, which stopped her laughter. He put his arm around her shoulder, pulling her into him. The motion both surprised and thrilled her. His presence made her realize how much she loved being near him and how much she had missed it since he had given her the cold shoulder in Peru.

"Are you okay Carter?" Amara's voice broke into Carter's daydreaming. Carter realized she was absentmindedly rubbing her shoulder where Jack had held her that day.

"Ya, I was just remembering the first time I came here," she said, shaking off her thoughts of the past, still struggling to understand her feelings about Jack.

"I have been here many times, and it is more beautiful each time." Amara paused, clearly holding back something.

Carter watched Amara carefully, wanting her to feel comfortable but unsure of the possibility after how she had treated her.

Amara leaned against one of the oversize boulders that stuck out from the ground, closing her eyes as she spoke. "It does not get easier. It hurts my heart every night and every morning when he is not in my bed with me." She blushed at her own words.

Carter walked over to her and pulled her into an embrace. Amara gasped for air as she choked on her own sobs. Her grief rocked Carter to the core, reminding her of her own. The two women stood atop the magical mountain in the fog and cried together until there were no more tears to shed. Carter didn't cry only for John. She cried for the loss of her own life, of things familiar. She cried because she was homesick and missed her other father, Peter. She cried for the strain between her and Jack, and her and William. She let herself cry because she knew that after this time, she would not be given that opportunity again and she would need to find her strength and move on.

When the tears ceased, they leaned against each other and watched as the fog eventually rolled away, as it always does, in silence. Hours had passed, and neither spoke a word. The sun moved slowly across the sky, and evening approached. She stood slowly and was about to say something when something caught her eye.

At first she didn't even think she had seen anything, as it happened so quickly.

"Carter? Did you see something?" Amara now stood near her.

"I—I, uh, don't know. I thought I did." She stared off into the distance, hoping to see the reflection again, but nothing happened. "Maybe just too much thin air." Carter brushed off her pants and stretched her legs as she stood.

"Thin air?" Amara asked, confused.

"Never mind," she said, chuckling. "We should be going, though. It's getting late." Then she saw it again and realized she only saw it when she looked from the corner of her eye instead of directly. "Amara, stand here." Carter directed her to stand and look at the door the exact same way she did, but no matter what she did, Amara couldn't see the archway.

"Is it the Gate? What does it look like?" Amara desperately wanted to see what her friend was seeing, but there was nothing there.

"Well, it's more like a threshold, or an archway. It's golden, and there are carvings on it. But every time I try to see more, it fades," Carter explained. They walked over to where the doorway was, but nothing happened. Then Carter walked back to her old spot and saw it again. And as the sun set, she saw it clearer. It looked like an arch, but it had to be the Sun Gate Amara had talked about. With illuminated clarity she saw the carvings in the arch. A carving of two snakes wrapped around a golden rod with golden wings stemming from it, reminding her of the logo of the American Medical Association.

Carter reached out, ran her fingers over the carvings, and flinched, surprised by its very warm temperature. She took a step forward, now barely outside the threshold.

"Carter, I do not think you should…"

Carter stepped through the threshold and felt the breath sucked from her lungs. As she stood just on the other side, she could still see Amara, but as if she were looking through a milky film.

"Can you see me?" Carter asked.

Amara tilted her head to the side as if she didn't understand her. The movement was extremely slow and disorienting. Carter looked around her, and everything looked the same but felt different. Something she couldn't put her finger on. Whatever it was, was uncomfortable to her. She felt as if she were being watched. The creepy, going-down-into-a-dark-basement type of watched. Shivers ran down her spine.

She's here. The whisper was barely audible on the breeze and nearly sounded like the wind itself. She spun around.

"Who's there?" Carter asked.

A whisper of air barely brushed her hair, but she knew it wasn't the wind. She shivered. She heard what sounded like hushed conversations in the background growing slowly louder. *Impossible*, she thought.

She quickly stepped back through the threshold. Her nerves were getting the better of her.

"Are you okay?" Amara asked, and Carter nodded. "You were in there forever."

Carter's eyebrows came together. "Forever? That was only a few seconds."

Carter looked up and saw the darkening sky. "No, Carter. That was at least an hour. I could barely see you. Were you talking to someone?"

"No, why?"

"I saw someone standing with you. I thought you were talking to someone."

Carter looked back at the gate but saw no one there. "Are you sure?"

"Yes, I am sure. Dark silhouette of a person, just behind you."

Carter rubbed her arms as she continued watching the gate, knowing they needed to get out of there quickly. Just before the archway disappeared, Carter recognized ancient carvings and read the word *Nahash*. And then the archway was gone. Nothing Carter did would make it show up again. Eventually she gave up as night started to fall, the air starting to cool and wisp around Carter's hair as they descended down the mountain.

Both women walked in silence back, contemplating the day's events. Carter replayed the experience with the Gate, trying to figure out the connection, feeling as if a piece of the puzzle was on the tip of her tongue.

CHAPTER 11

ᛁᚤ ᚲ ᚲᛁᚲ ᛄᛁ ᚻᛁᚤᛁ ᚳᚤ ᛁᛂ ᚳᚲ ᚲᛁᚤᚻ ᛄᛁ ᚲ ᚻᛁᛂ ᚲᛁᚤ

"IT'S NICE TO SEE YOU up and about." William stood in the archway between the kitchen and the living room, coffee mug in hand. Carter picked at the berries in the bowl, not looking up to acknowledge him. His voice made her tense, as she had been avoiding him since that night with Jack, the day she also lost her biological father. He seemed to want to be avoided anyway.

"Gotta live. Right?" Even she cringed at her own coldness. She rested her head on her forearm, hoping he'd leave, popping a dark berry into her mouth.

The silence was worse than the words unsaid. As much as she wanted to deny it, even after everything that had happened, she couldn't. She felt Will as much as she always did, and maybe even stronger now than before, the electricity buzzing around them—a current that wouldn't be ignored. The connection they shared was undeniable. Knowing when he was in the house, when he was around, made it harder for her to block him out. Even now, she knew he wanted to say something to her, but she wished he would just leave.

"Carter." His tone spoke a million words, words that hung wildly in the air between them. She wondered if eventually they would even need to speak out loud to communicate with each other. Finally she looked up at him, and his face reflected what she already knew he was thinking. Yet the silence continued to hang in the air between them.

"William." His name hung on her lips in a soft whisper, but she knew he had heard her. "Please." She shook her head at him, willing his anguish away, the anguish she could still feel on top of hers, compounding her sorrow, though it was a different type of anguish, one of regret and guilt instead of the pure torture she'd felt since John was ripped from her life at her hands. William's relief in seeing Carter finally talk to him was enough for him to walk quickly over to her, kneel down before her, and look up into her struggling eyes. He held her face between his hands, maintaining contact. Carter felt herself breaking inside and didn't think she could hold herself together anymore, if that was what she was doing.

"Carter, please. I'm sorry, if I—"

"If you what, Will? If you had known John was going to die?" Her voice broke on the last word. She wasn't sure how long they sat there just staring into each other's eyes, carrying on a conversation that no words ever could. She wasn't sure whether this was the Anunnaki in them or there was something more. She was grateful for it at this moment, and suddenly she wasn't sure why she had resisted this so long. Maybe she was punishing herself. Didn't she deserve it after all? There were now two deaths on her hands of people she loved and who had loved her back.

Stan and Rafe stumbled in out of breath, instantly breaking the tension in the room.

"Your vision on the mountain—we found out more info," Rafe said in between breaths, completely oblivious to what he had walked into. By the way Stan looked back and forth between William and Carter, though, he knew.

"I think you interrupted something," Paulo said as he walked into the kitchen with Jack. "You're not very observant for being on a protection force."

Carter blushed a deep scarlet red and avoided making eye contact with Jack. But that didn't stop her from feeling his eyes bore into her skull. Rafe just looked at William, still crouched on the floor, and Carter when it dawned on him, causing him to blush as well.

Stan cleared his throat as he pulled out a piece of paper, smoothing it out before laying it out on the kitchen table. Carter had told them about what she had seen on Machu Picchu when she got back. Immediately they went to work to find out more, everyone desperate for some lead.

Carter tilted her head as she looked at the familiar image on the paper. "That's what I saw. What is it?" Carter anxiously pointed at the rough draw-ing on the paper, guessing that either Stan or Rafe had quickly sketched out the haunting symbol.

"It's the symbol for the Brotherhood of the Snake," Rafe replied. "They opposed the enslavement of spiritual beings, and according to ancient Egyptian texts, its purpose was to liberate the human race from *custody*."

Carter raised her eyebrows. "Custody?"

"Enki wanted to free the human race," Stan said.

"Enki? He was the…" she paused, the puzzle pieces clicking togeth-er. "Enki was the serpent—Brotherhood of the Serpent." Carter recalled stories from the Bible that John had given her, as well as other texts she had been researching on their endless stay in Peru. "The Tree of Life and the serpent. The Bible says the serpent was overcome before it was able to complete its mission." Carter couldn't figure out one thing though. "The serpent represents the devil."

"The Brotherhood of the Snake later reformed itself and created false gods to deter humans from the Gods of Nibiru," Rafe explained.

"So, not the devil?" she asked.

"No, not originally. That was just a scare tactic," Stan said.

"It worked," Rafe said as everyone nodded in agreement.

"Nibiru, the planet of the Anunnaki?" William asked.

"Yes, the very one," Rafe replied.

"What did the Brotherhood of Snake call itself once they reformed?" she asked.

"The Vaticates," Rafe and Stan said together.

Her eyes widened, and she shivered. It all made sense. "What about that word I saw? Nahash?"

"We looked that up as well," Paulo said. "Nahash means to *decipher* or *find out.*"

"To decipher or find out? Find out what?" Carter asked.

"Find out how to free themselves." Rafe stared at the drawing on the table as he answered.

"From the Vaticates?" Carter didn't like the sound of that.

"Not exactly," Rafe continued. "From false gods. Once the human race is freed from false worship, they will experience a spiritual awakening." Rafe waved his hands through the air as if he were displaying something. "An awakening that will not only be spiritual, but physical. They will become closer to the perfect creation the Anunnaki meant to create in the first place—the true Tree of Life."

"So what exactly does this all have to do with me? How do I fit into the picture?" Carter looked around the table, letting the new information sink in.

"You are the daughter of Ashtoreth. Ashtoreth was the goddess equal with all other gods. Equal because she possessed the knowledge of how to speak with Enki, even after he was overcome. He must complete his mission," Stan said sadly, knowing how difficult that would be to accomplish, especially since they still weren't quite sure what they were accomplishing.

"I'm supposed to find out how to conjure up some god/alien guy so he can come and complete his mission?"

The guys nodded at her. William just watched her carefully.

"That's it?" She shook her head. "Not a problem," she said as her hands automatically went to sit on her hips. "All while preventing the Vaticates from accomplishing their mission to kill me."

"We found someone here at the college who can help us with some more information. Let the guys and me worry about Jibril for now," Stan said as he picked up the paper off the table.

"Carter?" William said as she stood up from the table. She looked at him apprehensively and reflexively looked back at Jack. He turned from her and left the room instantly.

Carter just frowned at William. "Not now," she said, not sure what exactly she was postponing.

✫　　✫　　✫

TENDRILS OF BLACK MIST CURLED *around her wrist, pulling and guiding her through the desert landscape.*

Thisssss way—*the darkness whispered to her mind, and she followed* reluctantly.

"*Where are we going?*" *she said out loud.*

You are clossssssse.

She followed the voice and felt the dusty and grainy floor beneath her, cold in the desert night air. She shivered slightly and felt affronted by the whispers deception.

You are clossssssssssssssse.

Carter frowned. The tendrils slithered around, gripping her wrist tighter, nearly closing off her circulation. She tried to pull away, but it only made it worse. Panic seized her as the tendrils slowly pulled her over the edge of the cliff and she plummeted into the endless pitch darkness, her scream caught in her throat. She was going to die.

When she hit the ground, she fell out of her dream, right onto her bedroom floor in Lima.

CHAPTER 12

𒂍 𒀭 𒂍𒀭 𒂍𒀭 ⟶𒅀𒐊 𒆷 𒐊𒂍 𒂍𒀭 ⟨𒅀⟶ 𒂍𒀭 𒆷 ⟶𒐊𒂍 𒂍𒀭

"THE APOCRYPHA IS A SET of books written between approximately 400 BC and the time of Christ. The word *apocrypha* means *hidden*. These books consist of one and two Esdras, Tobit, Judith, the Rest of Esther, the Wisdom of Solomon, Sirach, also called Ecclesiasticus, Baruch, the Letter of Jeremiah, Song of the Three Young Men, Susanna, Bel and the Dragon, the Additions to Daniel, the Prayer of Manasseh, and 1 and 2 Maccabees."

Dr. Nathaniel was met with stares and blank faces. Jack eventually had the courtesy to at least close his mouth.

"That's a mouthful," Carter said. Dr. Nathaniel, a Columbia professor and anthropologist as well as Amara and Sergio's friend, sat at the kitchen table with Carter, William, and Jack, explaining the copies of the texts in his hand. He shrugged at his audience indifferently.

"So why aren't they in the Bible?" William asked.

"The Protestant Church rejects the Apocrypha as being inspired, as do the Jews, but in the mid-1500s..." Dr. Nathaniel looked down at the notes on the table before him through his John Lennon round reading glasses barely balanced on the tip of his nose. "In 1546," he said at last, "the Roman Catholic Church officially declared some of the apocryphal books to belong to the canon of scripture. These are Tobit, Judith, one and two Maccabees, Wisdom of Solomon, Sirach, and Baruch." He waved his hands over the texts he had separated from his pile and sighed exasperatedly. "The apocryphal books are written in Greek, not Hebrew—except for Ecclesiasticus, one Maccabees, a part of Judith, and Tobit, and they contain some useful historical information." He leaned back in the chair and crossed his arms, slightly smug.

Carter watched everyone in annoyance. Her dream from the night before was making her feel grumpy and agitated. The last thing she wanted was to sit around a table discussing scriptures.

"Is the Apocrypha scripture?" Rafe asked as he ran his fingers through his coarse black hair.

"Protestants deny its inspiration, but the Roman Catholic Church affirms it. In order to ascertain whether it is or isn't, we need to look within its pages." Dr. Nathaniel looked at Carter over his spectacles, regarding her for the first time as if studying a specimen. Carter looked around the table and was met with similar expressions on William's, Stan's, and Paulo 's faces. Only Jack shared her look of annoyance.

Carter ignored them. They had a lot of pieces that could mean something, but they still didn't know how. They continued discussing anthropological sites in and around Peru but got no further with information.

When Nathaniel was halfway out the door, he abruptly turned back to them. "If you're looking for the messenger, you won't find it in there." He looked over Rafe's shoulders back into the kitchen at the books still sitting on the kitchen table and then glanced deliberately at Carter. His eyes bore into her, but there was a change in his eyes, almost as if she were suddenly looking at someone else. She nearly stumbled back at the abruptness and change in the doctor. He seemed … somewhere else. William glanced back and forth between Carter and Dr. Nathaniel.

"What messenger?" Jack asked, but Dr. Nathaniel still stared at Carter, as if he hadn't heard Jack. After several minutes, Dr. Nathaniel finally turned back to Rafe. The strange look in his eyes was instantly replaced with a distraught look that clearly belonged to Dr. Nathaniel again. He seemed startled to still be standing there. His forehead was beady with sweat, and his skin was flushed. As he looked around at the six of them staring at him with mouths gaping open, he paled. He shook his head and half stumbled out the door hastily, leaving everyone standing in the kitchen confused.

"What—was—that?" Carter finally asked after Rafe had shut the door.

CHAPTER 13

𒉿 𒀯 𒌋𒂀 𒉿 𒈠𒅀 𒀯 𒉈 𒂀 𒌋𒅀 𒉿 𒀯 𒈠𒉈 𒀯

THE WALK TO AMARA'S WAS quicker than Carter hoped. She wanted to pay her friend a visit, as she told the guys, but she also needed to get away. She was homesick. The embrace that Amara greeted her with made her feel as if they were long-lost childhood friends, and it made her miss Julia. Their relationship had made a near 180-degree turn since they had their strange encounter on the mountain with the Sun Gate. After chatting casually with Amara for a few hours over tea, Carter asked if she could use their house phone.

After punching in the numbers from her international calling card into the phone, she listened to the foreign dial tone ring three times before her dad—her step-dad, half-dad?—picked up the phone. She practically burst into tears at the sound of his voice.

"We're doing fine, honey, really. I mean, of course there's sadness, but life goes on. You need to find closure yourself." Peter was more intuitive than she had given him credit for. She had not mentioned how difficult a time she was having, but she didn't need to. This was the man who had raised her, who would tuck her in to bed at night and scare away the boogie monsters, who was both her mother and her father all at once.

"I know, I just don't know how," she confessed.

"It takes time, but you'll figure it out." Sensing a need for a change in subject, he continued. "Beth's sister, Virginia, moved into the house and is helping Beth take care of the furniture store. It's for sale," he explained.

"It's for sale?"

"Honey, that place reminds Beth of Carl too much. It's too painful for her. Your friend Mandy actually got a job there." He paused before continuing. "She's a bubbly one, isn't she?"

Carter laughed and agreed. Listening to Peter made her both happy and melancholy at the same time. She missed him greatly and wanted to get on the next plane home. If it weren't for their most recent lead, she probably would already be soaking in the sea air and dusting off her bookshelves or making chocolate croissants in the oven. She sighed heavily into the phone without realizing it. "How are you guys doing? Not finding anything?" He continued when she didn't respond, mistaking her sigh for something else.

"Well, we might have. I just miss home."

"I know you do, honey. You guys are doing something big. My baby girl is changing the world," he said as Carter wiped the tear that rolled down her cheek. She was happy that he hadn't stepped away from his role as her father, even though she recently just found out that John was her real father. She still needed him. "Hang on, someone's at the door."

Carter pressed the phone against her ear, attempting to hear who was on the other end through the static connection. She thought she heard a woman's voice. When her stepdad got back on the phone, she was quick to interrogate him. "Who's that, Dad?"

"That's Alexia. I met her at one of our meetings. We've partnered up in the business and are doing really well together. In fact, we are going to Costa Rica in March!" Carter couldn't remember the last time she heard this much excitement in his voice. In fact, she didn't recall *ever* hearing this much excitement. "When I got back home, I got to thinking. I love your mother, and that will never change. But we had a close call, and I don't want to live the rest of my life alone."

"Wow, Dad." She hesitated. "I'm happy for you." And she really was. She realized that his happiness, and things being okay at home, would make it easier for her to continue her mission here in Peru.

"You have one minute left on this call."

Carter cursed under her breath. "Well, Dad, I guess that's my cue. It was great talking to you. I'll try to call more."

"I'd like that, honey, but I know that's not easy to do. Don't worry about it if you can't. Love you."

"Love you too."

Carter stared down at the receiver in her hand for a moment longer, gathering herself before facing Amara. When she turned around, she found herself alone in the kitchen. Carter stuck her calling card back in her bag and went to find Amara to say good-bye.

"Would you like to go back up the mountain with me?" Amara asked as Carter stepped out onto the front steps.

It was a trek that Carter needed to make again to see if she could get answers to the threshold she saw. She felt as if there was more there now that she understood the patterns on the arch.

Carter took her time getting back, weaving in and out of streets, thinking about what her stepdad had said and seeing Amara looking happier than the last time she saw her. Carter found that after some reflecting, she was actually feeling a little better herself—ready to tackle this next project. She wanted answers. She needed answers.

CHAPTER 14

ᛣᛁ ᚲ ᛣᛁᛣ ᛣᛁ ᛞᛁᛁ ᚧ ᛁᛖ ᛣᚲ ᚲᛁᛁᛞ ᛣᛁ ᚲ ᛞᛁᛖ ᚲᛣᛁ

Μωυσέως _ερ_ βίβλος _πόκρυφος _πικαλούμενη _γδόη _ _γία

"Secret Book of Moses, called Eighth, or Moyseos, holy books citing esoteric eighth" Jack and Carter gaped at Paulo as he translated the foreign text.

"Don't tell me you speak...whatever that is." Jack waved his hand over the copy of what seemed like an ancient papyrus from Egypt, not hiding his discontent.

"It's a Leiden Papyrus from the first century," Paulo said indifferently. "I studied there briefly, at Leiden Library in Amsterdam."

Now it was Carter's turn to speak with discontent. "So you what—just happened to remember this information *now?*"

Paulo just shrugged at her question, ignoring the blood rushing to Carter's face.

William flipped over the photo and read out loud.

For I testify unto every man that heareth the words of the prophecy of this book, If any man shall add unto these things, God shall add unto him the plagues that are written in this book: And if any man shall take away from the words of the book of this prophecy, God shall take away his part out of the book of life, and out of the holy city, and from the things which are written in this book.

"And if any man shall take away from the words of the book of this prophecy, the Gods shall take away his part out of the book of life." Paulo finished.

They all three sat in stillness around the table of documents, absorbing who-knows-what. After only an eternity, Carter continued. "Apocrypha."

"Hidden," William said from the doorway.

Carter jumped and spun around.

"As long as the books are hidden, the messages will be withheld," William said.

"A conundrum," Carter said, half jokingly.

"So we need to just unhide the books?" Jack asked.

"It's not that simple, Carter. It seems Enki would need to complete his mission first, and then the Anunnaki here on earth can uncover the information successfully, and…" William stopped short.

"And change the future of humanity forever," Carter said, looking like she ate something sour.

CARTER WAS SITTING ON THE front steps watching the neighborhood kids kick around a soccer ball when William joined her. They sat in silence for quite some time before Carter finally spoke.

"When John died…" Her voice broke, so she took a deep, steadying breath. "When John died, I felt this hole inside of me." She paused, gathering her thoughts. William sat patiently next to her, not speaking or looking at her, but she knew he was just giving her the space she needed to frame her thoughts. "But there was always this place inside of me that held onto that small thread that there's something else out there. It made me doubt our mission—what exactly are we doing? Are we killing hope? Maybe it was better to let the church be." She felt William's intense focus on her face now, but she kept looking forward. "I know that's what my mom died for," she just said simply. "She saw Jibril's pain, the pain of everyone who lost someone they loved, and she couldn't take that away. William, she found compassion. Compassion is a human trait. Who are we to take this away?"

William didn't respond. Instead, he just let Carter work through her thoughts. Realizing her own revelation, Carter continued. "We're taking away the lies."

She turned to William, finally facing him. He searched her eyes as she did to him, looking for answers she didn't want to face herself.

"John is dead. There's nothing left of him except his memory here." She held her hand over her heart, her voice breaking. "That's the truth."

"The truth shall set you free?" William asked, half chuckling at the irony.

"The truth will hurt at first, right?" Carter spoke the words, still unsure herself.

"It's not just the people who are losing this, Carter." William took her hand in his and she let him, and the electricity there was stronger than ever, traveling up her arms now, coursing through her veins and charging all her nerve endings. "It's you."

Carter only managed a nod. They sat there for the rest of the evening, holding hands, again—never speaking. Slowly, words were not needed anymore. Was this what the truth was? Was this what the human race was missing? She remembered feeling things throughout her life, those moments when she connected with people and *felt* as if she were on a different plane with them. Was there more to it? The communication that Carter and William exchanged that night was mostly unspoken, but it reminded her that humans weren't exactly separate from the Anunnaki.

CHAPTER 15

ꗍ꘡ ꗔ ꗔꗍꗔ ꗍ꘡ ꗍꗑꗑ ꗱ ꗱꗍ ꗔꗔ ꗔꗑꗑ ꗍ꘡ ꗔ ꗍꗍꗍ ꗔꗍ

CARTER DIDN'T THINK SHE'D BE able to sleep that night with every-thing weighing on her, but she practically fell asleep before her head even hit the pillow. Somewhere, in the midst of her dreams and semicon-sciousness, she heard a distant telephone ringing. Fumbling through her room, she looked around until it dawned on her that she didn't even have a telephone. She paused for a beat, standing in the middle of her bedroom, listening to the strange ringing sound. She actually found herself literally scratching her head. Huh, people really do that, she thought.

She stumbled down the stairs into the hallway where the phone was relentlessly ringing away. First thing in the morning, she was going to tell Stan to install a voice mail system. *Men*, she thought—*they sleep through everything.*

"Hello?" she whispered into the receiver.

"Well, well, well, baby girl, it's been a while." Carter's heart hammered in her chest as adrenaline coursed through her veins. She suddenly felt vulnerable in the hall, exposed. She looked around quickly, not feeling alone anymore. "Aren't you going to say hello back?" The voice on the other end sent her emotions on a whirlwind.

"What do you want, Jibril?" she hissed into the phone.

"Now, now, is that a way to talk to someone who's only calling to pay his respects?"

"What?" she half whispered, half yelled into the phone, wanting to reach in through the telephone line to strangle Jibril—surprised by her own sense of violent thoughts.

"I was calling to give you my condolences." He sounded sincere and almost sympathetic, which made the hair on the back of her neck stand on end—a true psychopath whom she wanted nothing more than to completely obliterate.

When she cursed at him, her voice came out hoarse and rough, definitely threatening, she thought. She was repulsed by the cackling laughter on the other end of the line in response.

"That's what I love about you, Carter. You're so *very human* and so *very* wrong about your assumptions." She wanted to ask Jibril what he meant, but she refused to indulge him. "Dr. Nathaniel has no idea what he's gotten himself into."

Before Carter could respond, the line went dead. She replayed the last line in her head dozens of times but came to no conclusions. Then she decided it was just the rantings of a raving lunatic.

She went back up the stairs and found herself standing in front of William's closed bedroom door. She stood there for a moment contemplating what she was going to do and why she found herself here instead of at Jack's room. So *why was* she here? She was frozen in indecision when William opened the door, both finding themselves startled to be facing each other.

"William, I…uh…" She stammered to get the words out, not sure why she was there when she didn't even know what to explain to William.

"I felt you," he whispered, cutting her off. It took her a moment to register what he had just said.

"What?"

"I could feel your anxiety. It woke me up. Then I felt your anger—fear?" He searched her face now, as if identifying what he felt would still be there. Carter no longer could remember why she had even come to his room. All she could see before her was what she had fought to deny since she first met William. The electric charge sparked between them, and Carter felt her skin warm under his gaze. The darkness of the room cast shadows on William's chiseled features, striking Carter to her very core. The electricity that she could feel when they touched now sparked like a match being struck the few inches between them.

"I feel you now, too," he said gravely, and Carter felt her face flush. She knew he felt everything she wanted and desired in him because she could sense it in him. When he said he no longer wanted to be with her, it was a lie. She knew this now, and she just as much lied to herself about it as well, hoping she could distance herself.

He was trying to protect her from him, but she couldn't figure out why. She tried to sense what it was he was hiding, but she could not. The hunger in William's eyes as he watched her, felt her, was overwhelming. She yearned to reach out and close that distance between them, but she was frozen. There was nothing of her left to give anymore, not to anyone. She needed him badly, wanted him, but couldn't satiate her hungers and desires. The battle was raging inside of her; she wanted to give in to everything and just conquer their passion that felt on the verge of explosion. She bit her tongue to make her focus on something else.

William stepped forward, breathing down her neck, against her ear, and whispered. "Carter, stop this. I can't fight you anymore. Stop fighting me too, please."

His hot breath tickled her skin at the nape of her neck, and she could smell the scent of soap on his skin. She shook her head. "I don't know why I came here," she simply said. It took every ounce of effort and energy she had to turn from him and walk back to his room.

She needed to think. She couldn't think when they were together. But his energy consumed and whirled around her like a drowning cloud. He walked after her and grabbed her wrist, spinning her so fast that she was pressed right against him. He did it on purpose, she knew. She felt every contour of his muscles against her as he pressed her against the wall, one hand against the wall near her head. She felt his rapid breathing against her chest and saw the deep hunger in his eyes.

He closed the inches between them, and the heat electrified into a dizzying frenzy. His face hovered millimeters from hers, caught in each other's gaze. She could feel his ragged breathing underneath her, and she pushed against him, fighting the battle in her mind. Why was she fighting this battle? She didn't even remember anymore.

A tear escaped her, betraying the overwhelming fervor storming inside. William's face softened at the sight of the fallen. He tilted his head as he saw the tear fall.

"You love him." It wasn't a question.

He took a step back from her, then two.

"What we have is more than what two humans could ever have. There's more to it than what you see here, Carter. But you'll see it—and I'll be waiting."

"I should get back to my room," Carter whispered hoarsely, and William nodded. His eyes were still simmering as he watched her.

Neither of them moved, though, and she honestly didn't know if she had it in her to walk away. He was right—there was so much more to this than what she understood. That angered her more than it should have. What they had was out of her control, and she didn't like to be out of control. William felt the shift in energy and walked back into his room and gently closed the door.

She was thankful for that because she knew she wouldn't have walked away. At least she thought she was thankful for it.

CHAPTER 16

𒉌 𒋫 𒄑 𒂊 𒉌 𒁽 𒊩 𒅁 𒂊 𒋫 𒋛 𒂊 𒋫 𒁽 𒅁 𒋫

D R. NATHANIEL HANDED THE PHOTO to Carter.

"Adam and Eve?" Carter asked.

Dr. Nathaniel nodded. "It's an ancient Sumerian tablet, or rather a picture of one," he explained.

Carter mentally calculated.

"Sumer is between 4900 and 2900 BC," William said to Carter, either reading her conflict or understanding her lack of knowledge. She nodded to him, annoyed.

"The Adam and Eve story, so to speak, is in every civilization story. The gift of language from God. It's in the Quran, it's in Mayan texts, here you see it's in Sumerian text, and of course in the Bible." He paused, deciding where to go on with his story. "What do you know of Adam and Eve?"

"Traditionally? That if Eve ate the apple from the tree of life, she was disobeying God?"

Dr. Nathaniel continued. "But you're now familiar with the Brotherhood of the Snake."

Carter nodded.

"So now you know that the stories in biblical texts are not false, and not true. They're based on histories of your people, and the emrgence of humanity." He motioned to the center of the photograph. "That's the tree of life. The tree of life is the artificial development of hominids. The snake, which depicts Satan in religion, is Prometheus in Greek mythology, Enki in Sumerian. But as you know, it's not really Satan."

Carter kept nodding, remembering what they had just learned about Enki and the serpent.

"Prometheus, or Enki, was the Anunnaki who fell in love with Earth. He wanted to stay here and took it upon himself to advance hominids in their liking. Some of the Anunnaki were looking to develop humans enough to make them work for them, but Enki didn't agree with this. It was quite the battle," the doctor said.

"It's laughable that people think we evolved from apes," Dr. Nathaniel continued, looking as if he had eaten something sour. "If evolution happened the way humans would like to think it did, if survival of the fittest were true, then humans would not be here today. We are certainly not the *fittest*." He stared down at the photo in front of him, waving at it. "Scientists laugh at religious followers who don't believe in evolution and discount them for their faith. They don't know how wrong they have it."

"I don't understand," Carter said, thinking out loud. "This is logical; it makes sense. So why don't we think about this stuff like this?"

"Cognitive dissonance." William said.

"Cognitive dissonance is a large part of it, yes. A lot of it is also the lack of knowledge on time frame. It took millions and millions of years for hominids to learn how to stand up right alone, yet it only took a few hundred thousand years to go from that to building pyramids, learning language, building civilizations, learning astronomy, and becoming the homo sapiens of today's world."

"So humans weren't brought here or created by the Anunnaki?" Carter asked.

"No," Paulo said. "Humans were genetically manipulated."

"That's where I come in," Dr. Nathaniel said. "My studies are focused on the specific manipulations of human DNA."

"You lost me," Carter said.

"The missing link," Dr. Nathaniel continued, "is literal. The Anunnaki manipulated human DNA to advance their knowledge, their brains. They literally made them smarter. What would've taken billions of years of evolution took only a fraction of that time." Dr. Nathaniel reached across the table and took Carter's hand. "That's where you come in, my dear," he said. Carter felt the focus around the room disappear, and soon it was just her and Dr. Nathaniel at the table. It was as if things had suddenly become clearer. Things made sense that hadn't made sense before, as if they too were now communicating telepathically. Carter watched the curve of Dr. Nathaniel's lips move up into a smile. "Yes, my dear. You are the missing link. Not only did your people make us smarter, but they left a message there. One I've been on the brink of discovering. But I'm afraid that my brain is still not advanced enough."

Carter rested her other hand on top of Dr. Nathaniel's. "The Sun Gate," she said.

After Carter explained to Dr. Nathaniel what had happened at the ruins with Amara a few weeks prior, they decided to make a trek up together. Combining Carter's experience and Dr. Nathaniel's expertise, they had high hopes. Since their conversation she felt lighter in spirit. They would leave for Machu Picchu in three days. She thought this would be a great time to do some training with William. The only other time she had felt so connected was that first day in the training room. Since then, William refused to train her directly. She didn't think that would be the case now, and she was right. He was eager to train as well, and she wasn't sure if it was just that his craving to be around her was just as strong as her own.

William had found an abandoned apartment for them to practice in. The room looked like prewar era and hadn't been touched since then. The plaster was falling apart in the corners, revealing the brick and mud underneath. The wood floors creaked and were warped from wear and abuse. There were rectangular dark spots on the walls where paintings had hung for decades. Carter closed her eyes and imagined this room when it had been lived in. She felt the love and the family that had always gathered here—the comfort of the worn sofas, the nightly meals around the family dining table in the corner. She sniffed and could smell cooked potatoes. She heard the music from an old radio where an old man and woman had danced together, the laughter shared over practical jokes that the dad would play on the mom, and the kids giggling behind the sofa. This apartment, this home, was loved, and it caressed her like a soft, tender kiss. When she opened her eyes, she was even startled to find herself in the abandoned room, though the smells and sounds lingered. She turned to see William watching her.

"What did you see?"

"Everything," she said.

He just nodded and then turned and walked over to the CD player he had brought with him. He placed it on the windowsill and hit the play button. The music that came through was definitely tango, but it had an electric, modern feel to it.

She liked it but didn't understand the purpose. "I thought we were training."

"We are." He walked over to her and took her hand, feeling that electrical surge again. "Have you ever danced the tango?" he asked.

She laughed because she didn't think he was serious, but then by the expression on his face quickly realized he was—that and the hurt feelings that were surging through her from him.

"Sorry, no. I can't dance."

"Everyone can dance. We are all as one," he said, and she just looked at him quizzically. "Just follow my lead, but as you did that first day in training. Don't try to predict my next move, but feel it."

She took a deep breath to center herself, closing her eyes and taking in the room again. Soon, her body was responding and knowing what to do as long as she didn't allow herself to think. This was easy because her senses were consumed by the room, by William, and by the intoxicating music. When she opened her eyes, she locked contact with William and became consumed by their dance. He was right. She knew how to dance; it was impossible not to.

Not only was she able to follow his lead, as he put it, she was able to dance the tango with him. Their steps were perfectly mirrored, sensual, and graceful, as if they were each other's reflection. The rhythm of their heartbeats danced, as did their breath. The world ceased to exist in each step they took as the room around them brightened to a perfect clarity. Without the need to look around, she could see the fine cracks in the plaster, felt the small spider web in the corner of the windowsill, and felt the dirt basement beneath their feet. Yet at the same time, the only thing that existed was she and William dancing the most beautiful dance on earth. It was impossible to understand how this was happening.

It was as if she had been walking through a fog the last twenty-six years and had just broken through to the clearing. The song ended, and William let go of Carter's hand, breaking the spell. She looked around as if she had been shocked into awakening.

"What's happening?" she asked in a panicked tone.

"You're awakening," William said, concerned by her panic.

"That's what it feels like." Carter took a deep breath, trying to calm herself. "Why did it suddenly stop when you let go of my hands?"

"Because you thought it would."

"What?"

"You are in control over everything. Your thoughts are matter and can be measured. Not by any human device, but there is a very real definition to all our thoughts, and it manipulates the environment around us, which can be measured as well."

"What, like the force?" Carter asked, dumbfounded.

William chuckled. "Ya, pretty much," he said.

"What? You're serious? Is George Lucas an Anunnaki?" Carter couldn't take much more.

"No, no, he just got lucky." William kept trying to hide his laughter unsuccessfully, and Carter breathed out a sigh of relief. "Why, because *that* would be too much to handle?"

Her stare was relentless, and then they both broke out into uncontrollable fits of laughter, collapsing onto the floor.

Carter lay there staring up at the cracks on the ceiling. This place felt safe and she didn't want to leave, but she could tell by the way the shadows were getting long on the walls that soon they would lose their light.

"I don't know what you're thinking," William said indifferently.

Carter turned her face toward his voice, contemplating those words. "I'm not really thinking anything," she finally responded.

"Hmm." William abruptly turned and rested on his forearm, staring down at Carter. "Ready for your next lesson?" he said with childlike excitement.

She smiled, his giddiness spreading through her. "Definitely!" She hopped up and stood there waiting for whatever was next. It was when he was about to place his hands in hers that she saw the dark shadow dart across the room. She was so startled that she stumbled back and fell to the floor, feeling her heart race in her chest. She looked up at William to see if he knew what it was, but it was clear that he hadn't seen it. "What was that?" she asked.

He turned around to the direction she was pointing and then turned back to her. "What was what?"

"You didn't see that?" she said, her eyes practically bulging out of her face at the realization that this wasn't part of his next lesson. It was then that she saw another dark shadow dart across the room behind William toward the windowsill. "William!" she shrieked, staggering back to her feet. The dark shadows had a distinct human outline to them, but the limbs tapered into points and were wispy.

"Carter, calm down. What's going on? Talk to me."

Carter felt William's heart start to race as well, which only escalated her own panic. Feeling each other's thoughts and emotions didn't work out so well in high-stress situations, she thought.

"I saw shadows." She paused, shuddering at the memory. "Human shaped, two of them. They darted past you." It was the feeling that they weren't alone, that someone or something was listening to her that sent shivers down her spine and raised the hair on her skin. Carter kept thinking she was seeing things from the corners of her eyes, but anytime she looked in that direction, there was nothing there. She was on edge, and every little movement, or lack of movement, had her jumping out of her skin. She wanted to leave the apartment, but she was frozen in fear. Somehow, the idea of going back into the hallway and out the door seemed like an impossible journey.

That was when William jumped back and stood to the side of Carter. "What? What did you see?" Now she freaked out at his reaction.

"I thought I saw someone in the doorway watching us," he said, brushing his hands through his hair, clearly trying to calm his own nerves.

"Don't *say* that!" she whispered, feeling as if his words were only going to make it that much more true.

"Ok, we're just working each other up, feeding off of each other's energy. That's all. This isn't anything. We just need to get out of here into some fresh air."

"Who are you trying to convince? Me or you?" she said, clearly knowing exactly how scared William was as well. "Okay." She relented. "You go first," she said.

William furrowed his brow and pressed his lips together. For a moment Carter thought he was never going to move, but he started walking through the door, and Carter clung to his arm. They stepped out into the hall, and from the corner of her eye, she saw a ghostly white man standing at the end of the hall. She would have screamed if she hadn't stumbled over something that felt like a limb. From the corner of her eye, she could see the man taking a step toward her. Not wanting to look to confirm what she had stumbled over or confront the man at the end of the hall, Carter took off running full speed out the front door with her hands over her ears.

Getting out of the apartment onto the street was like being able to breathe again. Her safe haven apartment was suddenly a place she never wanted to go back to ever again. She stood in the middle of the road bent over with her hands on her knees, trying to catch her breath and calm her heart. She felt William standing there next to her, doing the same.

"What the heck was that?" he asked.

She looked to see him staring back at the apartment. Carter looked back over her shoulder at the apartment and the front door still wide open.

"Shouldn't we close that?" she asked.

"Yeah, we should," William said. Neither of them moved.

"What are you doing?" Carter asked.

"Hoping for a gust of wind or something that will shut it."

Carter stood there for a moment and then looked up at William's unchanging stance. "I don't think there's any gust of wind coming."

He started to chew on the corner of his mouth, and she felt him trying to build up the nerve to walk up and close the door.

"We can't just leave the door open. We have to close it," she said, hoping to encourage him to get this over with. They both stared at the front door again, trying to come up with a solution. As if in response, the front door opened further, and the wood floors creaked in the doorway, an invisible someone standing there. The porch creaked, and Carter knew whatever was in the house was now coming down the front steps toward them.

"No, we don't," William said, and they both took off running down the street. They ran the two miles back home without stopping and came bursting through the kitchen door, startling Jack, who was in the middle of reading through some of the papers from Dr. Nathaniel.

He sat there staring at the spectacle of William and Carter huffing and puffing in the middle of the kitchen, holding onto each other while they caught their breath. Jack's forehead scrunched up as he mistook their breathlessness. He ignored them and went back to reading the paper.

"We were just in a haunted apartment, or something," Carter explained.

Jack looked back up from the paper quizzically. "You were where?" he asked, and noticing William for the first time, added, "Are you *scared*?"

Carter felt William shift uncomfortably and stand straighter to her. She rolled her eyes.

"Um, well I don't know what we saw really," Carter said.

Jack turned to Will, but William just shrugged.

"Why don't you start from the beginning?" Jack said.

Carter and William took turns sharing the story from beginning to end. Jack sat patiently throughout the whole thing, nodding in some areas, asking a few questions here and there, but otherwise seemingly unfazed.

"Well, let's go back and check it out," Jack said, pushing his chair back from the table.

"I'm seriously not liking this country," Carter mumbled as she crossed her arms in front of her. "Are we really going back there?" she asked.

Now it was William's turn to shrug. She was going to have to adapt to the indifference that seemed to being running rampant among the men here in Peru.

They made the walk back to the apartment, no one saying anything. Carter wasn't sure what Jack hoped to accomplish, but her anxiety slowly increased with each step. She didn't want to go back; she didn't want to see the shadows again. The bottom line was that the shadows scared her, and she wanted no part of it.

When they got to the apartment, the front door was still open. Jack walked up the steps and right through the door, and Carter admired his courage. She watched in amazement as William followed right on his heels. If he was afraid anymore, he was doing a great job hiding it.

Carter huffed under her breath as she reluctantly followed them up the steps. The hair on her arms instantly stood up on end, and the feeling of being watched returned. She stepped between William and Jack, who were both looking around the room.

A sound of creaking floorboards nearly sent her running back out the front door. Jack walked through the threshold to the hallway looking for the source of the sound.

"Who's here?" Jack yelled to no one in particular.

"Don't ask that," Carter whispered.

"Why?" He looked at her.

"What if someone answers?" she replied.

"That's the point," he said.

The shadow passed in front of the doorway again, behind Jack.

"Jack!" she shrieked.

"What?" He turned around, but the shadow was gone.

"I saw that," William said. Just then the radio that William and Carter had left behind turned on to full volume, blasting static. William went to turn the volume down, but Carter stopped him.

"Wait." She tilted her head, listening carefully to the voices on the radio. "What are those voices saying?"

Jack shrugged. "Just caught in between stations."

"No," she said. "Listen carefully."

All three approached the radio to get a closer listen. "Sssssstttop," a voice spoke loudly over the other voices, and for some reason it sounded familiar. Carter felt as if she were falling through a dark abyss. "The vaticatessssssssssss." The voice hissed through the crackling speakers.

The radio abruptly shut off, and the rooms felt cold and empty. She knew they were now alone.

"You're not buying that crap, are you?" Jack asked.

"Jack, what I saw and felt can't be faked." She rubbed her arms, feeling cold. Jack shrugged and left the apartment. William and Carter followed, neither saying a word.

Later that evening Carter softly knocked on Jack's door. "Jack, I have to tell you something," she said as he opened the door. "That voice on the radio? I know that voice."

CHAPTER 17

ᛁᚤ ᚲ ᚲᛁᚲ ᛁᚤᛁ ᚺᛁᚤᛁ ᚾ ᛁᛖ ᛁᚲ ᚲᛁᛁᚺ ᛁᚤᚲ ᚺᛁᛖ ᚲᛁᚤ

C ARTER STARED AT HER DREARY closet, depressed. She had nothing to wear to dinner. Jack was taking her out under the pretense of a date so she could talk to him about what she thought the voice was. She knew it was just a cover so they could have some privacy, but she couldn't help but feel a thread of hope.

Carter was sitting on her bed wrapped in her towel when a soft knock interrupted her thoughts. She opened the door after wrapping the towel around her tighter.

She couldn't help but smile. Jack stood in the doorway wearing a neatly pressed soft gray suit and white button-down shirt. The suit sat on his well-built body perfectly.

"You look very handsome, Jack."

"Why aren't you dressed? Did you change your mind?"

"No…I uh…have nothing to wear." Carter frowned. "Hard to believe I was ever a fashion designer."

Just as she said that, Amara appeared in the door behind Jack with an armload of clothes.

"What are you doing here?" Carter asked.

"Well, I was going to buy you a dress since I figured you hadn't brought anything with you. But, well…I don't know anything about dresses," Jack explained.

"So he called me, and I have plenty of dresses," Amara said chipperly.

Carter stared in stunned silence.

"Well look at that," Jack joked. "We rendered her silent." He chuckled as he walked down the hall, yelling back, "I'll be downstairs waiting. Take your time!"

Amara ignored Carter's gaping expression and pushed around her, throwing the stack of clothes onto her bed. "I think blue," she said.

In less than half an hour, Carter was in a deep-blue wrap dress and barely there makeup. Amara watched approvingly as Carter pulled her hair up into a high ponytail, exposing her slender neck. She slipped the locket on that John had given her for her birthday in August, just after their arrival in South America.

"He won't be able to keep his hands off you," Amara said.

"It's not like that," Carter explained. "We're just taking a break from everything from one night." But Carter could tell by the expression on Amara's face that she didn't buy that story for a second.

Carter found Jack waiting downstairs just as he had said. When his eyes landed on her, his grin grew from ear to ear. She felt herself blush. When he held the door open to the waiting cab, Carter suddenly turned around, ran up the steps, and gave Amara a bear hug. "Thank you," she whispered. Amara looked at her friend, and they had a mutual understanding. The thank you was so much more than just the dress tonight, and the feeling was mutual. Maybe this country would grow on her after all.

They took a drive down to Lima to a quaint Creole restaurant. Carter had no idea how long they were there, but soon the servers were clanging plates around loud enough that it caused notice.

"Time to go?" Jack laughed.

Carter frowned, not wanting the night to end, not ready to return to their life of treachery. She hadn't even explained the voice yet, and Jack hadn't asked.

"We can go for a walk," he said, as if reading her mind.

They stepped out into the streets of Lima, and Carter saw Stan standing under a lamppost across the street from them. He gave her a nod as a greeting, and she smiled back.

"You think they were letting us go out without protection?" Jack said as he watched the exchange, giving his own hesitant smile to their guard.

"No, I suppose not," she said. As much as she understood the need for Stan's presence, it still put a damper on her night. It was difficult for Carter to find her joyous mood again, as she now felt that three was a crowd.

"Come on," he said, taking her hand and leading her back into the restaurant.

"Where are we going?" she asked, knowing full well they weren't heading back for more food. Even the servers looked stunned and slightly annoyed to see them return. Jack asked for another way out, saying an ex-boyfriend of hers was outside. One of the servers led them back through the kitchen and out the back door.

Carter knew that she should be stopping Jack from evading Stan, especially after John's death. But she so desperately needed an escape, a real escape. She needed a real human experience. The only problem was that part of her felt bad about eluding Stan because he was always really kind to her and just wanted to do a good job.

Jack sighed, and she wondered if maybe he was having the same internal battle. She was more in tune with Jack's energy now, but she wasn't as confident about his thoughts as she was with William. With William it was as if it were her own thoughts. Jack turned to look at her, and she thought she saw hunger in his eyes. Her body responded to it, warming to the inner depths.

They continued down the alley, and the nagging guilt gnawed at Carter, overlapped by her strong desire for escape. Jack led her to the edge of town, to the top of a hill that overlooked the homes below and their twinkling lights. It felt dangerous being exposed like this, but she didn't care—not at this moment.

The found a stone bench on the grassy knoll, and Carter noticed that Jack sat so that their bodies touched. He was so much harder to read than William and at times this frustrated her, but times like now she loved it.

"What are you thinking about?" Jack asked.

Carter blushed. "Just about how you're a hard person to read." At least it was partly true.

"You think I'm hard to read?"

Carter laughed softly. "I *know* you're hard to read."

"Don't you have some telepathic ability you're developing?"

"And even with that, I find you hard to read." It was honest.

"Why do you think that is?"

She thought about that, and she did not know. The silence dragged on, and she realized she would never answer the question.

"I didn't bring you out here to make out with you, ya know?"

Speaking of honesty. His blunt statement froze her, and she didn't know how to react.

"Um, thanks?"

Jack laughed. "No, trust me, I want to." He paused, realizing he said too much. "Carter, I'm not going to do anything until you know what you want."

She watched Jack's profile, wanting to tell him she knew what she wanted, but she didn't. He was right.

"Hey, don't worry. I'm not going anywhere. You already know you can't get rid of me." He laughed, but Carter could hear the strain in it. She leaned in to him as he wrapped his arms around her shoulders. She noticed how easily she fit in his arms and wished her heart could be loyal to Jack. But when William was around, she lost herself.

"Thanks, Jack, for everything."

"Hey, so are we going to talk about this voice, or was that a ploy just to get me out here all to yourself?"

Carter laughed, but a shiver ran through her body.

Jack pulled away to look at her. "Hey, you okay?"

"I don't know." She sat perfectly still, gathering her thoughts. She could hear sirens in the distance, a car horn blaring, laughter from women, and somewhere not too far, a dog barking. They were normal sounds of the town, she thought, but the voice in her mind was far from normal, and she had no way of explaining it.

Jack took her hand in his and squeezed it.

"Part of me thinks I'm losing my mind," she said as he turned to face her directly. "I keep having dreams, but I don't know what they are, yet they leave me feeling foggy all day. Now I'm having moments when I get completely disoriented and blank out. When it happens, I end up feeling really irritated and irrational—everything upsets me." She sighed heavily.

Jack remained quiet as he traced invisible circles on her hand with his thumb. She found it soothing.

"And then the other part of me thinks that something dark is seeping into my mind, and I can't stop it. Like, it's not really me that's losing my mind. That I'm being invaded."

Jack stopped tracing circles, and Carter watched as his body became rigid.

"You don't have to do this, Carter. We can take you home, take it slower. Too much has been happening, and we don't even know your involvement in everything."

"That may not be such a bad idea." The voice came from behind Jack and Carter near the bushes. She hadn't even heard him approach. Jack and Carter shot to their feet, and Jack was the first to speak.

"What are you doing here?" he asked.

"I come in peace." Jibril chuckled. "Wait, isn't that your line?" He pointed at Carter and then let out a boisterous laugh.

Carter frowned. They were in a dark park, and there was not a person in sight. They had walked into their own death trap, completely unarmed and helpless.

"What do you want?" she asked.

"You're alone," he said jovially.

"Maybe," she said.

"Well, I have some information that I thought you could use."

"Like hell you do," Carter spat.

Jibril just chuckled at her as if she were throwing a temper tantrum. "Well then, if you're so confident, I guess Ill be going."

Carter balled up her fists at her sides, grinding her teeth together. "What do you want, Jibril?"

Jibril handed her a black-and-white eight-by-ten photo.

"Is this your sister?" Carter asked.

Jibril nodded.

"I don't understand. What do I want with a picture of your sister?"

"I guess you've never met the great Gregory Moretti."

"Get on with it," Jack hissed.

Jibril turned to Jack, smiling. "I see you still are as joyous as ever, sweet cheeks."

Carter heard Jack grumble under his breath and didn't miss his fists balling up. She rested her hand on his arm, mentally begging him to remain calm. His posture relaxed slightly.

"Gregory Moretti is your boy William's father."

"Why are they together?" Carter asked.

"That's what I would like to know as well."

"You're telling us you don't know why your sister is with William's father? If that's even his father?" Jack asked.

"It's his father, and you will do your research to confirm it is."

"Why come to us," Carter asked, "if this isn't a setup?"

"Because you want to know, don't you? As do I." Jibril shrugged, as if it were the most obvious answer ever.

"After what you did to John, you can rot in hell, and so can your sister." Carter felt her face flush with anger.

"You think that I did that to John?" Jibril said.

"If you didn't, who did?" Carter asked.

"You didn't listen to a word I said when I called you the other night, did you? Just like you didn't listen the first time I called you before Bohemian Grove."

Carter felt her heart sink as that truth smacked her in the face. Jack tensed again next to her, and she was sure it was because she had been withholding information from him.

"It was the reptilians," Jibril said simply.

☆   ☆   ☆

STAN PACED THE SMALL KITCHEN floor endlessly while making calls to everyone he knew in Peru. Rafe crouched in the corner, rubbing his temples in frustration. Carter and Jack had been gone nearly twenty-four hours since Stan had last seen them, and they were making no progress in their search. They spoke to the server at the restaurant, who led them to the alley, and they even found a few people who had seen them running toward the edge of town. However, their trail went cold after that.

☆   ☆   ☆

CARTER STILL DIDN'T KNOW IF she could trust Jibril with what he had just said, and she was pretty confident that she shouldn't. But a huge part of her, mostly instinct, said that Jibril was being honest. Jibril said he would be in contact in twenty-four hours, though didn't say how. Carter and Jack had until then to decide what to do.

He was giving them twenty-four hours and the freedom to choose. Already he was out of character of the Jibril she knew.

"His sister is all he has left," Carter said as Jack locked the dead bolt to the room they rented behind the American bed-and-breakfast in Lima.

"I know," Jack said. "So he's going to be a little more desperate."

Carter nodded; Jack was already thinking along the same lines. "So what do we do? Do we just go back and act as if nothing has happened?

"I don't think we have much of a choice until we know more."

"Do you think William knows his father is talking to Amelia?" Carter asked, afraid of the answer.

"If that's even his father," Jack said. "That's the first thing we need to confirm."

Carter already knew it was his father. It had to be. They had already come up with an idea on how to check, and it would involve Carter flirting with William. Under normal circumstances that was not hard to do, but it meant she had to be deceitful, and she wasn't sure she could pull it off.

"And then what?"

Jack sat on the bed facing her, rubbing his chin. "Well, we need to come up with a story for why we went missing for so long."

"We can just say that we both needed a break from everything and went to the park and just fell asleep."

"They won't buy it."

"They'll have to." Carter thought for a beat. "And it's only half a lie."

"I've never known you to lie before," Jack said, his eyes suddenly intense.

"I've never known me to do a lot of things I've already been doing." And that much was at least the whole truth.

"I think that if we find out that William's father really is talking to Amelia, then we need to find out why," Jack said, and Carter nodded in agreement.

"I think we should also talk to Dr. Nathaniel."

"Why Dr. Nathaniel?"

"The night before Bohemian Grove, remember when Jibril called me in Santa Barbara?" When Jack nodded, she continued. "Well, he warned me about Bohemian Grove. I didn't realize it at the time, at least not until something he said tonight."

"Yeah, the phone call you didn't tell me about." Jack frowned.

"Yeah, sorry. There have been some distractions, you know. But anyway, the other night he called me, and when I got mad at him about John, he said I make wrong assumptions. Now I know what he was referring to, if that was true."

"Do you think it's true?"

"I do, Jack. I don't know why, but I do."

"I do too."

"Well, he said that Dr. Nathaniel didn't know what he was getting himself into. I think we need to speak with him, and I think we need to tell him about Jibril."

Jack stiffened. "I don't think that's a good idea."

"I don't think we have a choice. Who else can we go to?"

Jack frowned at her. She was right and he knew she was, but he didn't like the idea of telling anything to anyone yet.

"Jack?"

"Hmm?"

"Can I sleep next to you tonight?" She felt silly asking, but she needed him next to her. Her dreams were draining her, and she felt more lost than ever.

CHAPTER 18

𒌋 𒀸 𒆠𒀸 𒌋𒀭 𒈬𒉌 𒅖 𒅆 𒌋 𒈠 𒅂𒉌 𒌋 𒈬 𒊩𒅆 𒆠𒀭

NEITHER OF THEM GOT MUCH sleep. Carter kept thinking about what to expect when they returned, how she was going to get a picture of William's father, what Jibril had said, and the million other things happening in her life.

They both walked slowly back to the house, neither of them wanting to face anyone. So when they rounded the corner of the house and literally ran into Rafe, knocking him clear to the ground, it was no surprise that things were worse than expected.

"Where the hell were you guys?"

"We fell asleep in the park," Carter said, and by the look on Rafe's face, she knew he didn't buy their story for a second. Maybe she should have listened to Jack and come up with a better story.

Rafe dragged them into the house to a mix of reactions from Paulo, William, Stan, and even Amara. Amara was just relieved to see Carter and embraced her in a bear hug, reminding Carter that Amara was her only friend in the group who was just that—a friend. Stan had a look of relief, and Paulo looked angry. William, for the first time since Carter had met him, was unreadable. She couldn't sense any energy from him, and it confused her.

"What you did was not only irresponsible for yourself, but for your line," Rafe started in.

"Last time I checked, I was an adult who got to decide what I did or didn't do. Besides, Jack was with me." She turned to Jack, who just stood there watching everyone like a cat. It kind of turned her on. "And if you don't mind, it's been a long night, and I'm tired. I'm going to bed." Her own bravado not only startled her but everyone around her. She heard Jack mumble that he was getting rest too as he followed her up the stairs.

She paused in the doorway to her room. "Jack, I feel as if I'm always thanking you—for being here, for helping me."

"I'm here by choice." He smiled one his genuine crinkly smiles she loved so much. "That was nice downstairs."

She tilted her head at him, and he just kept smiling.

"I'm going to sleep for a few hours, and then we should go see Dr. Nathaniel," Jack said as he turned to leave. Carter nodded in agreement.

When they left to meet Dr. Nathaniel, the house was quiet—all except for Rafe. He surprisingly didn't ask questions or offer guard. Strange. When they called Dr. Nathaniel's home, he said he would be happy to meet them and gave them directions. He also mentioned that he had something to share with them anyway. Carter was curious.

Dr. Nathaniel's home was exactly what you would expect of a doctor and professor of quantum mechanics: a comfortable home with endless books. He had to move some books around just so Jack and Carter could sit on the plush leather sofas. Carter scanned the spines of the books, frowning when she couldn't even understand the titles.

"I wanted to show you something, Carter," he said as he shuffled through a chaotic pile of papers on a love seat. "Ah, here it is."

She took the paper from him and looked at the graphs. "I don't know what any of this means."

"I think I figured out what your role is in everything."

"You're kidding me," Carter said. Jack leaned forward on his elbows, trying to decipher the lines on the paper she held.

"Have you heard of the light particle theory?" he asked and continued after Jack and Carter stared blankly. "OK, so let's say you have a light beam." Dr. Nathaniel pulled out a penlight from his pocket and shone it into a crystal globe that sat on the coffee table. Carter noticed the light beam dispersed into three separate beams—two on the table and one above the globe on Dr. Nathaniel's dress shirt. "This is a theory of parallel universe."

"The light is?" Jack asked.

Dr. Nathaniel eagerly nodded. "Yes. Imagine that our universe has a source. Imagine our universe is just a membrane to a complex larger system. The source of this membrane is singular like this light beam here." Dr. Nathaniel pointed to the light coming directly from the penlight. "And the universe, our universe, is this beam here." Dr. Nathaniel now pointed to one of the light beams reflected onto the coffee table. "This light beam here represents another universe," he said as he pointed to the other beam reflecting on the table. "What's the difference in the two light beams here?" he asked.

"Nothing?" Carter was confident that wasn't the answer, but she tried.

"Exactly," he said.

She smiled.

"These light beams are parallel."

Jack nodded approvingly. "This is a theory?"

"It's a theory, correct. But it's quite plausible, and I also believe it's the key to what you are doing here," he said to Carter.

"Now you lost me again," Jack said.

"Carter, what did they say to you? The Anunnaki?"

"They said I'm the last of my line."

"But I don't think they meant it literally. You're the last of the line that Enki made, or genetically altered. You were a part of his mission that he never got to complete. Well, you figuratively."

"Genetically altered is what the tree of life symbolized," Carter recalled.

"Exactly. Who was at the tree of life besides Adam and Eve?"

"The serpent," Carter said as everything came together. "And the serpent is Enki."

"I still don't see how this has anything to do with a parallel universe," Jack said, and Carter nodded in agreement.

"Ah yes, that's the best part."

A knock on the door made all three of them jump.

"I'm not expecting anyone else; are you?" Dr. Nathaniel asked.

Jack and Carter shook their heads.

"You don't think?" Carter asked Jack. It hadn't been twenty-four hours yet.

Dr. Nathaniel got up to answer the door.

"I'm early."

Jack and Carter stood up at the sound of the familiar voice.

"I'm sorry; and you are...?" Dr. Nathaniel asked.

"I'm Jibril, and you must be the good doctor." There was a long pause, and Carter wished she could see around the corner to see the doctor and Jibril. She followed Jack as he went to the door.

"Ah, there are my two lovebirds," Jibril said from the doorway.

"We aren't lovebirds," Jack said. Though Carter wasn't sure if it was more to Jibril or to himself.

"Not yet," Jibril retorted. "I've come to find out what you know."

"Nothing," Carter said quickly.

Carter recalled sneaking into William's room earlier that day while he showered and going through his wallet. Fortunately, he had a folded-up photo of him and what looked like his parents—the same man in the photo with Amelia. Still, she wasn't ready to face the possibilities of what that meant—and certainly not with Jibril.

"Come in," Dr. Nathaniel said. Carter and Jack briefly stared at each other, and Jack shrugged. Like that, their decision had been made.

Jibril walked right into the living room and looked around, immediately honing in on the paper that Dr. Nathaniel had for them. It was suspicious, but when Jibril just stared at it confused and then tossed it aside, Carter's suspicions subsided.

Jibril then did the most curious thing. He sat cross-legged on the floor. "So, what are we talking about?" he asked casually.

"Parallel universe and light particle theory," Jack sarcastically replied.

Jibril nodded as if he understood what he meant. "So you think that Carter can contact the Anunnaki by parallel universe? What makes her the special link?"

Even Dr. Nathaniel's mouth dropped open.

"What? You think this one's the only doctor around here?" Jibril said as he pointed to Dr. Nathaniel.

"Get out of town," Carter said.

"Come sit next to me, buttercup." Jibril patted the floor next to him as he watched Jack. Jack responded by leaning against the chair back and folding his arms. Dr. Nathaniel studied Jibril and Jack curiously, as if they were specimens under a microscope. Perhaps they were. "So what's the link?" Jibril asked again.

"You're really a doctor?" Carter asked, curiosity getting the best of her.

Jibril nodded. "Well, not a doctor doctor. Not like a band-aid-type doctor. I have a doctorate in molecular biology and particle forensics. I haven't done much with it." He paused, regarding Carter. "You didn't think I'd climb the Vaticate ladder with a GED, didja?"

He had a point.

"Carter is the missing link," Dr. Nathaniel cut in, "because of her DNA manipulation."

Carter frowned. "All humans have gone through DNA manipulation, Carter. That's what the Anunnaki did. Yours just has a key—literally," Dr. Nathaniel said.

To an extent she understood this, but now that it had been explained, it seemed too simple. "So what's next?" Carter asked.

"I'll need a blood sample," Dr. Nathaniel said as Jibril nodded in agreement.

"And why exactly do you get to play a part in all this?" Jack asked Jibril.

Jibril leaned over, almost as if posing like a playgirl, and even went so far as to bat his eyelashes. Carter didn't know if she was entirely amused by Jibril or completely disgusted.

"Because you need me," Jibril said.

"For what?" Dr. Nathaniel asked.

"To restore the Vaticates to the Brotherhood of the Snakes' core mission," he said, once again shocking the trio.

"You want to restore the Vaticates?"

Jibril sat contemplating and then burst out laughing. Carter crossed her arms in front of her, annoyed at the inappropriate display. As quickly as he had begun laughing, he abruptly stopped and turned and sat on his knees, facing Carter. His eyes glistened with a depth of emotion Carter knew she would never understand—assaulted with pain, sorrow, anguish, and devastating sadness as if hit by a mac truck. It literally knocked her back. Jack and Dr. Nathaniel moved quickly to help her, but she held her hand out to stop them. She did not know how Jibril had done what he just did, but she was in no danger, she knew. It was his sadness she felt. It was his pain she felt. It was everything that drove him mad and sane at the same time. It choked her soul, and she knew with every fiber that this was the pain he lived with daily. When she finally looked up to meet his eyes and saw him staring intensely at her, she realized her decision had been made.

"What the hell is going on? Carter?" Jack's voice was barely contained.

"I'm fine." She took a deep breath. "Jibril was just sharing something with me."

Then, as if nothing else could shock the group, Jibril took Carter's hand in his delicately and kissed her palm. "You can bring me my son back. Not in the way everyone thinks, but you can help me."

"You just want a glimpse of him living a life in a parallel world to ours. You just want to see him alive one more time," she stated, understanding. "I don't know if I can do that," she whispered heavily, her heart sad with that fact.

"I know, but you can try, can't you? That alone will give me more than I've had since I lost him."

And for that brief moment, Carter saw the Jibril that was. She saw his life before it had so devastatingly changed for the worse.

"I can try," she promised.

And now she knew what faith was.

"You're so much like your mother," he said to her, and she knew exactly what he was referring to. It was the compassion that set her apart from her alien race and made her so human. Maybe she could bridge the gap between the Anunnaki and the Vaticates. Maybe her working with Jibril was the key.

Or maybe she was walking right into a trap that would end her race forever.

CHAPTER 19

𒀸 ⟨ ⟨𒂊⟨ 𒂍𒉼 ⊣𒅎 𒐊 𒅀 𒂊⟨ ⟨𒅕⊢ 𒂍𒉼 ⟨ ⊣𒅀 ⟨𒂍𒉼

I T HAD BEEN THREE DAYS since they first met with Jibril and Dr. Nathaniel and three days since Carter left a vial of her blood to be tested and observed. It had been an interesting three days since she spent that time hanging out with William, trying to learn more about his father. She had gotten nowhere. It turned out William was pretty tightly sealed about his father, and Carter didn't know whether it was because they weren't close or because William had something to hide. The lack of information frustrated her.

"You OK?" Jack asked.

"Yeah, just wish I were able to find out more information about Mr. Moretti."

Jack and Carter were waiting near the park for Dr. Nathaniel, Stan, and Paulo so they could make their way up Machu Picchu. William and Rafe decided to stay behind and do some more research on the Brotherhood of the Snake.

They made it to the top at sunset, and as always, the beauty took Carter's breath away. She showed Dr. Nathaniel where she had seen the Sun Gate, and they spent the evening looking around, trying different things to see it again, but there was nothing. They set up camp, and Carter fell asleep in her sleeping bag before everyone had even settled in.

In her sleep, the Gate glowed bright like a beacon, beckoning her. She knew she was dreaming but could still grasp her surroundings. She ran her hands over the golden arch and felt the grooves of the deep carvings.

"Carter?"

She spun around to the familiar voice. "William? What are you doing here? I thought you were with Rafe."

"This is your dream, remember?"

"So why are you in my dream?"

"I think the better question is, why am I here?" he pointed to the arch.

"I don't understand."

"I can see the gate too."

Carter sat up gasping, surprised by the cold night air. It had been daytime in her dream, and the pitch darkness of the mountaintop, lit only by the glowing embers of the fire, was startling. She desperately wanted to talk to Dr. Nathaniel alone but wouldn't do it with Stan and Paulo nearby.

She spent the rest of the night thinking about her dream, wondering if it was just a regular dream. Yet a huge part of her knew it wasn't. She knew it was something they were missing.

The nervous energy only continued to build up in her as they made their way back to the house the next morning. Stan and Paulo kept trying to reassure her, thinking her anxiety was from the lack of progress on the mountaintop. When they did finally get back to the house, Carter offered to walk Dr. Nathaniel back to his home and asked Jack to escort her. She hoped that no one would think anything of it and let her go. They did.

Dr. Nathaniel and Jack sat silent after she explained her dream. She began to think they thought nothing of her dream.

"We need to figure out how to get his blood sample," Dr. Nathaniel said.

"What are you trying to figure out?" Jack asked.

"I have a theory."

"Which is?"

"I'll let you know once I test his blood."

"I have an idea," Carter said.

CHAPTER 20

𒂍 𒐊 𒂊𒐊 𒂍𒅀 𒀝 𒅍 𒅀𒂍 𒂊𒐊 𒀀𒅍 𒂍𒐊 𒐊 𒀀𒅉 𒂊𒅀

G ETTING WILLIAM'S BLOOD SAMPLE WAS almost too easy. Carter told William that Dr. Nathaniel needed to compare her blood to normal Anunnaki blood and figure out if there was anything different about her DNA. Stan, the only other Anunnaki with them, wasn't around, so William was the only likely choice. It was almost too easy, and it made Carter realize that perhaps William wasn't hiding anything from her, at least not deliberately.

Dr. Nathaniel had just left with the sample when William walked up to Carter, pressing her against the kitchen counter. Their electric charge surged through her body, reminding her of all the physical connections they had.

"Are you okay?" William asked.

"Ya, why?"

"You just seem distracted lately," he said as he watched her lips. She felt that familiar warmth spread through her, settling in the bottom of her belly.

"Just thinking about everything."

He nodded, half paying attention to what she said. "I miss you, you know."

"William? I'm here every day."

"No, you're here." He took her hand in his, clasping it affectionately. "But we're not here." He pressed his palm against her chest, over her rapidly beating heart.

The door to the kitchen began to open, breaking their reverie. William stepped away from her quickly and went up the stairs, leaving her breathless and confused.

Jack stood in the doorway, completely aware that he had interrupted something. Almost happening was what scared Carter.

"I saw Dr. Nathaniel on the way up here, and he said he got the vial." Jack's tone was sad.

"Ya, it was easy to get." She flinched at how that sounded.

"I'm sure," Jack said and went up the stairs to his room.

CHAPTER 21

𒐫𒁹𒐈𒁹𒐈𒁹𒐫𒁹𒐊 𒈬 𒐊𒁹 𒐈𒐊𒐖𒁹𒐫𒐊𒁹𒐖 𒐫𒁹

SHE RAN THE ENTIRE WAY to Dr. Nathaniel's house after he called with the results. The shaking of his voice made her nervous, and he wouldn't delay any longer. When she got to his house, she was surprised to see Jibril had beaten her there. She wished Jack were with her, but Dr. Nathaniel thought it was better that she know the information first. She was curious, to say the least.

"What took you so long?" Jibril asked, chuckling. She frowned at him in response.

"This way." Dr. Nathaniel reappeared from a room at the end of a hall.

Jibril swept his arm out, letting Carter walk first. Normally she would appreciate the chivalry. But considering the source, she thought it was anything but, even after the way he had opened up to her just a week prior.

When Carter stepped into Dr. Nathaniel's lab, she gasped in awe.

"Dr. Nathaniel, this is amazing!" she cheered.

It was a lab from a movie. Beams of light shone through dust particles in the air, reflecting all different-colored vials and bottles. Streaming lights of colors bounced off the walls like a rainbow. There were hundreds of bottles and vials everywhere, stacked on top of old ancient books. Dr. Nathaniel watched Jibril and Carter take everything in. She picked up a book off the shelf, pulled open the cover, and looked at the print details.

"Eighteen eighty-six? You collect antique books?" Carter asked.

Dr. Nathaniel solemnly shook his head. Jibril gently took the book from her hand as he said, "No, you bought them new. Didn't you?"

And again, Dr. Nathaniel slowly shook his head.

"Eighteen eighty-six?" She paused, doing the math in her head. "I don't understand, how is that possible? No one is that old. And you don't even look like you're a day over sixty."

"That's part of what I want to explain to you," the doctor said. "But first, the reason why you came here."

He led Carter to a microscope on the table. "I have a slide already placed there. Please take a look."

She could tell it was a blood sample but didn't know what she was looking at. "I don't know what to look for."

"That's okay, you will," Dr. Nathaniel said. He gave Jibril a chance to take a look at the slide. He didn't seem to notice anything unusual about it, or if he did, he didn't say anything.

She looked at the second slide he provided. "It looks the same to me."

"Exactly."

Jibril looked at the slide and asked, "This can't be William's sample, is it?"

"It is."

Jibril looked at the slide again. "That changes things, doesn't it?"

"What does?" Carter asked.

"Your blood is identical," Dr. Nathaniel explained, as if it would mean something to her. Carter raised her eyebrows in question. "We picked up William's blood so I could try to identify how your DNA is different and see if we could unlock the key to that difference. What we found may even be better, at least for now."

"That might explain why Mr. Moretti has been meeting with my sister," Jibril said. Dr. Nathaniel nodded in agreement, but Carter could tell this was the first time he had considered that.

"I don't know what you two are going on about."

"Carter, you two have the exact same DNA structure."

"We're related?" Carter felt sick.

"No, no." Dr. Nathaniel jumped in quickly, but not before Jibril appeared completely amused. "It means that you're not the last living Anunnaki with the key."

"So they've been lying to me?" Carter asked.

"I don't think they knew. Well, maybe Greg Moretti did," Jibril thought out loud.

That was the first time Carter had heard his first name and wondered just how much Jibril knew about everyone.

"What are you thinking, Jibril?" Carter asked.

"I'm thinking that somehow Greg Moretti knows his son is unique..." Jibril stopped as he thought of something else. "Wait—what line are the Morettis? They shouldn't—ahhh, that's good, that's very good." Jibril started laughing as Dr. Nathaniel and Carter watched him curiously.

"Jibril?" Carter tried for his attention.

"Maybe William isn't really his son." Jibril smiled. "If his mom had an affair with someone in your line, then the DNA key would be there."

"Someone still alive?" Carter asked, still fearing that she was somehow related to William.

Jibril shook his head. "Doubtful."

"What male has been alive in the last thirty-five years from her line who could be William's real father?" Dr. Nathaniel asked.

"That shouldn't be too hard to figure out," Jibril said. "There have been fewer than a dozen just in the last eighty." Jibril went over to the computer again. "Mind if I use this? I can log into the Vaticates' log. They keep records of the lineage."

Carter was surprised that Jibril didn't argue when she and Dr. Nathaniel hovered over him as he searched records on the Vaticate computer.

"You guys know more about the Anunnaki than I do," Carter said.

Jibril nodded and laughed. "I think a five-year-old who does some Google research would know more, Carter. They aren't exactly forthcoming with information, are they?"

Carter blushed. He was right. They weren't forthcoming, and it wasn't right. There was no reason to hide things from her, and now she was wondering exactly how forthcoming they were with one another. It seemed the Anunnaki society and those who protected it might be even more corrupt than the Vaticates themselves.

The list that Jibril found for possible candidates for William's father was short, totaling three men—none living. This further confirmed their theory that no one knew that William was part of her line—no one except Greg Moretti.

Hutchinson H. Mead III
Clifford K. Hoffman
Leonard Daniel Summers

Non'iar to Carter. "Do you guys know any of them?" she asked.

"I know Clifford Hoffman," Dr. Nathaniel said. "We did our residency together in Chicago. I then went on to do research at Fermi. That's where I studied light particle theory."

"What year was that residency, Doctor?" Jibril asked mischievously.

Carter watched their exchange curiously and could tell Dr. Nathaniel was becoming visibly uncomfortable as he shifted around and ran his fingers through his hair repeatedly.

"There was something else you needed to tell me?" Carter remembered.

"I think you need to sit down for that one," Jibril said.

They went back to the living room, which was overrun with books—much like the rest of the home, Carter observed.

"I did residency with Clifford Hoffman after attending Northwestern University in Chicago in 1878. I was twenty-seven at the time."

"You're over 150 years old?" Carter gasped as Jibril chuckled.

"Sold his soul to the devil," Jibril sneered.

CHAPTER 22

𒌍 𒀭 𒌋𒁉 𒌍𒑐 𒌋𒉌𒉡 𒀻 𒄿𒌍 𒌍 𒌋𒁹𒉡 𒌍𒑐 𒌋𒉌 𒌋𒁉𒌍

C ARTER WALKED SLOWLY BACK TO the house, thinking about the last comment Dr. Nathaniel had made to her as she left.

Do not ignore your instincts. They are more than just intuition.

She also kept thinking about her most unlikely ally, Jibril. He promised he had nothing to do with John's death or Carl's—that he was at neither place during the time, and she believed him. He also didn't deny knowing of the incidents beforehand. She realized he still held back something important, though. The problem was she didn't know *how* important that something was and whether it was enough to keep her from working with him in the future.

She had learned more in the last few hours with Dr. Nathaniel and Jibril than she had from working with the Anunnaki in the last months. It was a fact she could not ignore.

"Carter?"

She looked up as Jack approached her. He frowned, and she knew he still thought about the last time he had seen her in an intimate space with

William. One thing she was relieved to find out was that she was not related to William. The three men who were candidates to be his real father were in no way related to her. At least there was that. That relief was mostly that she didn't want to think how close she had come to sleeping with a relative, but another part of it was that she also didn't know where her heart was. The conflict swam in her mind as she watched Jack's sad eyes.

"Hi Jack," she said sadly.

"You okay?" Regardless of what he saw, or whatever happened between them, she knew his first priority would always be her happiness and safety. That didn't make things any easier.

"I'm okay."

"You don't sound it."

She rubbed her eyes, exhausted. "I'm fine; I'm just tired. I'm going up to my room to take a nap."

✲ ✲ ✲

Jack watched as Carter walked into the house, closing the door behind her. He stood there for nearly an hour staring at the closed door. He fought with every part of his being, standing his ground. For what he really wanted to do was storm through the door and take Carter in his arms, shaking the reality into her that William was no good for her and that he was—he was what she needed. Yet a part of him did not even know how true that was. He could not tell if the growing hatred he had for William was just jealousy or something else gnawing at him.

✲ ✲ ✲

The dusty floor felt warm underneath her bare feet, a residual heat from the day's sun. With the large moon high in the night sky, the heat had long gone as the icy-cold air wrapped around her like a blanket. She watched her breath form ice crystals midair, yet her bare nightgown warmed her bones. She walked toward the light in the desert, which was drawing her like a moth to a flame. The blue and green spiraling light was the size of a large dinner plate, and Carter watched it, waiting. Through the light she saw the flame reveal her family on the other side—tall, beautiful, slender beings she hadn't seen in thousands of years. Her heart ached and yearned to reach out and embrace them. They did not see her.

She watched them in the golden kingdom of light and missed her home. They spoke in her mind.

No more, he whispered to her.

I know, she replied.

Why do you still seek? they whispered.

Because I still exist, she said.

We have lost her, they argued among one another.

I am being found, she reminded them.

She turned and faced the man beside her. *You created a key without permission,* she said.

"I made a mistake," he said out loud.

She nodded in agreement. "I am running out of time, Hutchinson."

He kissed her forehead. "I know."

✡ ✡ ✡

She knocked on Jack's door, realizing that the sun had not even risen. He opened it sleepily, rubbing at his eyes. He wore light cotton pajama pants and stood in the doorway in his bare feet and bare chest. The waistband of the pants hung low on his hips, and she couldn't pull her eyes away from the dips in flesh framing his hipbones.

"Carter?"

She blushed deeply, remembering why she had come to Jack. "I uh, I remembered one of my dreams," she whispered in a hoarse voice, her thoughts suddenly distracted.

"Do you want to come in?" He stepped aside.

When she did, she noticed the comforter in a twisted heap on the bed and his shirt on the floor. There was no place to sit except the bed or the dresser. She awkwardly chose the dresser. Jack sat on the bed, leaning on his elbows, brushing his hand through his hair.

She told him about the dream in the desert and then about her trip to see Dr. Nathaniel and Jibril. He seemed too calm as she explained it all and even surprised her when he didn't react to her seeing Jibril without any protection.

"Why are you so calm?"

"I trust you," he said.

She stood dumbfounded.

"What? Is that a surprise to you?"

"Well, actually it is."

Jack chuckled groggily. "So now what? What do you think we need to do?"

"I think we need to go to New Mexico."

"Okay."

Now Carter chuckled. Jack stood up and walked toward Carter and leaned in. Her heart sped up, drumming in her ears. Jack placed a light kiss on her forehead, lingering longer than necessary. "Now can I go back to sleep? Or do we need to leave now?"

"It can wait," Carter laughed nervously.

"Carter?" Jack said as she paused in the doorway. "So you think Hoffman is his dad?"

"I do."

He looked as if he wanted to say something else, so she waited. When he nodded, she turned and left his room, wondering what wasn't said.

CHAPTER 23

𒐊𒁹 𒐀 𒀗𒁹 𒐊𒁹 𒀀𒐊𒐊 𒈦 𒐊𒁹 𒐊𒁹 𒐀 𒈦𒁹 𒀀𒐊𒐊 𒐀𒁹 𒀀𒈦𒁹 𒀗𒁹

THE SUN FLOATED LIKE A kiss on the clouds. She leaned her head against the back of her chair, happy to finally be on a real airplane. Jack sat behind her, and she had the row to herself. Stan and Rafe sat in the seats to her right, fast asleep. Paulo was flying in to New Mexico later with Amara, who decided she had nothing left for her in South America and wanted to go. Paulo was helping her get a visa. Carter and Jack went to Dr. Nathaniel's house and let him know, and he said he would tell Jibril. Dr. Nathaniel would remain behind in Peru for now, working on finding the key.

The overhead "ding" from the airplane intercom startled her. The pilot announced their descent into Albuquerque, and Carter straightened up in her seat, slipping John's Bible back into her bag. She carried it with her because it made her feel he was still around. Ironic, she knew.

Carter moved to the seat behind her, ignoring the odd looks from William, who sat kitty-corner from her seat. She clutched Jack's hand, which was already damp.

He smiled at her but said nothing else. She knew his fear of flying was real, but she also knew that admitting it was harder. She would only sit with him and be there. A part of her was glad to be able to offer him at least something.

They rented an SUV and headed toward the Zuni reservation to the prearranged meeting point. They stepped out of the SUV and greeted the men in traditional native garb. Carter was amazed by the beauty of their clothes. Each piece was made with care and attention, with obvious endless hours of work. The man in the most elegant and adorned garb she guessed was the chief. She also knew by his posture that he was the leader.

Without realizing it, she found herself stepping toward this strange man. She was compelled to reach out to him, almost unable to retreat or contain her steps. He tilted his head like a curious animal as she stood mere inches from him.

"I know you," she whispered. She didn't know how. She couldn't place him, yet she knew him. With every fiber of her being, never having been so sure of anything in her life as she was at this moment, she knew this man. It was what he did next that sent her heart fluttering. He smiled. He smiled with his entire face. The creases at the corners of his eyes deepened, and the gray of his eyes sparked like a blue flame igniting. It was as if her soul had found what it had been searching for and did not know it had even been searching. He reached his hand out and cupped her face.

"Carter," he said as if answering an unspoken question. She closed her eyes against his touch, letting the bravado of his voice resonate in her mind.

"I know you," she repeated, trying to understand what was happening. She felt William standing next to her then, and she opened her eyes to see him watching this man in the same wonderment. As if what had been happening wasn't surprising enough, William embraced this Zuni man in a warm hug, and that set her back even more. The feeling of love was overwhelming to her—such an amazing and beautiful feeling that she never imagined could exist. Like love a mother would have for a child she followed from lifetime to lifetime. Something so profound it grew over centuries. Realizing then why part of this feeling was so familiar, she reached into her bag and pulled out the carved statue.

"I don't understand," Carter whispered.

"I don't either," William said.

"That makes three of us," Jack joined in, the only one not in awe of the incident. His eyebrows drew together, and he was annoyed.

"You all will," the chief said.

Three men dressed similarly stood apart from the group, as if on guard. Twenty feet behind them were two additional Zuni men on beautiful white horses, also donning what looked to be Zuni blankets, as they matched the pattern in the clothes of the men.

The feelings she got from them were also familiar and filled with affection, but not to the same extent as with the first man. Carter risked a glance back to see that William was only a few feet behind her, with Stan on his heels. She couldn't see the Zuni chief at all but knew he was somewhere in the group. She felt him—stronger than she had ever felt William. His presence was there as if he were standing before her eyes now.

They walked through the New Mexico desert as the sun began to set toward the reservation. The landscape was so vastly different that Carter kept finding herself in awe of it. The setting sun cast red, orange, and deep-blue shadows on the rocks and plateaus. She understood now why this was seen on so many postcards and backdrops. Carter reflected over the last year and the places she had seen, from the majestic redwood forest in northern California to the spiritual Machu Picchu ruins of Peru, and now to this red desert oasis.

"They are here with you," the Zuni man said over her shoulder. She didn't realize he was walking with her because she had been so enraptured by the scenery, yet his sudden presence didn't startle her.

Without turning to face him, she asked, "Who is here?"

"Your mother and father."

Carter's throat tightened in pain as she held back tears.

From the corner of her eye, she saw him wave his hand through the air in a sweeping motion. "What is death, when they live so strongly in your heart, in your eyes, in your memories? Death is an end. There was no end, only a change. You will learn."

"I didn't know my mother."

"You did. You just don't remember knowing her."

"I don't understand."

"You will. That is, after all, why you have come here. Is it not?" He smiled at her again. "And we will show you."

Carter stopped to turn to her new friend, searching his face—for what, she did not know. He gave away nothing. Eyes were on her as everyone stopped and watched them. The emotions coming off William were so strong she could feel them, surprised by the melancholy emotions he had. She ignored him, as she did not care why or what he was thinking at this moment; she would worry about that later.

"What is your name?" Carter asked, not knowing what else to say.

"Mankalita," he said, and then he gestured to the man to his right, who looked just as regal as he. "This is Onawa, my brother." Seeing Carter's expression, he chuckled softly.

"That's a mouthful," Carter said, blushing. "Can I call you Kalita?"

And the smile that took Carter's breath away the first time returned. "Yes, I think I would like that," Kalita said.

Onawa introduced the rest of the men to William and Carter. She desperately tried to put their names to memory, but it was impossible.

"This is impossible," Jack whispered to her as they started walking again toward the reservation, nightfall almost completely on them. Carter laughed softly.

✵   ✵   ✵

THE LAST OF THE SUN'S rays danced on the edges of the cliffs and mountains as the soft beat of a drum could be heard in the distance. William and Carter walked hand in hand over the last hill to the Zuni reservation. Firelight cast flickering shadows on the adobes of the natives and lit up the faces of the people sitting around the fire central to their village. Most of the faces wore expressions of seriousness, and others wore expressions of amusement from whatever stories were shared. It was a moment to behold, Carter thought. William squeezed her hand, mirroring her thoughts. They smiled softly to each other in recognition of the beauty before them. She realized then that both she and William were walking a path of familiarity, though she was sure he had never been to the reservation before. She turned to look at Stan, the only other Anunnaki with them, and he shared their expression. It meant something, she knew. She just didn't know what.

They gathered by the fire listening to ancient tales. Kalita promised understanding tomorrow, but tonight was for rest and observation, as he had said.

They stood there for what seemed like hours—or seconds; Carter had no way of telling time. Their eyes locked, and a whirl of emotions and desires swam through her. She couldn't tell anymore if it was the beat of the drum that sang in her ears or her own heartbeat. William brazed his fingers underneath her shirt and around her waist, pulling him to her. The static electric charge was subtle for once, but it sent pulses through every nerve ending in her body. She knew part of the pull to him was of her own accord, but she knew there was an unknown force pulling them together, just as it did that very first night in Bohemian Grove when his lips for touched hers. She felt drugged. She didn't know where Jack was.

The night when John was still alive, the complexity of her life was nothing more than a broken sewing machine and the start of a tangled love triangle. Then a knock on the door became the beginning of a new life and the end of some she loved. Carl was still alive, and the tragedies hadn't fallen on the woods in Northern California yet. She had just learned who she was and was yet to grasp it. All these thoughts whirled through Carter's mind as William pulled her closer to him, and with each breath, her sorrows were stilled. The fire, the jet lag, the desert night air, the euphoria of these people—they intoxicated her. She had no control over her sudden desires as William trailed kisses up her neck to her chin. The cool breeze left marks on the moist spots he made with his kisses.

"You want me," he whispered. The kiss was long and deep, and Carter thought she would lose herself forever in him. When they stopped, Carter gasped for air as if she had just resurfaced from the water—partially for air, but also from the energy between William and her becoming a void. He traced his thumb against her cheek. She didn't understand what was happening, but a small space inside her told her she needed to stop and get a grip. This wasn't her, this was something else getting a hold of her.

William ran his fingers through her hair, sending shivers through her body. She shuddered underneath his touch.

We have lost you—

The whisper echoed in her mind.

"No," she replied.

"What?" William asked.

We have lost you—

The whisper chanted, and Carter quickly pulled away from William's embrace. The whispers were a cold stone sober slap in the face.

"Stop," Carter said. "We can't do this."

William stepped in closer to her. "You want this."

"No," came the word on her breath. "I don't know what I want."

William stepped in even closer, hunger in his eyes.

Carter backed away from the fire, away from William and directly into Jack's arms. She jumped, startled by his sudden presence. How much had he seen? By the anger in his eyes, he had seen enough. Except the anger was not directed at her—it was directed at William.

If looks could kill.

"I'm uh…going to go find my bed," she stammered out.

Carter managed to pull her eyes away from William and Jack to those around the pit. A blush rose to her cheeks as she realized every set of eyes was on her—everyone except for Kalita, who watched the fire. She didn't realize how much of a show they had been putting on.

A woman stepped away from the fire with empathetic eyes. "I can show you where you'll be sleeping."

Jack followed on their heels. The woman left her by the adobe she would be staying in.

"I can stay nearby if you want," Jack said.

"No, that's OK. I'll be OK."

"Carter? What was that back there?"

"I don't know. I think…" she stopped. She didn't know what she thought.

"He didn't look as if he was going to take no for an answer."

"He would. It was just—I think it's this place. It makes me feel sort of drugged. I think it has the same effect on him."

That explanation didn't ease his tension. In fact, it made it worse.

"I'm going to sleep on the floor in there. I'm not leaving you alone," he said.

"What happened to trusting me?"

"I don't trust people on drugs." He moved past her into the candlelit adobe and pulled a woven blanket off a table and spread it out on the floor.

CHAPTER 24

𒐊𒁹 𒋡 𒁹𒌁𒀸 𒑀𒁹 𒀀𒁹𒁹 𒅗 𒑀𒐊 𒁹𒁹 𒅖𒁹𒀸 𒑀𒌁𒀠 𒀀𒐊 𒁹𒋡 𒀠𒑀𒐊 𒀸𒁹𒀸

C ARTER WAS SURPRISED BY HOW quickly she fell asleep. Jet lag took over, and she fell into a deep, dreamless sleep. When she woke, she saw that Jack was still fast asleep on the ground next to her, snoring softly. She smiled as she watched him for a few minutes.

She tiptoed around him, wrapping her blanket around her. She had no idea what time it was and didn't think there was a working clock around. When she stuck her head out the door, she saw the sun was directly overhead.

"Did you sleep OK?" Jack's voice came from behind her.

"Like a rock. Gotta love jet lag," she said. "You must've slept horribly. Jack, you really didn't have to do this."

He cringed as he sat up. "I slept fine. I'm just a bit sore." He stood up and brushed himself off. "So you know the chief?"

She nodded. "I do. I don't know how. But I'm as sure as I am my own name."

Jack nodded. "It seemed as if he wasn't surprised by that either."

"Well, we should be getting answers soon, right?" she asked.

He nodded.

Carter found one of the women from the night before and asked her about showering or bathing. Once Carter washed up and changed into fresh clothes, she felt human again. The jet lag finally wore off, and she didn't feel foggy anymore. Mara, the woman who had been helping her since the night before, showed her around their village, introducing her to several people. Carter liked it here. Mostly, she was just happy to be back in the States. After dinner they gathered around the fire again.

The fire flickered in front of them, and at first Carter thought she was just tired and her eyes were playing tricks on her. There were just flecks at first, but then she could see the flickering was taking on shapes. What unfolded before her was nothing short of miraculous as the shapes of fire formed into a perfect picture show of moving, silent images. It took only a short moment before Carter realized what she was watching was the history of not only of the Zuni, but of her own Anunnaki kind.

She saw images of a taller and lankier, though humanoid, species working with the Zuni of centuries before. Kalita began to narrate the images.

"Your people most recently came to this planet about four thousand years ago and helped take our kind to more advance places." Kalita spoke in his deliberate and enunciated native tone that Carter found soothing and calming. "There are stories that they helped our people mine for gold, but it is the gold you see flickering before you that your people gave to us. Not the gold you find in the earth." Carter watched as the fire reflected its own fire as the Anunnaki used flames to come to Earth, or what seemed like flames. "They gave us some of their blood, what you call DNA, to help us move thousands of years forward in our own evolution. They took a liking to us, our compassion for other beings, and wanted to help us. There was a great flood, and they helped our kind move below the earth for many years until we were able to come back. It was at the time of the flood that we started sharing our stories in our simple ways. Some of those stories were passed along by our friends and became the religion of the Egyptian pharaohs, the Book of the Dead. The story has changed from people to people, but not for us. The story is the same." Kalita watched as the flames changed, showing the shapes of the pyramids and the pharaohs, even of Christian prophets. His eyes, for the first time, seemed sad and thoughtful.

Carter turned briefly to see Jack, William, Rafe, and Stan all mesmerized. "They have not been back since the time of the flood, as they said they wouldn't. It is difficult to travel when they are on this side of the stars." As Kalita spoke, the fire turned into the familiar shape of the Milky Way Galaxy. He poked a stick into the fire. "We are here," he said and then moved the stick to the other end of the galaxy. "They are there." Kalita turned to Carter. "But there is a way," he continued. "To bring them here, to finish their mission and free the people of their prison." The fire flickered, bending, forming the shape of the serpent Carter had become familiar with.

"When will they be back?" William asked.

"Soon. The time has come." Kalita deliberately looked at Carter, sending shivers down her spine, even against the warmth of the raging flames.

"They gave us life in a different way." The images flickered back to the Anunnaki and the Zuni again, except this time they were giving someone a goblet to drink, someone who looked very much like Onawa. Carter's eyebrows furrowed as she struggled to make sense of these latest images.

"That is my father," Onawa said, reading the confusion on her face.

"I thought you said they were here four thousand years ago," she said.

"Yes, as Mankalita says, they gave us life." He spoke slowly, unsure of himself, or rather unsure of whether he should be sharing this information. "That is the gold that many look for today. It is gold, and fire, and Anunnaki blood. We are almost immortal, like the stories in the book of the white man of a six-hundred-year-old man."

Carter felt William tense behind her, struggling himself with this information. "You mean you're..." She couldn't even bring herself to form the words.

"Yes," Kalita said. "We are over a thousand years old. And so you shall be as well."

Carter remembered Dr. Nathaniel's story the day she found out he was over 150 years old. He had been given a virus by the Anunnaki society in the late 1800s as a test—a virus that would manipulate his DNA to withstand mundane diseases and degeneration, making him live longer than normal. He had figured out years later that he was still aging, only he aged a tenth of the pace of normal humans. "How do I know you?" she asked Kalita.

"This is your second life." He pointed back to the fire of the Anunnaki handing Onawa's father a goblet, the tip of his stick swirling around the Anunnaki. "This, is you," he said with melancholy.

Carter found herself standing inches from the fire, not even affected by the heat, as her mind fought, yet she knew and understood this new knowledge, almost like an ancient memory. She realized then that that was exactly what it was. She looked nearly identical to her prior self. "Why you?" she asked. "Why do I feel a connection with you then, and not with Onawa?"

"Because you gave your life for me, to save me with your blood as I was dying. It has forever bonded us, through many lifetimes. I am your brother in blood."

"Why am I here?" she asked.

"Because you are the final tablet to the key to help bring your people back, to open the sun gate. Because your mind is different now, in this new body, because you now have human in you, we are unsure how we will do that. You possessed the knowledge before, but we don't know how you will possess the knowledge now."

"What do you mean the *final* key?" William interrupted. Carter watched him carefully, wondering if he knew he was the key as well.

"There are three tablets of a map that were spread about the world when the Anunnaki left. We have two of them. The third the Vaticates have stolen from us, and the fourth is Carter. She is more like a key to the tablets, though."

Carter nodded in understanding.

"We do not die, we just become a part of the energy around us— we change, we never die. What the Anunnaki have done was make this time in this body longer, for on earth the air makes our lives so short that we cannot gain much knowledge. It is the extent of the lives of the Anunnaki that gives them the knowledge they need to grow. Time makes the people wise; without time, we were lost." Turning back to Jack, surprising him, he said, "But we can bring the energy together to see in brief moments those we love so dearly we can not ever let go completely. It is because of this love that they will never be completely changed until what holds and binds them to this earth has changed as well."

"We can see the dead?" William asked.

Comically, Kalita just responded with a shrug. "There are ways."

Kalita stood slowly, and Carter watched him in a new light, realizing his age only made him seem larger than life.

"It is time, my family, to get some rest. We will have plenty of time to talk tomorrow when your friends from the south come."

Carter nodded. Amara and Paulo were arriving in the morning to join them.

CHAPTER 25

ΣΥ ⟨ ⟨Σ⟨ ΣΥ ⊢ΥrΥ ττ ΥΣ Σ⟨ ⟨Υr⊢ ΣΥ ⟨ ⊢ΥΣ ⟨ΣΥ

CARTER WAS REFOLDING HER CLOTHES in her suitcase when she felt William's presence outside her door. She turned, waiting.

"You can come in," she said.

He opened the door. "I wanted to see whether you were asleep or not. Your energy was so calm I couldn't tell."

She smiled, reflecting on that. She had been calm since their arrival in New Mexico. She wasn't sure whether it was from being back home in the States, their progress, or just being around Kalita.

William stepped toward Carter, warming her by his presence. He ran his fingers up her arms, raising her flesh with goose bumps. Carter closed her eyes against his touch, struggling to gain her balance. He was always intoxicating to her, but she was learning more and more that it was a strange chemistry they had more than anything. Her thoughts continued to drift back to Jack. Her eyes shot open.

"William?"

"Hmmm?" He nuzzled against her neck as she pulled back.

"William, please."

He stepped back. "What's changed?" he asked.

"Everything."

"It's Jack?"

"William, what we have is a connection I don't understand. It feels out of body, and I don't know how much of it is me or this weird cosmic thing going on with us. I don't want to be with someone because it's chosen, or because of lust. You and I both deserve more than that." She knew it stung, but she felt it through their bond.

He stepped away from her, leaving the adobe. Carter stared at the closed door for a long time. She thought about going after him to try to make things better but decided she would give him time first.

She definitely needed to talk to him, though—he needed to know about his father, that he was also a key, and that he may possibly be in danger because of it.

☆   ☆   ☆

Carter stood staring down at the two tablet pieces in front of her, bewildered.

"I'm confused. I thought that there was no God. I thought that gods were just the Anunnaki being a higher power." She did air quotes around "higher power" as she spoke, not bothering to hide the irritation from her voice. "And 'higher power' just meant smarter than humans, more advanced."

Kalita nodded patiently. "You're referencing the story of the Bible, or any human religion. But this…" he motioned to the tablets in front of Carter. "This isn't a religion."

"I don't understand," Carter said, and felt Jack shift next to her. She struggled to read his energy but could not. He was still the most difficult for her to read.

"The deity you understand through human religion is mundane," Stan said.

"But the deity that exists to the Anunnaki is more profound, and not so simple to explain as an omnipotent being." There seemed to be a distinct pause in time, and Carter thought she was imagining it as she looked around. Yet the expression on Jack's face perfectly matched hers. He furrowed his brow and looked around as well, and they both stopped when they got to Kalita's face.

"What's happening?" Jack asked.

Carter turned back to Kalita. "Are you doing this?" She waved her hands through the air. "You were saying that the Anunnaki deity is not as simple as an omnipotent being." She turned to Stan, glaring. "What IS the Anunnaki deity?"

"Not, an omnipotent being, Carter—*the* Omnipotent," Kalita said carefully.

Carter put her hands on her hips, frowning at her friend. "Do you mind speaking English?"

"The Omnipotent is a collective consciousness," Kalita said simply, and Carter just stared at him.

"Like the Force?" she asked, annoyed.

"The what?" Kalita looked at her quizzically.

"The Force? Don't tell me you don't know what the force is. Aren't you like a gazillion years old?"

Kalita tried to take Carter's hand and she pulled away, still aggravated.

"Kalita, I'm sorry. I..." she fiddled with the hem of her shirt as she felt his eyes boring into her. "I don't want this."

"What do you mean?"

"This." She waved her hands through the air and felt it move like Jell-O around her. They were still frozen in time. "Can you put everything back?"

Instantly the room went back to normal.

"I'm sorry. I thought you'd like to see the extent of—"

Carter cut Kalita off. "No, I don't want any of this. This is wrong. All of it. Manipulating time? Collective consciousness? Maybe the Vaticates are right. Maybe we're not ready for this. And I'm not even *human*! What makes you think humans can handle this?"

Carter stormed out of the large covered area they had met at and walked fast toward her own adobe.

Jibril was sitting on her bed waiting for her, and she nearly screamed, forgetting that she was actually not supposed to be afraid of him anymore. Of course, he seemed amused by her reaction. He quirked his head to the side like a listening puppy, his lips curling up in a half smile.

"Bad time?" he asked.

"Did you fly here from South America to be an ass?" she asked.

"Bad time, then."

"Wait. Do people know you're here?"

Jibril pursed his lips together in a sour look.

"OK, if they don't know you're here, how'd you get in?"

Again, the sour look. "Carter, you don't usually ask stupid questions. Two in a row?"

"So why are you here?"

"Finally, a decent question." He smiled. She glared. "Your boy is in trouble."

Carter tensed up. "Who?"

"William. The Vaticates know about him. I'm guessing my sister told—she's always been really bad about being a tattletale." Jibril crossed his legs and leaned to his side. "Where is he, anyway?"

Now it was Carter's turn to have the sour look. "I don't know."

"Uh oh, you broke the boy's heart. Didn't you?"

"How do you do that?"

"Do what?"

"Figure things out so easily?"

"I'm a genius."

"Okay," Carter crossed her arms. "Seriously, do you read minds or something? Energy?"

"No. I'm a genius."

"You're serious, aren't you?"

"Why wouldn't I be? Have I ever lied to you before?"

She thought about that for a moment. She jumped nearly a foot when Jack walked in. She realized he was worried about her and had come to check up on her but he stood motionless as he stared at Jibril. Jibril wiggled his fingers at Jack.

"Hey, Buttercup, I see you've been getting sun. It looks delicious on you," Jibril sang.

"You're going to get us in a lot of trouble if you get caught here," Jack said.

Jibril clucked his tongue. "Carter, your lover here is quicker on his feet than you."

"Did you really come all the way here to tell us William's in danger?" Carter asked.

"Well, you wouldn't answer your cell phone. Ah—yes, that's right. You guys are living like the Amish here—ya know? No cell, no electricity, no showers. It's awfully dusty; doesn't this bother your sinuses? I much prefer the humidity—"

"Where's Dr. Nathaniel?" Jack asked.

"He's on the verge of a breakthrough with his DNA tests. That's another reason we need to see William. He needs to know pronto." Jibril snapped his fingers to emphasize.

"See William?" Jack asked.

"Yes, we need you two back in Peru."

"Like hell," Carter said.

"So where is William, anyway?" Jibril said, ignoring Carter.

"I don't know," Carter said. Jack turned and looked at Carter curiously.

"What happened?" Jibril asked, always too observant.

The shuffling of feet and hushed conversation alerted all three of them—sort of. It alerted Carter and Jack. Jibril sat there carelessly watching the two panic. Carter watched in complete surprise when Jack cradled Jibril and slid him under her bed.

"What?" Jack whispered. "He wouldn't have budged."

"I bet he enjoyed that," Carter whispered back.

"I did. Thank you, Jack. I always knew you felt that way about me," Jibril said too loudly.

When she heard the shuffling at her doorstep, she did the only thing she could think of. She kissed Jack. He froze at first but reciprocated quickly. She heard the opening of the door and Amara's startled voice.

"Oh, I am sorry! I—"

"Amara!" Carter pulled away quickly from the still-stunned Jack and ran to Amara's arms and embraced her.

CHAPTER 26

𒂍 𒀸 𒀊𒀸 𒂍𒅀 ~𒅕𒅀 𒀹 𒅄𒂍 𒂽 𒀊𒅀~ 𒂍𒅀 𒀸 ~𒅀𒂍 𒀊𒅀

C ARTER WALKED WITH AMARA AS she left Jack to deal with Jibril. She saw everyone beginning to gather at the nightly fire. Fortunately, she didn't run into Stan, Rafe, or Kalita.

"So you and Jack are—"

"No, no—it was um…I thought you were someone else," Carter tried to explain.

"I don't understand, Carter."

"Yeah, it's hard to explain." She wanted to explain to her friend that they were working with Jibril, but she didn't think that Amara would be as forgiving. After all, Amara was still mourning the loss of Sergio.

"So what is happening here?" She pointed to the fire.

Carter explained the nightly fire gathering and realized she was excitedly talking about it. She loved that time with everyone. She loved the sense of community and unity.

Everyone soon formed a circle around the fire, and Jack approached, smiling. She wished she could read his mind because that smile could mean anything in regard to Jibril. Suddenly, she was concerned for Jibril's safety.

"What did you do with him?" Carter asked in hushed tones.

"With who?" Jack asked.

She frowned at him.

"Oh, he's still in your hut."

"Adobe."

"What?"

"It's an adobe."

"Oh, whatever. Anyway, he's there—probably napping."

"Is he safe there?"

"I don't know. Maybe I should have laid out some paper and a bowl of water."

She smacked Jack on the shoulder.

"You two act like a married couple," Paulo said, appearing out of nowhere.

Carter realized she still hadn't seen the rest of the group from earlier in the day and wondered if they were avoiding her. Good, she thought.

"Have you found William?" she asked Jack, changing the subject.

"Oh, I saw him earlier. He went into town with Rafe and Stan," Paulo said.

This made both Carter and Jack tense up.

"Why, what's wrong?" Paulo noticed the change in their stance.

"Nothing, um—why did they go into town?" Carter asked nervously.

"They had to make some calls."

"William too?" Jack asked.

"I guess. He said he needed some air." Paulo looked up at the night sky. "I don't know what all this is called, then."

Carter knew exactly what William needed. He needed to get away from Carter, and she may just have put him in danger by doing so.

"It'll be fine, Carter. He's with Rafe and Stan."

"Do you know when they'll be back?" Kalita asked. He watched Carter as he asked. He had an expression that Carter couldn't read, but she felt as if she were being scolded.

"I think they were coming right back. They left hours ago. They should be back soon."

On cue, she saw Rafe approach the fire. They must had left right after their meeting and her storming out. Rafe ignored Carter and Jack and sat at the opposite end of the fire. She wanted to know where Stan and William were.

"Where's Stan and William?" Paulo asked.

She could kiss Paulo.

"They're calling it a night and went to sleep."

Carter relaxed. "That was a close call," she whispered to Jack, and he nodded. "We need to talk to William first thing in the morning." She suddenly thought of something. "Wait, where's William sleeping tonight?"

Jack shrugged. "You can sleep in my hut."

"Did you feed him?"

"I left some biscuits by the bed."

"Jack?"

"No."

"Really?"

"He had a sandwich with him. He's fine. Stop worrying about him. He never worried about us when we were locked up," he whispered agitatedly.

"Where did you get the ingredients for that, anyway?" She pointed to the box of Graham crackers propped up on the rock in front of him, wanting to change the subject before Jack got upset.

"Paulo brought them with him."

It reminded her of that night in Santa Barbara when they made a bonfire by the beach. She realized she knew then where her heart was, but she just ignored it.

She made her own chocolate, graham cracker, and marshmallow sandwich, enjoying the crackling of the fire.

"You're smiling," Jack said.

"I guess I am."

"Want to share your happiness with me?" he said, chuckling softly. He took the last bite of his s'mores and wiped his hands on a napkin.

"Can we go for a walk?"

He nodded, standing up. "You're not going to eat that?"

Carter looked down at her half-eaten sandwich and handed it to Jack. He chowed down as they walked away from the fire. The moon was full, casting a light over the desert landscape.

"I remember how much you liked those things when we were in Santa Barbara," she said. Jack stiffened, and she wondered what memory he was thinking of. She replayed that night in her mind, but nothing distinctly stood out.

"What did you want to talk about?"

"How do you know I want to talk about something?" Carter asked.

"Whenever you want to go for a walk, it's usually because you have something on your mind."

She nodded. Now that they were alone, she suddenly became nervous, which was silly because she was never nervous around him. Except now—now that she wanted to tell him what was on her mind, what had been on her mind for a long time

"Hey, you okay?" He turned to face her, and his brows drew together in worry.

She shivered and wrapped her arms around herself. He pulled her in, wrapping his arms around her body. She continued to shiver.

"I'm fine," she whispered against his shirt. Feeling him this close to her warmed her. Her breathing became warm and heavy, and her heart drummed heavily in her chest, reminding her of its existence. Carter threaded her fingers through Jack's and felt him freeze and then instantly relax.

He lifted her chin with his fingers and gazed into her eyes, and the moon cast vivid lights against the green of her iris. Her presence intoxicated him, and he knew his fight to stay away from her was nearly exhausted, a battle he could no longer fight. As she leaned in closer to him, he wondered if perhaps she had lost her own battle. He didn't care anymore. He didn't care if she still loved William even though it killed him. He was so desperate for her at this moment that he would not think about tomorrow until tomorrow came. He moved his hand along her jawline and felt her shudder underneath his touch. It delighted him that he had that effect on her. He cupped his hand at the back of her neck and pulled her face close to his as he leaned in, gently brushing his lips against hers.

His breath was warm against her lips, and she yearned for him to bridge the gap and close the kiss. When the moment lasted too long, she leaned in and pressed herself against him, losing herself in the hunger of their kissing. In one swoop he lifted her up, cradling her before sitting her down on the desert floor.

☆   ☆   ☆

THE PALE MOON CAST LUMINOUS shadows over her trepid, quaking skin. Carter arched her back, giving herself to him in more ways than just the physical. She shivered, and not just from the desert night air. The dust from the ground rubbed against her bare shoulders as he trailed kisses down to the hollow of her throat, and heat welled in the bottom of her belly. She raked her fingers through his hair and pulled him to her, kissing his lips desperately.

This was right, she knew. It wasn't lust or centuries of love; it was stronger than that. Stronger than what had been written in the stars for her. A love she could no longer ignore or deny. For whatever coursed through her alien blood and whatever screamed at her to be with the one she had always been with, it was this. This moment that meant everything to her. This was what she chose, from the bottom of her heart to the tip of her mind. She knew, she knew with everything she was and had been and everything she would be, she knew without a shadow of a doubt.

She shivered in fear, she shivered in lust, she shivered in the pleasures that Jack's kisses sent traversing through every nerve ending in her body and soul.

"Yes, I want this," she whispered into his ear. He hovered over her, holding her face to his, and looked into her eyes. She nodded. "Yes, Jack. *You* are who I want—not just tonight, Jack. I want you forever."

His eyes lit up with a joy that overcame him as he pressed his lips against hers, smiling. She giggled in response, surrendering in their delight.

"You are so beautiful," he said, smiling.

She rolled over on top of him, and her hair fell over her shoulders. He ran his fingers through the ebony cascade as he sat up, causing their bodies to press closer together. He bunched her hair in his fist behind her neck and pulled her head back, kissing the curve of her throat.

"I will love you until the end of my life," he whispered to her.

"I will love you forever," she said.

Her heart ached with how much she realized the truth of this.

"Come on, I want to show you something." Jack took her hand and led her across the plateau.

"Where are we going?"

"A place I found recently. You'll love it. We'll be able to find it easily since the moon is full."

They didn't have to walk more than a quarter mile, but it felt as if they were worlds away. The oasis took Carter's breath away.

"How is this possible?" She stared in awe at the waterfall that fell into the perfectly clear pool below the red, jagged rocks.

"Underwater rivers run through these plateaus."

The moon cast a beautiful light across the water, and she thought it looked like something straight out of a postcard. Green, lush palms framed the water, and she walked down to the water, knelt down, and dipped her hand in, almost to see if it was real. The water was cool and refreshing.

"Want to go for a swim?" Jack spoke against Carter's neck, and his warm breath sent delightful sensations through her.

She took her sandals off and stepped into the pool until the water reached her bare thighs. The coolness was refreshing against the warm desert night air. The edges of Carter's skirt wafted on the surface of the water around her, billowing out in deep crimson layers. Jack took his shoes off and stepped into the water following in her wake. The mist from the waterfall sprayed their skin, making them seem almost reflective.

He placed a tender kiss on her bare shoulder and let his lips linger there for a moment, enjoying her scent. She turned to face him and meant only to give him a light kiss, but the heat became intense quickly, and their kisses deepened. Jack lifted the hem of her skirt and cupped her thighs, pulling her closer to him.

They sank deeper into the water until it was just below their shoulders. When Jack kissed Carter, she could feel the last year of everything they had been through. The unspoken words of pain, of love, and fear. His kisses were both desperate and soft. He pulled the straps of her dress off her shoulders and the dress down to her waist. A sweet shiver traveled down her as he pulled back and looked at her body, smiling in hot desire.

She leaned back as he tugged her dress down and off her body, slowly and deliberately.

"Your turn," she whispered as she slipped the rest of his clothes off, tossing them onto the rocks by the pool. Jack lifted her up in his arms as the warm water cascaded off them like a slow song.

"I won't let you go," he whispered into her ear as he trailed kisses down her jaw and her throat. She sealed her eyes shut as tears of joy slipped from her eyes. Sighs of happiness and pleasure lifted from her lips.

"I'm counting on that."

He watched her with hunger and pleasure in his eyes, covering her with tender kisses. A low growl escaped his throat as he kissed the spot between her neck and ear.

"The Gods are watching and smiling on us tonight," she said, smiling—knowing.

"I know," he replied as he took her into the water.

Never in her life had an emotion been as intense as her love for him was. She felt as if she were his celestial guardian, as he was her protector of love and life. His name escaped her lips in soft whispers. He looked down at her lips with a hunger that sent her emotions on high.

Moving from the pool to the edge that framed the water, he laid her on the cool, flat rock, repeating his kisses and love again—running his fingers through her wet, tangled hair and kissing her swollen lips. The night swept them away, their love swept them away—and for once, the whispers in the air remained silent as Carter and Jack fell deeper in love with each passing moment.

"Jack?"

"Hmmm?" They lay with their bodies tangled, watching the waterfall.

"I don't want to go back."

"Go back where?" he asked.

"To anywhere before you." She smiled as she sat up. "Sometimes I become so sad when I think of what I've already lost. The life I knew was taken from me, but the life I was given is so much better."

He lifted his head up on his arm and pushed the hair away from her face. "You like this life?"

"I think I do."

"The danger?"

"Not so much the danger. But who else gets to embark on a journey that can free the human race? Who else gets to meet people who have lived for over a thousand years?" She watched his face as she spoke, and he listened intently.

"Tonight, was that human? Or was that alien?"

"I don't know." She continued to watch him. "What are you thinking? You look worried."

"Carter, you are basically a god, and a really damn important one. I'm nothing but a mere human. You really don't think you'll want this with me from here on now? William is meant—"

"Stop."

"Carter, really. I need to be realistic."

"No, you're ruining things."

He frowned at her. "Carter—"

"Jack, stop. Please. I'm begging you. What William and I had was nothing but some weird alien connection. My heart has never been with him, and it never will be. Do you hear me?" Her voice broke, and she knew she was close to losing her control. He needed to see where she stood, what she felt. If only he could feel his energy like— "I just thought of something."

She sat naked in front of him with her legs crossed. Closing her eyes, she focused. She focused on her instincts and listened to the whispers.

"She is listening," they said.

She smiled. She was.

"Carrrrrterrrrr," the whisper dragged out.

"Carter?" Jack's voice broke through. "I heard that."

"Keep listening, Jack. Close your eyes and listen." She felt the missing piece inside her form together like a lost memory coming to fruition.

He took her hands in his, and she felt his trust course through her.

"Yessss," they whispered.

"We can bring the energy together to see in brief moments those we love so dearly we can not ever let go completely. It is because of this love that they will never be completely changed until what holds and binds them to this earth has changed as well." She repeated Kalita's words from the night of the fire to Jack, now understanding what they meant.

Her hands warmed, and she felt an electric charge there, one she had never felt without William. She touched Jack gently, and he jumped slightly.

"What was that?"

Carter opened her eyes to look at him and saw they were enveloped in a dull and quavering light. She looked around them in awe.

"What is this?" he asked. She laughed in delight as she saw him smile.

"It's euphoria."

"This is what you feel around me?" he asked, understanding that she brought her energy out for him to feel.

She nodded excitedly.

"How did you do that?"

She shrugged, and he burst out in laughter. The light dulled out completely, but he still felt the effects of it.

"What were those whispers?" he asked.

"Those are my relatives," she said.

"You figured out how to connect?"

"I'm getting there," she admitted.

CHAPTER 27

ᛁᚳ ᚳ ᚳᛁᚳ ᛁᚳ ᛁᚳᛁ ᛁᚳ ᛁᛁ ᛁᚳ ᚳᛁᛁ ᛁᚳ ᚳ ᛁᛁᚳ ᚳᛁ

T HE SUN WAS RISING OVER the mountaintops when they headed back toward the village. Kalita met them near the edge of the village.

"Good morning," Kalita said.

"Yes, it is," Jack said, and Carter elbowed him, blushing.

Kalita looked at Carter curiously as her blush deepened. Was it written all over her face?

"You found a connection," he said excitedly.

"What?"

"You connected. How? I have not seen that light in a millennium."

Carter looked around. "What light?"

"The one around you two. It is a trace when someone connects."

"I did, but I don't know how."

Kalita nodded. "That's progress, though. Maybe we can try again tonight." Kalita turned around and walked back where he came from, and Carter thought she recognized more bounce in his step.

Jack reached down and gripped her hand, and she nuzzled against him as they walked back toward her adobe. "Carter, last night—"

"Was perfect," she finished.

"It's just yesterday you were really upset about everything."

"And I still am, but I mean with everything we've experienced, I'm allowed a breakdown once in a while, aren't I?"

He nodded and leaned in to kiss her on the forehead. She pulled him down into a deeper kiss. He was hers, and she was his. She wasn't going to let a moment of that pass.

A shiver crawled up her spine, and energy seemed to strangle her senses. "William," she whispered against Jack's mouth.

Turning around, she saw him glaring at them both. This wasn't what she wanted him to see, not this soon.

"I was right," he said.

"No, William, please." She paused as Jack gripped her hand tighter. She looked up at him, pleading.

"William, we need to tell you something," Jack said.

"I'm pretty sure it's obvious what you need to tell me."

Jack frowned. "It's not about us, it's about *you*. You might be in danger."

Although William continued to glare at them, Carter felt his energy shift. The sun was almost completely over the mountain's horizon, and it was casting strange orange lights on William, making him look angrier than she felt. Underneath the layer of heat she felt from him, she felt the layer of fear.

"I think you should come back to my adobe. It'll be better if we all explain it to you together," she said.

"Who's we?" he asked.

That was what she didn't want to explain to him out in the open.

"It's better if we talk in private," Jack said as he let go of Carter's hand. She was grateful for that, only because it was harder on William to see, and they both needed him to be calm if he was going to face Jibril.

They walked slowly back to the adobe, and an awkward tension filled the space around them. Just before they opened the door, Carter stopped.

"William, I know you're upset with me right now. But I need you to have an open mind with what you're about hear."

William nodded solemnly as Carter led the way into her adobe.

William was about to sit down on the bed when he changed his mind suddenly—looking awkwardly to Carter and Jack. "OK, what do you have to tell me?" he asked.

"Well, I met with Dr. Nathaniel in Peru." She felt horrible about omitting the information about Jibril, and by the look on William's face, he knew she would be holding information back. Carter mentally cursed their energy connection. "About the blood sample you gave him."

"Oh?" William asked, standing straighter.

"It turns out that I'm not the last of my line to hold the key," she said quickly.

"What do you mean?"

"It means that you also hold the key within your DNA to connect with the Anunnaki at home. I'm not the only one."

"That's impossible. My parents aren't in the same line as…" He stopped abruptly, recognition forming in his mind. He looked to Carter as he pieced the puzzle together. She realized it was more than the information that she was giving him at this moment that helped him. He was remembering something more.

"My real father isn't Greg Moretti."

"You figured that out quickly," Jack said. Carter looked at him curiously.

"I always had some sort of feeling, something unspoken between my mom and him. The way he treated me, but I could never figure out why or what it was."

Carter thought he was accepting the fact too easily but wasn't sure if it was because he had already suspected it.

"Wait, are we—is that why you and I..."

"No, no." Carter quickly jumped in as Jack shifted uncomfortably next to her. This was not the conversation she wanted to have. "No, we narrowed it down to four possible people, none of whom are related to me at all."

William sighed loudly, and again Jack shifted. Carter dared a glance at him and saw the pulse in his neck throbbing and his jaw clenching tighter. The tension in the room got worse.

Blushing with visible anger, William turned to Carter and asked, "What does this mean exactly?"

"Well, it means your life is in danger now too."

He stared over Carter's head after she said that, and she wondered if he had even heard her.

"I need to speak to Greg," he finally said.

"Your dad?" Carter cringed as soon as she said that, and William responded with a sour expression. "What are you going to say?"

"I don't know," he said. "I'll play it by ear. I haven't seen him in almost eight months, so it'll be interesting to see how he reacts to me. I also think I need to pay a visit to my mom."

"Maybe we should come," Jack said. Carter looked at him, surprised by his suggestion. Granted, it was a good one—but Carter thought Jack would try to get away from William as soon as possible.

"What about the tribe here?" she asked.

"You should stay here," Jack said. "It's safer for you. I don't think coming with us is wise.

"Like hell."

"What are you guys planning?" Rafe appeared out of nowhere.

"Nothing," all three of them answered in harmony.

"I'll see you tonight," Jack whispered to Carter and kissed her, lingering just a moment longer than necessary before leaving. Carter blushed at the public display, and especially blushed when she saw William's reaction. She felt her heart sink into her stomach when she saw William press his lips together and frown. He turned and walked away from them.

Carter was exhausted and decided to take a nap before their nightly gathering. Just before she drifted off to sleep, a memory tugged at her mind.

And Adam knew Eve his wife, and she conceived, and bare Cain, and said I have gotten a man from the LORD—Behold, thou hast driven me out this day from the face of the earth; and from the face shall I be hid; and I shall be a fugitive and a vagabond in the earth; and it shall come to pass, that every one that findeth me shall slay me.

It had been months since she had read that passage in the Bible, but something about its meaning swirled in her mind. She decided she would need to go with Jack and William to meet Gregory Moretti. They needed her there. Besides, she needed to get back to civilization so she could call Dr. Nathaniel and see if that passage meant anything to him.

CHAPTER 28

𒐊𒁹 𒀸 𒀊𒁉𒀸 𒐊𒁹 𒍣𒅀 𒀀𒐊 𒐊𒈨 𒀊𒁉 𒀊𒅀𒐊 𒀸 𒀀𒅀𒈨 𒀊𒁹

"**Y**OUR LIPS POUT WHEN YOU sleep."

Carter shot up in bed. "What the…"

"Forget about me?"

"As a matter of fact, I—"

Jibril pressed Carter's lips together before she finished her sentence. "Shhhh, you're so much prettier when you're not talking."

Carter frowned at him as she smacked his hand away. "I don't like you being here while I'm sleeping."

"Most people don't sleep in the middle of the day—unless you're a vampire now and not an alien."

Carter got up and walked to the other side of the adobe, putting as much space between them as possible.

"So you're off to see Greg Moretti, are you? With your little love triangle as well, to boot. Now, *that* I have to see. Besides, I have to make sure little Jack doesn't get all flustered around William."

Carter's mouth fell open.

He continued, ignoring her. "I take it you'll leave in the morning. After you try another one of your communication things tonight. Now *that* was pretty impressive to see, especially with you two naked."

Carter turned a deep scarlet and remained stunned and speechless as Jibril got up and casually walked out of the adobe. Either he didn't care if he got caught, or he just knew he never would.

She eventually regained her composure and went to the fire to meet with the rest of the group. She knew Kalita was going to ask her to try to communicate again, but she just didn't know how. She knew he would also ask what she was doing when she did earlier, and she didn't know how to explain that. She found Jack already sitting around, roasting a marshmallow.

"Where's the rest of the s'mores?"

Jack looked up at her with a simmering gaze that made her hotter than the fire did. "No more chocolate."

"What about dinner?" she asked.

"Already ate—worked up an appetite from last night. I've been eating all day," he said and smiled wider as she blushed again. "You've been doing that a lot lately."

"Doing what?"

"Blushing."

"Yeah, I wonder why."

"Go grab a plate and come back and join me. I'll save you some marshmallows."

When she returned with her food, Jack wrapped his arm around her. She loved how comfortably she fit in his arms—as if they were made for each other.

"Someone paid me a visit while I was napping," she said between bites. She felt Jack go rigid next to her.

"They aren't doing a very good job of keeping an eye on you, are they?"

"I don't think they'd expect a raid here in the village. It's in the middle of nowhere, and you can see for miles around. Hard to sneak in without being seen."

"Yet he managed."

"He manages to do a lot of things I don't understand," Carter said, agreeing.

"He paid me a visit too."

"Oh?" she asked.

"Well, he was mostly being his stupid, annoying self. But right before I kicked him out, he said I should listen to your dreams more."

She frowned. "Did he explain why?"

"No, he said that and then walked right out of my hut. What did he say to you?"

Carter explained to Jack what Jibril had said, and Jack frowned the entire time. "Carter, I'm not comfortable with you coming with us. It's dangerous."

"All the more reason for me to go—so you can keep a close eye on me."

She knew that was a cheap move on her part, as he couldn't resist looking after her, but she knew she needed to go with them, no matter what.

He kissed her head. "Okay. I have a feeling I don't have much of a choice anyway."

"What about the others?"

"If they know, they'll come with us." William appeared behind them, and Carter wondered how much of their conversation he'd heard. She also wondered why she couldn't feel him approach.

"If we sneak away, they'll look for us," Jack said.

"I have an idea of how we can get away," William said.

Carter watched Kalita approach the fire and sit opposite them. She excused herself, wanting to ask him something.

"Kalita?"

He looked up at her with kind eyes. "Your stay is short," he said.

She nodded. "How did you know?"

"I sense it in your energy."

"Will I ever be able to get that good at sensing energy?" she asked.

"You're already better. You just have to awaken that memory."

"I need to ask you something," she said. "If I came back from my previous life, then what about the others? What about John? My mom?"

Kalita nodded. "I often wonder that myself."

"You mean you don't know?"

"No," he said. "It's never happened before, that we know of."

"So it probably won't happen again?"

"I don't think so, Carter. I think there's a specific reason you came back."

"I just don't understand how that's possible."

"That's one of many things you will help us find out," he said solemnly.

"When I figure out how to communicate?" she asked.

"On that note," Paulo said as he walked up, rubbing his palms together, "I heard you managed some form of communication last night. Please, do tell!"

Kalita mercifully interrupted. "Carter, you were with Jack when you communicated?" She nodded, and he continued. "Then perhaps it's best if you work with him again. Perhaps he has a calming effect on you and allows you to open up."

She turned back to see Jack watching her through the fire, and she heated up at the thought. "Yes, I think that's a good idea."

"What? No! I want to see you try," Paulo exclaimed.

Kalita frowned at him. "Paulo, we will—in time." Kalita clapped him over the shoulder hard and led him away from the fire toward the table of food.

Just then Carter felt Jack's arms wrap around her waist. "What was that about?"

"We have a mission tonight," she whispered.

"Oh?"

She turned around in his arms and kissed him deeply, still in awe that she could so freely be with him after all they had been through. It made her realize just how much she had been missing out on.

CHAPTER 29

𒂖 𒀹 𒂊𒀹 𒂖𒀹 ⸗𒁲 𒀸 𒄿𒂊 𒂖𒀹 𒀸𒁲⸗ 𒂖𒀹 𒀹 ⸗𒄿𒂊 𒂊𒀹

THEY WALKED BACK TO THEIR now-favorite spot, and Carter took her shoes off and dipped her bare feet in the cool water.

"It's so beautiful here."

"What do you think Kalita meant about seeing a trace?"

She had completely forgotten about that. "I don't know. I didn't notice anything."

"There are a lot of strange people around," he said.

Carter laughed in spite of his seriousness. He raised his eyebrows as he watched her. Jack stripped down and then jumped into the water, purposely splashing her as much as possible.

Jack took her foot in his hand and started massaging it underneath the water.

"Kalita seems to think you can help me communicate again."

Jack ran his thumb along her ankle, down her foot, and underneath the arch. She became more relaxed with each stroke.

"What do you think?" she asked.

He ran his hand up her leg to the inside of her thigh, making her gasp softly.

"I think you're overdressed for the occasion."

Jack pulled her into the water, fully dressed. The clothes stuck to her skin and created a wave of fabric between them—creating interesting sensations. They spent their second night in a row in the desert, lost in each other and their own moments. The night passed with no communication, and Carter didn't care.

Before the sun rose, they made their way back to the village.

"I think you should stay with me," Jack said. "I don't like the idea of Jibril sneaking into your hut."

Carter could barely keep her eyes open by the time they got back to Jack's bed. She stripped down, slid in next to Jack, and had another dreamless sleep.

✡ ✡ ✡

SHE DIDN'T KNOW HOW LONG William was calling Jack's name from the door, but by the sound of his irritated tone, it must had been a while. She nudged Jack awake, not wanting to alert William to her presence—though he probably already felt her energy. She could feel his energy buzzing with anger, annoyance, and—disappointment?

"What is it, William?" Jack hoarsely asked.

Unfortunately, William took that for an invitation to come in. He stopped abruptly in the sunlit doorway upon seeing Carter wrapped in nothing but a thin sheet.

"I didn't invite you in," Jack hissed through clenched teeth.

"I see that," William said in a similar tone. "Did you two forget we have something we need to do? Or were you going to sleep the day away?"

Jack frowned. "When are we leaving?"

"When you're ready." William turned back toward the door and paused for a moment before leaving. "I wouldn't have forgotten today so easily," he said with his back to them both. She wasn't sure exactly who he was saying that to. He walked out, closing the door behind him, without saying anything else. Carter wrapped the sheet around her tighter.

"He's purposely trying to make you feel guilty," Jack whispered to Carter, wrapping his hand in hers.

"It's working," she said.

☆ ☆ ☆

KALITA AND ONAWA ESCORTED JACK, William, and Carter back to the main road near the reservation, where a cab waited for them. The entire time, Carter expected Jibril to make a sudden appearance again.

"How did you manage this?" Carter asked William, who sat in the front seat.

"Easy. I told them we're visiting my dad," he said. He paused and looked out the passenger window. "My dad always has protection detail around him—now I know why."

"William, maybe your dad has a reasonable explanation for talking to Amelia."

"I don't want to hear it, Carter. Not from you."

Carter's heart drummed faster as his words stung her. She felt the anger rolling off him and seeping into her pores.

"This is going to be a long trip," Jack mumbled.

"No one said you had to come," William said.

Jack looked at Carter curiously, and she responded to his confused expression.

"We have better-than-human hearing," she reminded him gently. Jack pressed his lips into a thin line in frustration.

"So where are we going?" Carter asked.

"Chicago," William said.

Carter shifted uncomfortably in her seat, remembering that Dr. Nathaniel had studied in Chicago. She couldn't help but think there was a connection. By the look of concentration on Jack's face, she guessed he was thinking the same.

CHAPTER **30**

⟨Y ⟨ ⟨Ξ⟨ Ξ⟨ ⊢YⲨ Ⲩ Yᴱ Ξ⟨ ⟨YⲨ⊢ Ξ⟨ ⟨ ⊢Yᴱ ⟨ΞY

T HE THREE OF THEM HAD separate seats on the flight to Chicago, and Carter was sure William did this on purpose when booking their trip. Still, Carter managed to switch seats with the kind woman sitting next to Jack. Jack crushed Carter's hand.

"Maybe you should take something when you fly?"

"I didn't know I'd be flying so much," Jack replied.

"I bet Dr. Nathaniel would prescribe you something."

"I don't think he's that type of doctor, Carter."

"With all these resources, I'm sure we know someone who's a doctor," she said.

"My dad's a doctor," William said, standing next to Carter's seat in the aisle. He was frowning at them.

"I didn't know that," she said, trying to not look uncomfortable by his sudden presence.

"He studied at Northwestern," he continued as he handed Carter a book. "You left that in my room," William said, and turned back to go to his seat.

"In his room?" Jack asked.

"Don't."

"Don't what?"

"Don't play his games," Carter said through gritted teeth.

Jack pressed on regardless. "Did you leave that in his room?"

Carter looked down at the Bible in her lap. "I don't remember where I left it." She frowned at her lack of memory and began absent-mindedly rubbing her temples in frustration.

"It's so good to see a young Christian woman," the lady in the seat across the aisle from Carter said, pointing at the Bible in Carter's lap.

Carter just nodded.

"Especially a woman who is so devout. How often do you read the Bible?" she asked.

"It feels like all the time," Carter answered truthfully.

The grayed-hair woman beamed. "That's lovely," she replied. "I read it all the time too." She leaned forward to look around Carter. "This must be your husband. Is he devout as well?"

Carter smiled. "Jack, why don't you answer the nice lady?"

"No," he answered in a grunt.

"Sorry, he's just in a bad mood. He gets really annoyed that I carry the Bible around so much," Carter said to the lady.

Her bushy gray eyebrows came together as she frowned at Jack, clucking her tongue. "You should be so lucky to have a lady who's so devout to Christianity. She is a *true* woman of God."

"Ya, I'll say," he said.

"Well, it's good that you at least recognize it," the lady continued, and Carter smiled.

"You have no idea," Jack said as he smiled back at Carter, all appearances of apprehension gone from his face.

"You two are a lovely couple," the lady continued. "I can see you were meant to be together."

"You have no idea," Jack whispered again, pulling Carter in for a soft kiss.

A ding sounded from overhead as the captain announced their descent into Chicago O'Hare International. With that sound, Jack tensed and paled. Carter frowned, feeling helpless. She squirmed as she felt the bone-crushing grip on her hand. She made a mental note to ask Dr. Moretti for a prescription for Xanax when they got to William's parents' home.

William was waiting for them as they exited the plane, still frowning.

"Well, ready to go meet my fake dad?" he said nonhumorously as they walked to the taxi stand. Carter sighed in response.

The trip to William's parents' home took nearly an hour in Chicago traffic. Carter looked through the taxi window at the passing scenery. Every place they visited was vastly different from her former home in Santa Barbara. At first the travels were daunting and made her homesick. Now she realized the possibilities were endless. She was without a home, and it didn't bother her the way it should.

"You like it?" Jack asked.

She turned to look at him and saw that he was watching the scenery over her shoulders as well.

"Have you been here before?" she asked him.

He shook his head.

"William? Did you grow up in Chicago?"

"I did," he said and paused. "I still live here. My condo is back on Lakeshore Drive."

Carter was more surprised at this than she should have been. She and Jack were currently without a home, but why would William be? They were thrust into his world, not the other way around.

"Do you like it here?" she asked.

"I do, a lot."

It was the first time in days that Carter had heard an inflection in his voice that wasn't anger.

"My brother lives in Michigan," he started. "So my parents don't really have anyone besides me here."

"You have a brother?" Jack asked.

Carter didn't know anything about William, and that saddened her. All this time he had taken the time to help her and understand her, and she realized she had never even taken a moment to get to know him. This wasn't who she was. This new life had become such a distraction to her that she had lost a large part of herself that made her the woman she always was.

"Ray. He's three years younger than I am."

Carter sat in silence, stunned by her epiphany. Jack gripped her hand, squeezing it tightly.

"You don't have to feel guilty, Carter. We've all been busy. Besides, your guilt is suffocating in this car."

They pulled up to a sprawling estate nestled in perfect landscaping. The front gate was wide open, so the cab pulled right up to the front door. William paid the cab driver, and they found themselves standing on the gravel drive.

"The alien business pays well, huh?" Jack asked as he leaned back, looking up at the three-story Victorian architecture.

William huffed under his breath, softly chuckling.

"It feels weird here." Carter spoke the words before she realized what she was saying.

"It does," William agreed.

"I don't feel anything," Jack said.

William walked up the steps to the front door and rang the doorbell. They stood for a few minutes as William continued to ring the bell.

"Maybe they went shopping or something," Jack asked.

"They have a housemaid. Someone's always home." William's voice was strained.

"What do you want to do?" Carter asked with growing concern.

William turned the doorknob, and the door easily opened. Carter's heart pounded.

"William, should we call the cops?" Carter asked.

"I don't know," William said, and Carter could feel the turmoil and conflict in his energy. It was the first time that she could feel anything from his energy, and she wondered if he had been blocking her the last few days.

"Let's look around the property first," Jack offered, and William nodded.

"Good idea," William agreed.

"Should we split up?" Carter asked apprehensively.

Jack and William both stared at the front of the house, as if it would provide the answer.

"Yeah, I'll go around the east side, and Carter, you go around the west. Jack can check the rest of the property to see if we find anything suspicious or telling." William turned and looked behind him at the still-open gate. "I'm going to close that. If someone opens it and tries to leave or come in, we'll hear it."

Carter nodded as she made her way around the house, stepping through the plush green landscaping. It was difficult not to be distracted by the opulence of the estate. She tried to imagine William growing up here with his younger brother. She wondered what William's parents looked like and half expected to run into them somewhere on the property—thinking that perhaps they just didn't hear the doorbell ringing. After all, how could you possible hear the doorbell from all corners of this immense mansion?

The rustling of trees alongside the eastern end of the house startled her, and she stood frozen. William appeared through the maple trees, looking flustered. It took a moment for Carter's heart to slow to a normal beat.

"Anything?"

"No." William shook his head. "I don't think anyone is here, but I'm picking up something strange."

"What do you mean?" Jack asked as he joined the duo behind the house.

"There's energy in the house, but I don't quite understand it," William said. Carter instantly tried to tune into what he was feeling. She couldn't feel anything herself, but felt it through him. Anguish.

Her heart sank. Something was wrong, and she was afraid to find out.

"I think it's time to check out the inside," Jack said.

William led the way back around to the front of the house and up the steps. He took a deep breath before stepping through the threshold. Carter held her breath, waiting for someone to come at them. No one showed.

"It's so quiet," Carter said. The inside of the home was grander than the outside. Her flats clicked against the black-and-white marbled floor, which opened into a grand lobby. A single, dark-wood-floored staircase lined with cream-striped carpeting led up to the second floor. In the center of the lobby was a round oak table with a large vase filled with a beautiful arrangement sitting in the center. In front of the vase was a single car key.

Carter looked to William curiously.

"I don't know whose that is. It's not my parents', and it's not Yolanda's."

"Yolanda?" Jack asked. Everyone spoke in hushed tones.

"Our housemaid."

"There's no car in the drive," Jack pointed out.

William frowned. Glass shattered from a room somewhere in the house.

"That's the kitchen," William said as he hurried along the hall down the east corridor. Jack and Carter followed on his heels and practically crashed into him when he came to a sudden stop in the kitchen.

A trail of blood, as if someone had been dragged, smeared nearly the entire length of the vast kitchen. The trail continued around the center island. Whatever happened had either started there or ended there.

The trio carefully walked toward the island, not making a single sound. Carter's heart was in her throat as she saw the lifeless body.

"What was she doing here?" Jack asked.

"Is she alive?" Carter said.

William leaned down to feel for a pulse. It seemed as if he hovered there for minutes. "No." He looked up at Carter and Jack. "Who is she?"

"Jibril's sister," Jack said solemnly. Carter began to panic. She knew Jibril was on their heels; would he think they had done this?

"Amelia?" William asked, familiar with her in an indirect way.

Carter and Jack nodded. "Who killed her?" Carter asked William without realizing what she was implicating.

The rage from William's energy nearly blasted her back. "William, I'm sorry—I didn't mean—I thought maybe you would have an—I'm sorry—I just didn't—" Carter fumbled over herself. "I'm sorry."

"What do we do now?" Jack asked.

"What if the killer is still in the house?" Carter asked.

CHAPTER 31

𒐊𒀀 𒐊 𒐊𒌋𒀀 𒐊𒀀 𒐊𒌋𒐊 𒌋𒐊 𒐊𒐊 𒐊𒌋 𒐊𒀀 𒐊𒌋 𒐊𒐊 𒌋𒐊𒀀

"N O ANSWER?" JACK ASKED WILLIAM.

"None. It goes straight to voice mail," William said.

"We need to call the police," Jack said.

"Let's call Stan," Carter suggested.

"I think that would be a great idea, if it weren't for the fact that they're still in the middle of nowhere," Jack said.

Carter felt deflated. "What if we call Jibril?"

"Jibril?" William asked abruptly. "Even if we wanted to call him, how would we manage?"

Carter wasn't sure whether this was the time to tell William about their nonaggressive relationship with Jibril.

"Jibril is unstable anyway. I'm not sure we'd leave here alive if he came and saw his sister like this," Jack said.

William watched Carter and Jack carefully and then suddenly turned to Carter. "What aren't you telling? I can feel it on your energy."

Carter looked at Jack, who shrugged. She spent the next twenty minutes explaining what had been happening since Peru, not leaving out a single detail.

"So he could already be on his way here?" William asked angrily.

Carter apprehensively nodded.

"He's going to think we did this," he said. Again, she nodded.

"OK, let's call the police," William said, running his fingers through his thick hair.

Carter had barely completed dialing 911 when they heard another crash from the kitchen. She dropped the phone and ran into the kitchen behind Jack and William.

Jibril had knocked a vase off the countertop. Carter guessed he had done it without realizing when he found his sister. The image of him standing there, staring at his sister, stunned, was the most human and normal that Carter had ever seen him.

"What happened?" Jibril asked in hushed tones.

Carter felt a slight relief that he didn't immediately accuse them.

"We don't know," Jack said.

Jibril leaned down on the floor and placed his hand softly on his sister.

"Who did this?" Jibril asked.

"We don't know," Carter repeated Jack's words.

Jibril looked at the three of them callously, lingering last on William. "Where are your parents?"

"I don't know."

"You guys don't know anything, do you?"

"Their phone goes directly to voicemail," Carter said, trying to explain. Jibril just nodded, watching his sister. Sirens sounded in the distance, which put everyone on alert. "I forgot I called 911. I didn't say anything. They must have just traced us."

"What do we say?" Jack asked.

Everyone frantically looked around at one another. "The truth," was all Jibril said.

Carter nodded, hoping she wouldn't have to say much at all.

The police arrived and immediately pulled each of them into separate rooms, questioning them extensively. Why were they visiting? How did they all know each other? Where were William's parents? How well did they all know Amelia? Carter found herself repeatedly saying she didn't know or giving extremely vague answers. After what seemed like hours, William came into the room with an older, graying man in a charcoal suit with a deep-red tie the color of blood.

"If you are to question my clients any further, you will need to take them down to arrest them and charge them. Considering we've established their alibi with the taxicab company and the airport, there is no possible way they were responsible," the man said.

Soon after, Jibril and Jack joined them in the sitting room while the police continued searching the home. Mr. Harold Moretti, William's uncle and also the Moretti family attorney, sat with the four of them and waited out the police search. Coroners came to remove Amelia's body, and Jibril sat stone silent. He had not said a word since their first encounter. Carter imagined it was the quietest he had ever been.

Her mind flashed back to the night in Santa Barbara when Carter's stepfather, Paulo, explained to her about Jibril's son. She remembered Paulo also saying that Amelia was his only family left. Losing his son had nearly driven him mad, if he wasn't already mad—and she could only imagine what this would do to him. She shivered in fear.

The energy rolling from William pressured Carter and gave her a headache. William's mind was in turmoil and confusion. He was also scared, something she had never felt from him before.

Detective Flores seemed to be the only one who didn't suspect them from the beginning—which meant that Carter instantly liked him. He had the right instincts, and she found herself drawn to watching him go through the crime scene. Hours passed, and they all continued to sit in silence, watching everyone come and go. Finally, the detective approached William.

"Mr. Moretti—"

"Please, call me William."

"William, your parents' room was ransacked. Can you think of anything that someone would want to steal?"

"Look around you, Detective. Can you think of something they wouldn't want to steal?" William's voice was cold and hard—a tone Carter wasn't used to hearing. It resonated of money, and she wondered if that was something instilled in him to command business and attention.

"I can see that. It seems that what they were looking for, they knew they would find in the bedroom. Otherwise, why is the rest of the house not in disarray?"

"Your guess is as good as mine, Detective. In fact, I'd wager your guess is probably better than mine."

Detective Flores nodded. "Well, we will be here the rest of the night tagging and securing everything. This home is officially a crime scene and will be locked up. I assume you have somewhere you all can stay?"

"They can stay with me," Harold Moretti said.

The detective handed William his business card. "If you hear anything from your parents or remember anything else—"

"I'll call you," William said.

As they stepped out in the drive, Harold Moretti abruptly turned on his heels. "I know who you are," he said to Jibril, who didn't look the least bit concerned about this. "And I'm not sure why my nephew and his friends are in cahoots with you. But I'm sure they have good reasons. However, *you* are not welcome at my home."

Carter cringed and felt Jack tense next to her. Jibril had just lost his last living relative, and she didn't think he should be alone—if not for his own safety, then for everyone else's. She didn't know whether he would have a change of heart over who was at fault and do something rash.

"You are a brave man," Jibril whispered. "You are a brave, brave man. For a man without a thing to lose and has everything to gain," Jibril hissed through his teeth. His words sent a shiver down Carter's spine.

Before walking down the drive, he turned to Jack and Carter. "Everything is different now."

CHAPTER 32

𒂍 𒐕 𒌋𒂍𒑴 𒂍𒉿 𒅗𒐊𒆳 𒅀 𒂍𒉿 𒂍𒐊𒅗 𒅗𒌋 𒂍𒉿 𒈠 𒅗𒐊𒅀 𒌋𒂍

"HOW DID YOU KNOW TO come for us?" Carter asked as they got into Harold's blue BMW.

"I called him," William said.

"I was at my office downtown. If I had been home, I would've been here in ten minutes. I didn't even get the message until an hour after Will had left it."

The drive to William's uncle's home was brief. The home was a stark contrast to William's parents'. In every way that their home was classic and Victorian, Harold's was modern and angular. Long, horizontal lines made up the Frank Lloyd Wright-esque home, whereas Greg Moretti's home was curves and depth. She wondered about the brothers. How similar and how different were they?

William's aunt greeted them at the door. She looked young, barely older than William. Her long blonde hair hung loosely around her shoulders, framing her perfect blue eyes. She hugged Jack and Carter tightly.

"I was so worried about you guys. Harry called me on the way to Greg and Christy's home and told me what happened. Are you OK? Did you hear from them yet? What did the police say?"

"Allison, perhaps we should let them settle in first. They've had a long day."

"Of course, you guys must be hungry. We have some pizza in the fridge."

Pizza was not what she had expected. Caviar? Brie and crackers? Not pizza.

"Pizza sounds great," Jack said. Carter smiled for the first time all night.

They all sat around the kitchen table while Jack, William, Carter, and Harold ate leftover pizza. Allison easily filled the silence with stories of how she met Harold and one of her own sisters who had moved to Chicago from Wisconsin. Her family was very close, and Carter admired that.

When they had finally finished eating, Harold jumped in. "Last I heard from Greg was a week ago. He said Ray needed some help with a contractor who was giving him some heat on unfinished work on his house. I called and spoke to Ray, and that was it."

"How often do you guys talk?" Carter asked.

"Once a week maybe, sometimes twice. We're both incredibly busy, but we still try to make time to connect."

"Do you know why Amelia could be there?" William asked.

Jack shifted in his chair, and Harold watched him curiously. Carter realized he was incredibly observant, and they would need to be on their toes.

"That is something I'd like to know as well," Harold said.

Carter couldn't feel Harold's energy at that point and noticed she couldn't sense William's either. They were hiding something, and she needed to find out what.

"You kids have had a long day; I think you should get some sleep. We have tomorrow to talk about this. Perhaps a good night's sleep will put a fresh perspective on things," Harold said as he stood up from the table, taking his plate to the sink.

"William, can you show Carter and Jack to their rooms?"

William led them down the hall to the far end of the house. "Jack, this will be your room." He opened the door to a sparsely decorated room. William turned around and walked back down the hall without waiting for a response.

"Where's my room?" Carter asked.

"Upstairs."

Carter turned and frowned at Jack. She wanted to say something and stay with Jack but thought better of it. They were in William's family's house, and she didn't want to aggravate William any more than he already was. Jack nodded at her, as if agreeing with her thoughts.

She followed William up the stairs. "This one is my room." William pointed to the first door on the left. Her room was just next door. He was doing this on purpose. Carter didn't know if she should be flattered or annoyed with him. At this point she was too tired to care.

"William?" she asked as she stood in the doorway, "is there a way we can get a hold of the guys back at the reservation? I think they should be in the loop."

William nodded. "Yeah, I was thinking the same thing earlier. I'll talk to Harry in the morning and see if he can think of anything."

Carter stepped farther into room as William hesitated in the doorway. She thought he would say something, but he just walked away. She heard the door to his guest room open and close.

Her guest room had an off-suite bathroom, and she poked around until she found some towels. By the end of her shower, she was already half asleep. She crawled into bed naked, too tired to look through her carry-on for her pajamas. She hoped for another dreamless night.

☆　　☆　　☆

THEY SHOULD OIL THAT, CARTER thought as she heard the slow creaking of the opening door. Her eyes shuddered open slowly, still heavy with sleep. The light of the moon cast slivers of light through the window, and that was when she realized it was still the middle of the night.

She abruptly sat up in her bed, realizing that someone was entering her room. Her mind was foggy as she struggled to remember where she was.

Harold Moretti stood at the side of her bed, inches from her, looming over Carter in the most menacing way. Carter gasped as she shrank back in her bed. Harold tilted his head, looking at her as if she were the prey and he were the bird about to go in for the attack.

She quickly leaned over to the nightstand and flipped the lamp light on. When she sat back in her bed, Harold was gone. She looked around her now-lit-up room and saw no traces of him. Her bedroom door was shut. Carter sat frozen in fear for several minutes before getting up. When she opened the door to peer into the hallway, the familiar creaking crept up her skin.

It wasn't her imagination.

Carter thought about going to Jack's room, but the dark hall frightened her like a child. What had happened? She didn't understand. She softly shut the creaking door again, creeped out by its sound. She locked the door and stood there for a moment, looking around her room. There were no traces of him anywhere.

Suddenly feeling overly exposed after sleeping naked, she went through her bag looking for her pajamas and quickly slipped them on. The Bible John had given her sat on top of her clothes, and she quickly grabbed it, hugging it to her tight.

She knew it was silly that an object could bring her comfort, but it made her feel safe. She thought she could still smell his scent on the book and realized that John had been a place of safety and comfort for her since the moment she met him. She felt that emptiness more than ever after what she had just experienced. She crawled into bed and read through the passages of Genesis again. She fell asleep with the light left on.

CHAPTER 33

𒂖 𒄿 𒍈𒄿 𒂖𒀀 𒀸𒅀𒄿 𒀀 𒅆 𒂖 𒄿 𒅖𒄿 𒍈𒀀

CARTER AWOKE IN THE MORNING to Jack sitting on the bed next to her.

"Morning, sleepyhead," he said.

"What time is it?" she asked.

"Just a little past ten."

She saw the open bedroom door behind him and panicked. "How'd you get in?"

His misread her tone.

"No, I mean...I locked the door last night."

Jack turned around to the door. "Are you sure? It was unlocked."

"I'm positive." Carter paled.

"What's wrong?"

Carter told Jack what happened the night before, and Jack frowned. "I don't think we should be here," Jack whispered.

William appeared in the doorway, and seeing Jack sitting on Carter's bed, he frowned. "There are muffins and juice on the kitchen counter for you guys." He turned around and left in a flash.

"I agree, but what about William?"

"I think he's safe here with his family."

"Are you sure? What if his uncle knows that William isn't really..." Carter was afraid to say it out loud. There was no one around, but she couldn't shake the feeling that the walls had ears.

Jack nodded. "We'll have to think of something," he said.

"Maybe we should call Dr. Nathaniel. Maybe he's figured something out."

"We need to call him anyway. He needs to know about Amelia," Jack said.

Jack sat on the bed quietly while Carter dressed and brushed her teeth and hair. Surprisingly, no one met them in the kitchen as they expected.

"Where'd everyone go?" Jack asked.

"They're out back," Allison said, appearing in the kitchen doorway. "Grab something to eat and come out and join us. The detective called again."

"Thank you Mrs. Moretti," Jack said politely.

She smiled at him, but something seemed off. Carter wondered if Jack noticed it too.

Jack piled three large muffins and a croissant on a plate and then poured a large glass of orange juice.

"Hungry?" Carter asked.

"Starving." He smiled, leaned down, and kissed her softly on the lips. "Apparently love does that to a guy."

Carter raised her eyebrows at him. "What did you say?"

And for the first time since Carter had known Jack, she saw him blush. "You heard me."

"I'm not sure I did." her smile grew larger.

"I said, love does that to a guy." He paused and brushed the tip of her nose with another soft kiss. "What, can't handle that?" He walked out onto the back porch, leaving Carter standing there with her glass of orange juice in hand.

"Huh," she said to no one in particular.

"*Leaveeeeeeee,*" the whisper hissed in her mind.

The glass of orange juice shattered to the floor into a thousand fragments. Everyone came running into the kitchen.

"Sorry, I shouldn't have washed my hands before picking up that glass," Carter said nervously. She bent down to pick up the fragments of glass, and Allison was there in a flash, startling her with her quickness.

"Sorry, didn't mean to startle you. I thought you were used to Anunnaki speed by now."

Carter just smiled in response as William stepped forward. "Is that why you dropped the glass? 'Cause your hands were wet?"

Jack and Harold turned to look at William curiously as William continued to frown at Carter.

"Yeah, why?"

"So there was nothing that scared you?" William asked accusatorially.

"Was there supposed to be?" Jack stood tall next to William as he spoke in a grave tone.

"I think we're all on edge, son. No need to jump at anything," Harold said as he smiled at Carter. His smile sent shivers down her spine as she remembered him the night before. He had been in her room, but she didn't know how.

The phone rang, and they all jumped slightly. Yes, they were definitely all on edge. Harold picked it up and immediately handed it to Carter.

"Are you guys OK?" Stan asked.

"As OK as we can be," she answered honestly.

"We're at the airport. Our flight leaves in thirty minutes. We'll be there as soon as we can."

"That was Stan. They're on their way here," Carter said to everyone, but mostly Jack. He nodded knowingly.

After the broken glass was cleaned up, they went back out on the porch.

"Leaaaaaaaaaaave now," the whisper came again. Carter stumbled into Allison, startled.

"Are you OK?" Jack asked, seeing Carter turn white.

"I'm OK." She looked around at Harold, Allison, and William already sitting around the table. She knew they had to leave, but she wouldn't leave William behind. She knew his life was in danger and knew that these people had something to do with it. She sat down stiffly, smiling. "Sorry, I just keep seeing flashes of Amelia's body in my mind."

"Understandable, dear," Allison said too kindly.

"You said the detective called?" Jack asked.

Harold nodded. "He did. He confirmed there were no prints in the house and nothing out of place except for Greg and Christy's room. They don't know what was missing. The safe there wasn't tampered with. They're doing an autopsy today, and we should get results back in a few days. It looks as if she died from blunt force trauma, though, is their guess."

"So now what?" William asked.

"They're searching for Greg and Christy. As of right now, they're suspects."

Carter watched and felt William's energy fall. She did not know what their relationship was like but imagined that whatever it was, this was a huge blow for him. She wanted to reach out to him but thought better of it.

"There was something I wanted to see," Carter started. "Maybe William can drive us to Fermilab. I think it'd be good to get away from everything anyway."

Harold stood up abruptly, "I don't think you should go anywhere," he said through clenched teeth.

"Why's that?" Jack stood up, matching Harold's bravado.

"Well, um…what if whoever got Amelia is after you guys?" It was the first time Harold had ever stammered.

William stood up now too. "That's all right. I don't mind taking them. I'm curious myself."

Carter watched as Harold pressed his lips together, his breathing increasing.

"*Gooo nowwwwww*," the whisper screamed in her mind, scratching at the surface like sharp nails against flesh.

Carter screamed, stumbling back over the chair she sat on.

"Carter!" Jack and William both yelled, running to her side.

"I'm OK," she panted as she struggled to catch her breath. "I just…I don't know what happened—my head is pounding."

"We should get you to a doctor," Jack said, concerned etched in the creases of his features.

"No, I'm fine—it was just a sharp pain. I overreacted. I'm fine. We should go, though."

Jack and William both pulled Carter up.

"Are you sure? Maybe she should be lying down instead?" Allison asked.

Jack and William looked at Carter. "No, we're going."

Allison frowned at them, and Carter thought she was going to try to stop them before they left.

"Here, take this cell phone. We'll call you if we hear anything else," Harold said as he handed William the phone.

✶   ✶   ✶

"I DIDN'T THINK WE'D GET out of there," William said as they drove away from the mansion.

"You and me both," Jack said.

"They were acting strange," William continued. "I have a feeling that whatever my dad was talking to Amelia about, Harry knew about as well."

Carter released a breath she didn't know she was holding.

"I think we should stay in my condo tonight," William said.

"What will your uncle say?" Carter asked.

"I don't think he'll say anything, as it's my condo. Why wouldn't I want to stay there?" he said. "Carter, what happened? Why did you scream? I know that was not a headache. I felt something strange in your energy."

"I don't know," Carter said. "I just felt a sharp pain in my head, felt like claws." It was a half-truth.

William put the Fermilab information into Allison's Range Rover's GPS system.

"Only fifteen minutes," William said.

They drove the entire way in silence. Carter kept thinking about the whispers in her mind. It was the first time since that night with Jack that she had heard the whispers. She had no idea what or who they were and really wanted to get on the phone with Dr. Nathaniel soon to talk to him.

"You've gotta be kidding me," Jack said.

"Is that it?" Carter asked.

The three of them gawked at the laboratory, which looked more like an architectural masterpiece. Two curved buildings faced each other like a dancers' embrace, surrounded by a man-made mirror lake.

"It's nice to see our tax dollars going to good use, I suppose," William said.

"Not exactly what I picture a Department of Energy building to look like."

"Looks like we're in luck," Carter said, pointing to the *Public tours today 12-2* sign near the entrance. "That starts in fifteen minutes."

They followed the sign around to the laboratory entrance and registered for the tour. The inside of the laboratory was more impressive than the outside. The two buildings surrounded a massive, lush courtyard.

The tour started in the lobby, where the physicist explained they'd be going through the four different parallel universe theories. Carter looked at Jack and William, stunned by their dumb luck. Carter, William, and Jack, surrounded by twenty-something science geeks, were directed through room after room of labs and strange things that Carter knew she'd never understand. She imagined Dr. Nathaniel would be in his element and wished he were with them to help explain what they were listening to.

They listened carefully throughout the tour as the scientist went through the first two levels of parallel universe theories, and neither made sense for what would work. Then, when he spoke on the third level, Carter knew that was the right one.

"Level-three parallel universes are different from the others posed because they take place in the same space and time as our own universe, but you still have no way to access them. You are continually in contact with level-three universes—every moment of your life, every decision you make, is causing a split of your 'now' self into an infinite number of future selves, all of which are unaware of one another," the scientist said.

"I don't think completely unaware of one another," Jack whispered into Carter's ear.

"Though we talk of the universe 'splitting,' this isn't precisely true. From a mathematical standpoint, there's only one wave function, and it evolves over time. The superpositions of different universes coexist simultaneously in the same infinite-dimensional Hilbert space. These separate, coexisting universes interfere with one another, yielding the bizarre quantum behaviors."

"Excuse me?" William raised his hand.

"Yes sir?" the scientist asked.

"Have we done anything to try to connect with these universes?"

A soft chorus of hushed laughter sounded through the brainiacs in the group, but William didn't seem perturbed.

"As a matter of fact, yes."

Silence.

William's smug smile said it all.

"There was a reporter for the *Dallas Morning News*, Tom Siegfried, who explained it best: 'Imagine a mansion with a secret room—the perfect setting for a mystery. Now imagine that the room is vastly bigger than the mansion itself—and contains more mansions.'" The scientist watched William, Carter, and Jack as he explained. A pin drop could be heard. Every pair of ears and eyes was astutely attuned to this scientist.

"You lost me," William admitted, and Carter noticed several heads bob in agreement.

"We have realized that nature may be concealing extra dimensions—not of sight or sound, but of space itself. Space's hidden dimensions."

"Right, like level three?" William asked.

The scientist nodded. "Hidden dimensions can't be seen because only gravity can go there. Part of those studies includes studying things on a fraction of a molecular level."

"What?" Jack asked.

"Think of a molecule—so small that you can't see it. Think of a fraction of a fraction of that molecule. The answers lie there—and that's what we're studying here." The scientist waved his hand around him at the room. "At our very own Fermilab."

"What have you found?" William asked.

Carter felt as if they were on the verge of being handed the information they needed.

"We are built of particles that cannot fall off and probe the extra dimensions," the scientist concluded.

"All but you guys," Jack said to Carter and William.

"We need to get a hold of Dr. Nathaniel," Carter said.

"You don't think he already knows this?" Jack asked.

The phone buzzed in William's pocket. He stepped outside the room to answer it, and Jack and Carter continued to listen to the tour. The scientist explained the fourth level of parallel universe, but Carter only half listened.

William came back into the room just as the group was split up looking around at one of the molecular observation machines.

"Stan and his team just landed. I gave them directions to my condo, but we should head out now if we want to meet them there. I live on the other side of town, and it'll take us some time to get there."

Carter nodded. She walked up to the scientist and thanked him for his time. They excused themselves as they got back into the car to head to downtown Chicago.

As they got in the car, William handed a small note to Carter with a phone number on it. "That's Dr. Nathaniel's number in Peru. You should call him when we get to my place."

"We can't call him now?" Carter asked.

William shook his head. "I don't want to use Harold's cell phone to call."

32

"Wow, this is beautiful!" Carter exclaimed as they pulled onto Lakeshore Drive. "I can't believe that's a *lake*," she said.

"Lake Michigan," William explained.

"It's big," Jack said.

"I could get used to this," she said.

"Wait until wintertime before you say that." William explained how cold it got near his condo during the winter, especially considering he faced the lake. He explained something called *lake effect snow*, and Carter didn't think she wanted to learn what it really was.

When they pulled up to the condo, William parked next to his Audi in the parking garage.

"You brought it back?" Carter asked.

He nodded. "Yeah, one of the guys towed it back to Chicago. I like my car."

She stared at the car, remembering the times she spent in there. They were nothing but fond memories, and it made her almost miss them. William shifted uncomfortably in his seat, and she struggled to change the thoughts in her mind. She knew he was sensing her thoughts.

They walked into the lobby, where Stan, Rafe, Paulo, and Amara waited for them. Seeing them all together without John broke Carter's heart all over again.

The lobby security greeted William. "Welcome back, Mr. Moretti. It's been a long time."

"My friends will be staying with me. I'd like to add their names to the list for full access to anything they need," William said as he turned to Stan and the team. "Did you guys want to stay with me as well? It'll be a tight squeeze, but we can work—"

"No, no, it's fine. We already have four rooms booked at the Omni."

"OK, then please add Carter and Jack."

The security guard took down Carter's and Jack's information, handing them key cards to the facilities as well as spare keys to William's condo. William's condo was on the top floor—the whole top floor. Carter and Jack stood in the doorway, stunned.

Floor-to-ceiling windows wrapped the entire thirtieth-floor penthouse. Deep plum drapes framed windows that overlooked Lake Michigan on the east and the city to the west. The furnishings were modern and rustic, masculine and comfortable. A dark wood baby grand piano sat in one corner of the living room, and deep-brown leather sofas formed a U shape around it. Wood carved statuettes were placed perfectly throughout. Two hallways led from the living room.

"You can come in," William said to Carter and Jack.

"This is amazing, William. I had no idea…" Carter didn't know why she should. It was clear she didn't know much about this man.

"No television?" Jack asked.

William walked over to the coffee table and picked up a remote and aimed it against the stone cast wall. He pressed a button, and the painting dissipated, turning into a flat-screen television.

"Nice," Paulo said.

Paulo, Rafe, and Jack sat on the sofa and started flipping through the channels.

Stan and Amara approached Carter as William went into the kitchen and opened the fridge.

"You OK?" Stan asked.

She nodded, sitting on one of the barstools alongside the kitchen island.

"There's something we need to tell you," she said.

William pulled out a cheese, crackers, and deli meat platter from the refrigerator. Amara stood next to Carter, rubbing her back comfortingly.

Carter frowned. "Where'd that come from? We've been gone for months."

"The complex supplies a housekeeping and house-sitting service. I called this morning and had them stock up the place and clean," William said as he placed the platter on the coffee table alongside a six-pack of beer. He pulled three from the pack and came back to the kitchen island where Carter sat. He handed one to Carter and one to Stan. "You might want to sit down for this," William said to Stan.

"Uh oh," Stan said.

Carter told Stan about Jibril and Dr. Nathaniel working with them in Peru. He remained quiet the entire time, but he turned several shades of red throughout the story. At one point, Stan crushed the beer can in his hand, spilling foamy beer all over the kitchen island top. He even ignored the guys on the sofa yelling at the basketball game on television.

"Carter, what were you thinking?"

Carter straightened her back and lifted her chin. Her voice became deeper as she spoke in as serious a tone as any of them had ever heard. "It was the right thing to do, and you will support him and us in finding out why his sister was working with Gregory Moretti."

The three men from the sofa fell silent and turned to pay attention to the conversation for the first time.

"Carter, after what he did to your father?" Rafe spoke from the sofa. She could hear the pain in his voice, and it made her bravado falter.

"It wasn't him," she said.

"So he says," Stan replied.

"I believe him," she said in a sterner voice.

"Carter, no offense, but it's not as if you've been doing this for a long time. Jibril is conniving. He knows how to get what he wants. You were vulnerable and—"

"I believe her, which means I believe him," William said, cutting off Paulo.

"What?" Stan and Jack both asked. Everyone now stood around Carter and Stan in a sloppy half circle except William, who was still on the other side of the island, leaning against the kitchen counter with his arms folded across his chest.

"What's so hard to believe? It's not as if you can fake energy. She picked up on his energy and knows the truth. We need to trust her."

Carter stared at William with her mouth hanging open as Stan ran his palms across his face in frustration.

"It would've been nice to know," Paulo finally said.

Carter just frowned.

"I know what we should do," William said in a chipper tone. "There's a great steakhouse just down the street. I'll call and make reservations. We need a break anyway."

"Before you do," Carter said, "can we try calling Dr. Nathaniel?"

William showed Carter how to connect internationally on the phone and then called the steakhouse. The phone rang a dozen times before

Carter gave up. She had barely placed the phone back in the cradle when it rang again. Without thinking she picked it up and answered, hoping that Dr. Nathaniel had noticed the missed call.

"What the hell are you guys doing there?" Harold hissed through the phone. His voice sounded like a pair of snakes slithering in her ear. She pulled the phone away from her in disgust.

Stan grabbed the phone from her. "Mr. Moretti, such a pleasure. It's been so long. We thank you for hosting Carter and Jack last night, but it's easier for our detail to watch them downtown. I asked William to host them until we head back."

Carter watched Stan in awe. She tilted her head, trying to listen to Mr. Moretti's response. But it sounded as if he was whispering. William frowned.

"Thank you, sir; that won't be necessary. We'll call you as soon as we hear anything."

Stan disconnected the phone before Harold could respond.

"How—how did you know?"

"I'm not human, Carter, remember?"

"Yeah, but still—"

"He's old," William replied.

"Old?" Amara and Carter both asked.

"Yup, just like a lot of the Anunnaki—old as dirt." William chuckled as he stepped out of the kitchen. "Time for steak!" He yelled.

"And more beer," Jack said.

CHAPTER 34

ᛒᛁ ᚲ ᚲᛒᚲ ᛒᛁ ᛁᛁᛁ ᛁᛁ ᛁᛒ ᛒᚲ ᚲᛁᛁ ᛒᛁ ᚲ ᛁᛒ ᚲᛒᛁ

DINNER WASN'T WHAT CARTER EXPECTED. It was normal. They didn't talk about aliens or murders or anything that had been the crazy part of her life. Stan didn't say much about his age when Carter pressed, but she wasn't giving up on finding out. They talked about everything normal, from movies to music to childhood stories. These were her friends, Carter realized.

Amara linked arms with Carter as they walked back to the condo, telling her about Paulo trying to learn to ride a horse on the reservation and falling off.

"I AM hath sent me unto you." The whispers screamed into her mind, tearing her from the arms of Amara.

Carter clawed at her face, struggling to remove the scratching sensations from her mind—not even realizing that she was screaming. The whisper came into her mind over and over.

"I AM I AM I AM I AM."

She gasped for air, struggling to breathe. The words drowned her mind, and she feared she would never see the light of day again.

Then, mercifully, the darkness covered her like a blanket.

✫ ✫ ✫

THE WARM HAND STROKED HER palm in soothing circles, and she felt the softness beneath her body.

"Mmm," she murmured.

"She's coming to."

Carter tried to open her eyes, but the piercing headache begged her not to.

"Carter?"

The voices sounded familiar through the fogginess, but she couldn't place who was speaking to her—or where she was. Last thing she remembered, she was—

She opened her eyes, "Oh my..."

"How are you doing, honey?" Amara asked softly.

"Headache," Carter managed to say.

Rafe handed her four blue ibuprofen pills as Amara and Jack helped her sit up gingerly. Stan stood next to the bed with a cup of water in hand. He reached out and handed it to her, concern etched across his forehead.

"We need to take you to the doctor," Jack said.

Carter looked around at everyone standing around the strange bed. She assumed she was in her guest room. She saw her suitcase in the corner.

"How'd that get here?"

"Messenger brought it while we were at dinner," William said.

"Messenger?" Carter asked.

"Yeah, Chicago has them everywhere. It wasn't a big deal," William said.

"Messenger," Carter repeated.

"Carter? Are you OK? What's going on?"

"What did I do?" Carter vaguely remembered screaming but didn't know what else had happened.

"You just kept saying 'Ahya' over and over again," Rafe said.

"Ahya?" Carter didn't remember that, and the word meant nothing to her.

"Ahya is another name for Enki," Stan said.

"What? Really?"

"You scared us to death. You just started screaming as if someone were stabbing you. It took everything to get you up here. Several people said they were going to call the police because they thought we hurt you," Jack said, his eyes large with concern.

"How'd you manage to get us up here?"

"William compelled them," Stan said, his brows furrowed together.

"He what?"

William shrugged. "I didn't know I could do it, either. So I'm just as surprised as you are."

"Is that an Anunnaki thing?" Carter asked.

"It hasn't been—not that we know of at least," William said.

Carter explained the whispers. She also told them that the whispers had been there for a while but had become more frequent and, recently, painful. Unfortunately, no one had any answers.

"The first time it was painful was this morning in Harry's house?" William asked.

Carter nodded.

"What do you think it is?" Jack asked.

"A warning is my guess," Stan said.

The ibuprofen finally started to kick in, and Carter didn't feel she would vomit from the pain anymore. She pressed her fingers against the bridge of her nose.

"Still hurt?" Jack asked.

"It's better now."

"This one was worse than this morning, wasn't it?" Jack asked.

"It was, but this morning felt more urgent. I don't know, but I feel I can sense the emotion behind the whispers. This one felt like a different person," she said, unsure of what she was saying.

"I don't understand," Stan said again.

"The whispers almost have a personality behind them. I mean, it's always the same unidentifiable voice, like twenty people whispering together through a pipe or something. But there's something about the energy behind them. They don't need to say much for me to understand their intent." Carter looked around as the last of the headache subsided and her mind became less foggy. "This morning they were scared for me. Tonight, it was as if someone who wasn't supposed to be there got through, although I don't think they meant to hurt me. Like ... being loud on the radio."

"I heard those whispers too," Jack said.

Everyone looked at Jack, surprised.

"When I was with Carter in New Mexico."

Stan turned to Carter, and she blushed in response.

"She was able to envelope us in that energy, and I heard the whispers too. It's almost like a bad telephone connection," Jack continued.

"Maybe that's essentially what it is," William said as he rubbed his chin.

"You don't get these whispers, though?" Rafe asked William.

"No, why?"

"Well, because you both have the gene, right? So I figured you'd both have a similar connection."

"Hmm, that's a good theory," Stan said.

Carter looked to the clock and calculated the time in Peru. "I'm going to try Dr. Nathaniel again. He would be able to help us with this."

"You stay in bed; I'll try him." William left the room to try Dr. Nathaniel.

Carter leaned her head against Jack's shoulder and shut her eyes. The day had drained her considerably.

"I think we should call it a day and let Carter get some rest," Amara said. Everyone except Jack left the room after hugging Carter. She was half surprised by the affection from her friends.

"Are you going to be OK?" Jack asked.

Carter nodded. She could barely keep her eyes open as it was. "I feel good here, really."

"My room is just down the hall."

"Your room? You're not staying here?"

"I want to, believe me. But this is William's home, and I wouldn't want him doing that to me."

Carter leaned in and kissed Jack. "I love you too, ya know."

Jack laughed loudly. "Good thing, 'cause I'm not going anywhere," he said as he left the room, shutting the door behind him.

Carter pulled her suitcase up on the bed and pulled out her pajamas and toiletries, laying them out on the bed.

She heard a soft knocking on the door. "Come in," she said.

The dejected look on William's face told her what she didn't want to hear. "No answer."

"That's weird, right?"

"He could be teaching or researching someplace. It's hard to say." William watched Carter as the worry lines etched into her features. "Carter, he's been around for a long time. He can take care of himself."

She nodded. He was right, she knew. But she would still feel better if she heard from him.

"I always wanted to bring you here," William said. Carter looked up to see him staring out the windows, admiring the city lights. "I just didn't think it would be like this, in separate rooms." When he looked back to Carter, he had aged twenty years. The lines were heavy on his face, and his mouth turned down in a deep frown. "We were meant to be together, and I know that now more than ever. It was written in the stars for us, and you can not ignore that."

William turned and walked out the door, shutting it closed. He was right. Her heart was with Jack, and her soul was with William. Her heart had won, and she hoped her heart would remain stronger.

✶   ✶   ✶

CARTER WOKE IN THE MORNING with the sun shining in on her. She had forgotten to close the shades over the large windows. She sat up in bed, staring at the city in awe. She stayed in her pajama pants and camisole when she went to the kitchen, realizing that she'd most likely be the only one awake.

She found some tea in the cupboard and boiled some water. Folding her legs underneath her, she sat at the breakfast table and watched the city come to life. Sighing deeply, she realized this had been one of her only moments of solitude since that night that John had swept her and Jack away into this new life. She realized it was most likely one of her last as well.

She sipped at her tea, enjoying the silence, and thought of the night before. She wished John were around. He would know what to do. Just when her cup was empty, she felt the energy shift in the room.

"Your calmness feels good," William said in a sleepy voice.

"It's hard not to be calm here," she admitted.

"You're welcome whenever you like."

She shifted in her seat uncomfortably.

"William, I don't—"

"I know, Carter."

He walked back down the hall and disappeared into his room. She washed the cup in the sink and went to the phone, calling Paulo first and then Julia. Both were beginning to feel like strangers to her, and it made her sad. These were people she saw on an almost daily basis, and here it had been nearly a year since she had seen Julia. The last call she made was to Dr. Nathaniel, and she sighed heavily when there was no answer.

"Still nothing?" Jack asked as he walked into the kitchen, fully dressed. Carter raised her eyebrows at him. "I don't want to get too comfortable here," he said.

She frowned. She was already too comfortable here.

"I'm starting to get really worried about him, Jack."

"Do we know anyone else there who can go check on him?"

She thought about that. "No, but maybe Amara does. She was there a lot longer than we were."

"Good idea. When are they coming over?"

Carter shook her head; she didn't know. William reappeared dressed as well.

"They're on their way here," William said.

Carter walked back to her room and laid out her clothes before hopping in the shower. By the time she got out and dressed, everyone was already sitting around in the living room.

Jack was telling everyone about the level-three universe they had learned about at Fermilab. Stan was nodding along as he listened.

"We're getting closer, I think," Stan said. "But we still have a long way to go."

"Amara, is there anyone you know back in Peru? We haven' t been able to get a hold of Dr. Nathaniel."

Amara thought for a moment. "I do know someone. My neighbor. Nice lady—I think she can help us. I'll get her number from my suitcase, and we can call later," she said in her broken accent.

Just then the phone rang, and Carter jumped. William was next to the phone, and he looked at it momentarily. "Blocked number; that might be him," he said as he handed the phone to Carter.

When Carter spoke into the receiver, she heard only static.

"Dr. Nathaniel? Is that you?"

The sweet honeybee voice spoke through the receiver as if transmitting through water. "Carter? Honey? Is that really you?"

"Who is this?"

"Well, it's your mother, of course."

CHAPTER 35

꜓Y ꜔ ꜔Y꜔ ꜓Y ꜒YꜛY ꜔Y꜓ ꜒꜔ ꜔YꜛY꜓ ꜓Y꜔ ꜛY꜓ ꜔Y

T HEN, IT WAS AS IF a million serpents' tongues licked through the earpiece into her ear, threatening to suck her into the darkness.

William yanked the phone from her hand and threw her into Stan, who stood just a few feet away from her. He ripped the cradle of the phone from the wall with such force that the cord ripped from the phone-jack.

"What was that?"

Stan clawed at his own head, yelling as he thrashed from side to side. William fell to the floor in a heap as he pounded at his head repeatedly.

"What the hell is going on!" Rafe yelled as he ran to try to help Stan. Paulo and Amara tried to help William.

Jack turned to Carter. "What's happening?"

The dark licked at her mind; the hissing seeped into the edges. Her head throbbed, but she knew it wasn't to the extent of what William and Stan were experiencing. "I don't know exactly."

"Can you stop it?" Amara yelled.

Just as suddenly as everything began, it stopped. Soft moans of agony escaped Stan and William, but it wasn't as bad as it had been.

"What—was that?" Stan said huskily.

"How'd you stop it?" Jack asked.

Carter shook her head. "I didn't. I didn't do anything."

"You must have," Paulo said.

Stan and William were helped to their feet, and both had bloodshot eyes.

The phone rang again.

Everyone looked at the dismantled phone on the floor with wide, disbelieving eyes. Jack picked up the shattered receiver and thrust it out over the balcony as everyone watched in abject terror.

"Your eyes!" William said in shock, looking at Carter.

Carter ran into the bathroom and switched the light on. When she looked at her reflection, she stumbled back into the wall behind her. All seven of them had crowded into the bathroom behind her, staring at her reflection.

"What's happening?" she asked in a mousey voice, afraid of her own reflection.

Her jade irises had been replaced by swirling serpents, swimming around her pupils. From a distance, her eyes would seem normal. Up close, the two serpents swirled around each other in an endless spin. She squeezed her eyes shut, and the residual licking sounds echoed in her mind.

"I can hear that," William said.

"Hear what? I don't hear anything," Paulo said as Jack, Amara, and Rafe nodded in agreement.

"I hear it too," Stan said.

"Whatever's happening is happening because you're all Anunnaki."

222

Carter pressed her palm against her forehead against the pressure.

A knock at the door caused everyone to jump. Rafe ran to the door and looked through the peephole.

"No one there," he said.

"No, one of the security guards would have called before they let anyone up."

Rafe stared at William. "Maybe a neighbor?"

"You need a key card just to access this floor on the elevator."

The knock came again, so loud that it splintered the door. Rafe, Stan, and Paulo pulled their guns out and held them to their sides.

Stan and Paulo approached the door from the sides, and when Stan nodded, Rafe threw the door open. They filed out into the hallway with their guns pointing in opposite directions.

Jack and William stood near Carter, flanking her and Amara, taking guard. Rafe remained at the door with his gun drawn as Stan and Paulo checked the area near the elevator. Carter's heart drummed in her ears loudly, and her palms were sweaty.

The knock pounded loudly again, but this time it wasn't the front door.

"Where was that?" Jack asked desperately.

"That was Carter's room," William said.

Stan and Paulo returned to the penthouse and ran toward the sound in Carter's room. They reemerged into the living room mirroring each other's confused faces while everyone stood, unmoving.

"Nothing," Stan said.

Rafe closed the front door again.

"What the hell is happening?" Paulo asked.

"The same thing that happened at my house in Santa Barbara," Carter said, frowning.

The air became charged with static electricity.

"OK, that didn't happen at my house," Carter said.

"What's happening?" Amara asked nervously, scooting in behind Carter.

A visible fissure formed in the air right in the middle of the living room. It was like looking through water. Carter, Amara, Jack, and William stood on one side of the fissure while Rafe, Stan, and Paulo stood on the other side. All seven of them slowly backed away from the growing phenomena until they could not back up anymore.

Sounds of conversation traveled through the fissure into the living room—conversations that were muted and muffled, sounding as if there were a wall between them and a party.

"I can't make it out; can you?" William whispered to Carter.

She shook her head. "I can sense something, though."

Stan edged around the perimeter of the living room, avoiding the fissure in the middle, until he was on the same side as Carter. Rafe and Paulo followed suit.

"I don't think that whoever's there is aware of us," Stan murmured.

"No, I don't think so."

A vase on the coffee table fell to the floor, crashing into a thousand pieces. The conversation abruptly ended. Stan raised his arm in front of Carter in a protective manner, the way her father used to do when he had to slam his brakes on the car—as if he could physically keep her from going through the windshield.

"They can hear us," Jack whispered.

The front door swung open, causing all seven of them to jump.

"*Carrrrrrrrrrrrterrrrrrrr,*" whispered the wind that blew in through the door.

The fissure seemed to respond to the whisper because it began to hum with energy. A light-blue, electric glow outlined the vibrating air in the middle of the room and slowly grew until it was nearly ten feet wide and six feet in height.

Carter watched the energy shift in colors from the blue to a soft, dusty pink to a light lime green. Carter watched the door from the corner of her eye and felt the wind caress her skin softly.

"Carter?" William whispered, pulling her in closer against him.

The wind continued to caress her cheeks lovingly, and she felt a familiar sense in it. Without realizing or understanding why, she stepped toward the fissure. Jack pulled her back while William and Stan stared into the light, mesmerized.

Stan stepped forward, reaching out to the fissure. He pointed his forefinger against the light, testing it. His fingertip had barely touched the edge when the fissure snapped closed, disappearing completely. Stan jumped back, grasping his finger.

"You OK?" Paulo asked frantically.

Stan held his hand out where the tip of his finger had been seared off. Then, as they all watched with their own eyes, his fingertip regenerated itself. In under a minute, it had been completely healed—as if nothing had happened.

"It's gone," William said as he stood where the fissure once was. "I don't feel anything. All traces of it are gone."

Carter felt a deep saddening by its departure. She hadn't realized the euphoria it had brought to her, and now the lack of it made her feel completely empty.

"That sucks," Stan said.

Jack, Rafe, and Paulo turned curiously to Stan, eyeing him as if he had lost his mind.

"Are you OK?" Amara asked, looking at Stan's finger, which he still held out in front of him in wonderment. He nodded.

"OK, what the hell is happening?" Jack asked. "Do any of you know?"

"I don't know, exactly." William still stood in the middle of the living room. "But it felt familiar."

Stan and Carter nodded. "Some of the voices I almost recognized," Carter said, finally sitting down on the sofa with an exasperated look. She ran her fingers around her neck, stretching her head back.

"Yeah, familiar to me too," Jack said. "Carter, one of those voices sounded like yours."

Carter tilted her head to the side as she thought about that. William went into the kitchen, frowning, lost in thought.

"He's right," Rafe said. "One of those voices did sound like yours, and I could have sworn the other voice sounded like William's."

Now Jack frowned as he watched Carter, hoping for some explanation as to what was going on. William returned with a dustpan and a broom and began sweeping up the broken vase. Amara joined him on the floor helping, mindlessly picking up the larger pieces and dropping them into the small shopping bag he was using.

Stan sat on the coffee table facing Carter. "Carter, what else did you feel?"

"I felt good," she said, watching him carefully. It was the first time anyone had looked her in the eyes since the mysterious serpents decided to take up residence in her irises. "I felt really good."

Stan nodded in agreement. "Yeah, I did too. It was almost like a drug," he said. "William, what about you?"

William continued to clean up the pieces, and Carter almost repeated Stan's question, thinking William hadn't heard them or wasn't paying attention.

"Yeah, I felt the same way."

A phone rang in the distance, and William's head popped up. "That's my office phone."

Stan took off and returned with the phone before anyone even had a chance to react. Their Anunnaki speed was still disorienting to Carter, even though she had used it herself at times.

"Do you recognize this number?" Stan asked as he handed the phone to William.

He shook his head. "No, but it's a local number."

William answered the phone and visibly relaxed when he heard the person on the other end of the line. Carter didn't realize she had been holding her breath until she let it out. William nodded a few times but didn't say much as he listened intently. Carter felt the instant change in his energy and stood up instinctively—as if a threat were nearby.

"What is it?" Jack whispered to her.

"I don't know. He's worried—um—or I don't know exactly."

"Yes, Detective, I understand," William finally said. Everyone exchanged looks of apprehension. "Yes, sir. We'll be there in about twenty minutes."

William hung up the phone and turned to everyone already staring at him at full attention.

"Amelia's body is missing."

CHAPTER 36

𒀉 𒀼 𒍦 𒀉 𒈾𒅍 𒍦 𒀉 𒐋 𒅖 𒀼 𒈾 𒀉 𒀼 𒈾 𒍦 𒀼

"I'LL RIDE WITH STAN," CARTER said, eyeing the Audi longingly. She could feel Jack's eyes boring into her skull. William looked at her sadly but just nodded in response.

Jack, Carter, and Amara rode in Stan's rental Jeep Cherokee while Rafe and Paulo rode in William's Audi. Stan drove behind William, following him to the police station.

"Are they going to let us all into the police station?" Jack asked.

"No, we'll wait in the car outside the station. But we don't want any of you traveling alone, and considering what just happened, it's probably best if we all stay together as much as possible," Stan said.

"What do you think happened to her body? You don't think Jibril—"

Stan shook his head. "I don't know, but for some reason I don't think Jibril had anything to do with this."

Though Carter agreed, she did not say anything. She wanted to see what the detective had to say first. They pulled up to the police station just as it began to rain. Carter pulled her sweater around her tighter, feeling colder against the cool rain.

When they stepped through the doors of the police station, Harold Moretti was already waiting for them in the front lobby. They interrupted him midpace, and the look on his face showed he was not happy—though Carter wasn't sure whether it was from the three of them leaving him high and dry or from their current situation with a missing body.

He let out an exasperated sigh and shook his head at his nephew, and William just shrugged in response. Carter could suddenly picture William as a little boy. She imagined he mostly always did his own thing and just nonchalantly shrugged off his deviance to his parents and family. Before Harold could say anything, a door opened, and Detective Flores stuck his head out.

"Thank you for coming on such short notice," the detective said. He opened the door wider and stood to the side. "We can chat in my office."

William followed the detective, with Carter, Jack, and Harold behind him. Even though Jack walked between her and Harold, Carter felt uncomfortable with her back to him. She knew Harold wouldn't pull anything in the middle of the police station, but all her instincts screamed at her to face him. She suddenly became worried that the freaked-out whispers would return and didn't know how she'd explain her behavior then to the police.

Detective Flores's shoebox of an office was overstuffed with paperwork and files. There were only two chairs in front of his overflowing desk, and he excused himself to fetch more chairs. As Carter sat in the seat closest to the window, she couldn't help but think about Dr. Nathaniel. Except instead of files and paperwork in an office, it was piles of books in his home. As she thought of Dr. Nathaniel, apprehension ate away as her stomach twisted in knots. She realized that the last time she had spoken with him was in Peru. It had been over two weeks since she had heard from him. The last person who had seen Dr. Nathaniel was Jibril, and that thought made Carter feel sick.

"What's wrong?" William asked.

Jack and Harold turned their attention to Carter, but thankfully the detective returned with the other two chairs before she could answer. William and Harold shifted their attention back to the detective, but Jack continued to watch her with concern etched across his features.

"Amelia Dekkers's body was found missing this morning when the medical examiner, Dr. Asha Bankowski, checked in." Detective Flores spoke in a bored monotone as he read through his notes out loud. Carter imagined that there wouldn't be much that would pique Detective Flores's interest anymore, including a missing body. "Dr. Bankowski was also the medical examiner who closed up last night. We already questioned the security guard on night duty and checked all security cameras. There were no unauthorized entries." Detective Flores leaned back in his seat and let out a sigh. He looked up and held eye contact with Harold for a few seconds before briefly looking at Jack, Carter, and William. "We have been unable to get a hold of the victim's brother since the night in question."

"We haven't spoken or heard from him either, Detective," Carter said.

The detective nodded. "That's what I imagined." The detective paused and looked around at the four of them again before leaning forward in his chair. "OK, look. I've been doing this for a long time, and what's confusing me isn't the homicide or even that we suddenly have a missing body. What's confusing me is why I was called into a meeting yesterday with the captain, the mayor, and an Agent *Smith* of the Federal Bureau of Investigation about this very case."

Carter swallowed a lump in her throat. She turned to look at Jack and William, who stared straight ahead at the detective with blank looks on their faces. Harold Moretti just nodded curiously as he rubbed his chin, as if this were the most fascinating information he ever heard. His energy, which the detective could not detect, said otherwise. Harold Moretti was hiding something, and in the process of trying to act indifferent to the detective, he forgot to block his energy from Carter.

"Ms. Robinson, they were specifically curious about you, though," the detective said, suddenly focusing all his attention on her. Carter saw Jack shift uncomfortably next to her from the corner of her eye and felt William's energy shift, though he showed no physical reaction.

"What do you mean?" she asked nervously, wishing she could remain as indifferent as the boys were.

Detective Flores continued to watch her, and Carter felt as if she would burn under his stare. She wasn't sure what he was searching for while he looked at her, but whatever it was, he seemed satisfied with the result because he visibly relaxed as he continued. "Who are you guys?" he asked.

"I'm not sure what you mean," Harold said.

Detective Flores looked to Harold curiously, and Carter felt the detective's shift in energy. He did not like Harold and didn't trust him, she sensed. The detective's instincts were right on par, she thought.

"I've been doing this a long time, Mr. Moretti, and I've seen a lot of homicide cases, and never has the mayor gotten involved, let alone the FBI, on any old case. In fact, I can't think of a single time when I've even spoken to anyone at the bureau. Obviously, this is no regular homicide case, and you're no regular folk either. So what I want to know is who you are and what makes you all so special, especially you." The detective looked to Carter again.

"Detective, your guess is as good as mine," Harold said coolly.

"Is that so?"

"Yes, sir. I'm just as curious as you are."

The detective leaned back in his chair again and tapped his pen against his chin. He then turned to Jack suddenly.

"You didn't tell us you are active duty, Senior Airman Freeman."

"You didn't ask," Jack said. Carter saw the muscles tense in Jack's neck and jaw and knew that the detective would have noticed it as well.

"So you're just hanging out with these guys?"

"I'm on leave."

"For eight months?"

Jack shifted in his chair, sitting up straighter.

"May I ask the relevancy of these questions, Detective? I'm not sure that Mr. Freeman's service duty is under investigation, is it?" Harold's tone took on a different lilt, the distinct lilt of an attorney acting officially.

His tone never fazed Flores. "No, his service duty is irrelevant—for *now*." Flores stood up, walked around his desk, stood directly in front of the four of them, and crossed his arms. It was an intimidating stance, and Carter was sure it was on purpose.

"That's all for now. I'm going to ask that you all remain in town for the time being, in case I have more questions."

"Of course," Harold said, standing up.

William, Jack, and Carter stood up as well and followed Harold out the door. Carter hoped that the detective would remain behind in the office, but he followed closely behind them. Just as they were entering the lobby and Carter thought they were done, the detective stopped them.

"Just one more question," Flores said. All four turned back to face him. "Is there a reason your main phone number is disconnected, Mr. Moretti? Is there something wrong with your phone?" Flores asked William.

"Oh, yes. My housemaid must have done that."

"Really? Because it seems that the line itself has been severed. We've already contacted the phone company."

"Oh, um, hmm. I'm not sure. I'll look into it when I get home," William said.

"Good idea," Flores said, clearly not believing William.

William nodded awkwardly, and they all left the building. Carter was thankful that at least the rain had stopped.

"So why *was* your phone line disconnected?" Harold asked.

"Like I said, must have been the housemaid."

"You're lying."

"If that's what you want to believe, then that's what you will believe," William said, frowning at his uncle. "Have you heard from my father?"

Carter and Jack stood to the side as William and his uncle seemed to have a silent standoff. Carter leaned unconsciously into Jack, who wrapped his arm around her shoulder protectively. She felt the distant sounds of warning whispers in her mind and willed them to remain silent. *I know,* she mentally spoke to the whispers, hoping they could hear her thoughts. It seemed to work because the whispers quieted even though Carter could still feel a cord of connection with them, as if they were silently listening.

"Maybe you should tell me what's going on, Uncle."

"What do you mean?"

"Where's my father? I know you know."

"If I knew, don't you think I'd tell you?"

William just watched his uncle, searching for an answer. "Perhaps."

Stan mysteriously appeared behind Harold, startling him—and Carter. She didn't even hear the car door open or close. Harold spun around to face Stan.

"Mr. Moretti," Stan said, nodding and giving Harold a charming smile.

"Mr. Capshaw, it's been a long time. We haven't seen you at any of the meetings."

"We've been busy," Stan said, squaring his shoulders.

"Yes, that you have, and my condolences on the loss of your boss."

Carter frowned at Harold. She had never received any condolences for the loss of her father. She knew it was a childish reaction, but she couldn't help it; it was like a slap in the face.

"The loss was greater for Carter. She deserves the condolences more," Stan said, placing his hand on her back supportively.

"Of course, Ms. Robinson knows she has my deepest regrets," he said, smiling.

Stan and Jack led Carter back to the car as William walked to his Audi without saying another word to Harold.

"I'm starving," Stan said as he got into the car.

Stan sent a text to William, and they were on the road. They pulled into Portillo's, and Carter had no idea what type of food they had.

"Portillo's?"

"No, Portillo's, not the Spanish spelling. You say the *l*."

"OK Stan, Portillo's. What is it?"

"Only the best hot dog you'll ever eat."

Carter's stomach twisted into knots. Between Detective Flores and Harold Moretti, she didn't think she'd ever eat again.

"Hot dog?" Amara asked.

"Don't tell me you don't know what a hot dog is?" Jack asked, bewildered.

"No, it's a dog?"

Stan, Carter, and Jack chuckled, and Amara frowned. "No, not a real dog. It's just called that. This is beef," Jack explained.

"Americans are strange," Amara said, smiling.

Carter and Amara sat at a table while the boys ordered food. Carter tore a napkin to shreds as she explained to Amara what the detective wanted.

"He may be a good detective," she said. "But he could never guess the truth. And even if he did, no one would ever believe him."

"That's true," Carter said. "I'm living it, and I barely believe it."

Stan returned with a tray stacked high with foil-wrapped hot dogs and beef sandwiches. Jack followed with a tray with seven sodas, and William followed with a tray topped with French fries. Amara and Carter burst out with laughter at the comical sight.

"Are we feeding a small country?" Carter asked.

"Check this out," Stan said, holding his hand out to Carter. "Feel my fingertip."

"Uh…" Jack stared at Stan.

"Not like that you, jackass," Stan said to Jack and then started laughing out loud.

"He said jackass, and you're Jack!" Paulo said, joining in on the boisterous laughter.

"Wow, you guys are making me feel like I'm back in college," Carter said, but laughing regardless.

She reached out and felt Stan's fingertip with her thumb and jumped at the electric charge she felt.

"What did you feel?" William asked.

"Same thing I feel every time I touch you," Carter said and instantly regretted it. She made the mistake of looking at Jack, whose face fell. "I mean, that weird electric charge."

William ignored the exchange between Carter and Jack, thankfully, and reached out to touch Stan's hand as well. "I have an idea," he said. As he unwrapped the foil from a beef sandwich, he looked at Carter. "I think that might have been level three."

"Parallel universe?" Jack asked, and William nodded.

"Yeah, that's great," Carter said. "But what does it all mean?"

Silence fell over the group as they ate the rest of their meal, undoubtedly tossing ideas around in their heads. If the ideas were anything like Carter's, they weren't coming up with anything worthwhile.

"I don't know," Jack said as they all got back in the cars. Carter turned around, wondering if he was responding to a question she hadn't heard. By the looks on everyone's faces, she hadn't. Jack was losing it, she decided. "I don't know what it all means. But I do know that we're getting closer to finding out. It seems that whatever we're doing is working."

Carter tilted her head to the side, thinking about that. "We haven't really been doing anything, though."

"True, but you were able to open up communication with Jack that one night. What were you feeling when that happened?" Stan asked as he pulled out of the parking lot and headed back toward William's condo.

Jack cleared his throat. "That's a little personal," he said.

"Oh," was all Stan managed. Carter blushed in response.

"Well, this isn't awkward or anything," Jack said, and Amara, Stan, and Carter nodded in agreement.

"Maybe it helps that you were in New Mexico?" Amara asked. "I mean, how can anyone think with all the chaos happening here in this big city?"

Carter remembered the time on Machu Picchu and how she was able to see the Sun Gate then. "I think you're right, Amara."

"So what do we do?" Jack asked. "Detective Flores was clear that we can't go anywhere."

"And where would we go anyway? Back to New Mexico? To Peru?" Carter thought of Dr. Nathaniel and felt anxious. The last thing in the world she wanted to do was go back to South America, but she also wanted—no, needed—to know what was happening with Dr. Nathaniel. He might need their help.

"We can take care of Detective Flores," Stan said. "But what about Amelia? I think it's important we find out how she was killed and what happened to William's parents."

Carter sat back in her seat and looked out the car window as they pulled into the parking garage to William's condo. She liked Chicago, she decided. She sighed heavily as she thought about what they could do or where they should go and guessed the others were thinking the same. What she really wanted more than anything, though, was a nap.

"I don't think we should go to New Mexico," Jack said. "It seems we got all the information we could get while we were there."

"Except the tablets," Carter said. "The tablets are still there."

Jack and Stan nodded.

"But Dr. Nathaniel has more information on the DNA," Amara reminded them as they all walked toward the lobby door.

Stan was catching Rafe, Paulo, and William up on their conversation as they stepped into the lobby area.

"Detective Flores," Jack said. Carter stumbled into Jack as he abruptly stopped in the lobby. "What's going on here?"

Detective Flores wasn't alone. He was accompanied by eight officers and a very angry-looking Jibril. The officers put Carter, Jack, and William against the lobby wall and handcuffed them.

"You're all under arrest for the murder of Amelia Dekkers. You have the right to remain silent. Anything you say can and will be used against you in a court of law. You have the right to an attorney. You have the right to have your attorney present with you during questioning. If you cannot afford an attorney or do not have an attorney, one will be provided for you. Do you understand your rights?"

"I understand," William said.

Detective Flores repeated the Miranda rights to Jack and Carter individually. They said they understood as well. Rafe, Paulo, and Amara stood in the lobby watching in shock. Carter wasn't sure what was happening with Stan, but guessing by everything going on, she thought he was probably already somewhere calling in some favors or something.

"Can I call my uncle?" William asked.

"You can certainly try, but your uncle is nowhere to be found," Flores said.

Jack and Carter exchanged looks of apprehension. She looked over her shoulder and saw Jibril leaning against the security counter with his arms crossed, looking quite smug. She thought of Amelia on the kitchen floor covered in blood, she thought of Jibril's anguish with his son, she thought of William's missing parents and uncle, and a haze started to cloud her eyes as her own desperation clawed its way through her mind. She was on the verge of a psychotic break, she knew. Too many things were happening with no resolution, and she didn't understand how they could continue to tumble down this path without any answers. The more they learned, the more questions she had. No one knew anything, and she was angry. She looked at Jack, who leaned his forehead against the wall in near servitude and thought of taking him away from Santa Barbara, of taking him on this whirlwind of chaos. She turned to see William pale and looking sick. She had broken his heart, and then his world had continued to collapse. By the time she turned back to Jibril, her vision had gone red. She didn't know what he saw in her expression, but he stood up suddenly, alert. He took one step toward her and then another. William's head popped up like an animal hearing its prey. He turned to Carter and gave her one long look before his face flushed with anger.

"Where do you think you're going?" an officer said to Jibril.

Jibril never broke eye contact with Carter, but he stopped moving forward. She saw him calculating his next move, felt it.

You bastard, she thought. *I hope you can hear this somehow.* He didn't react to her thoughts.

Hadn't they lost enough already? He was only making it worse.

Yessssss, the whisper came. This time the whisper was solemn, alone.

She became fueled by the energy swirling within her. She realized all this time she had a wall up—a wall she didn't even know she had put up.

Yesssss, the whisper came again, anxious. *Yesssss,* another whisper joined in, sounding familiar. The familiarity tickled her mind. She knew that voice, knew it well, but for some reason her mind blocked out whose voice it was.

She felt a sharp burst of energy from William so strong it nearly pushed her back, as if it had physically hit her. She turned to William and saw that his eyes were also now swirling with serpents. The ferocity of anger and anguish rolling off of him pelted her, and the energy around them started to physically transform.

"What the hell?" one of the officers asked.

Carter saw Jibril's eyebrows come together in confusion. First time for everything, she thought.

"It's happening again," Jack whispered to Carter.

"What's happening?" Flores asked, overhearing Jack.

The fissure returned, larger and more profound than before. Every officer in the lobby, the security guards, and Jibril all backed quickly away from it. They formed a sloppy circle around the fissure, watching it in awe.

Carterrrrrr, the whispers came again, more urgent.

Carter did the only thing she could think of at that moment. She jumped into the fissure.

CHAPTER 37

𒂠𒀸 𒋫𒀸 𒂠𒀸 ᐅᛁᛁ 𒊏 𒁹𒂠 ᐳᐊ 𒀸ᛁ ᐳ 𒂠𒀸 𒀸 ᐳᛁ𒂠 𒋫𒀸

T HE TIGHT VACUUMING SENSATION SUCKED the air out of her lungs but lasted so briefly that by the time she could register its discomfort, it was already gone. She landed so hard on the floor that it jolted every bone in her body.

"Ow," she said out loud to no one.

Getting up off the floor proved difficult since she was still handcuffed. She looked around at the familiar surroundings, but it felt different.

"You've got to be kidding me," she said again to no one.

She awkwardly managed to stand upright as she looked around the living room still overflowing with books. The tight whispering and sucking sound startled her, and she turned around just in time to see Jack and William come crashing through the fissure simultaneously, landing on the floor in a heap.

"Hey," Jack said to Carter hoarsely as he caught his breath.

The fissure sealed shut behind them.

"Where are we?" William asked from the ground.

"Dr. Nathaniel's home, I think," Carter said.

"You think? This is his home; looks just like it," Jack said.

"Looks like it, but doesn't feel like it," she said. "It's missing something, and it feels creepy. His home never felt creepy to me before."

"It feels stale here," William acknowledged.

"We need to get these cuffs off," Jack said as he stood up more grace-fully than Carter had managed. "How'd you know to do that?" Jack nod-ded his head toward where the fissure had been.

"I didn't," Carter said.

"Wow, well that's reassuring," William said sarcastically, now sitting cross-legged on the floor.

Carter walked down the hall to where Dr. Nathaniel's studio office was and started rummaging through drawers. She found a pair of thick wire cutters, an ice pick, and a handsaw. She managed to carry the wire cutters and ice pick back out to the living room and handed them to Jack. "Do you think these would work?"

"They might, if my hands were in front of me and I could see."

"So what do we do?" Carter asked. "What are you doing?" she asked William, who was turning several shades of red.

After about a minute, William pulled both hands apart and held them out in front of him.

"How did you do that?" Jack asked.

"Anunnaki strength," William said. "We're normally not that strong, but something about going through that weird portal made me feel I could do it."

Jack and Carter both focused on trying to remove their own cuffs. Jack managed to remove his in about two minutes, and Carter took about five.

"Well, that's pretty cool," Jack said, and Carter nodded in agreement.

Carter walked to the end table by the door and picked up the phone there, holding the receiver to her ear.

"Nothing," she said.

Jack walked up to the window and looked out, pulling the shades back. "It's early morning here, but there should still be people out. There's nothing."

"OK, now really, where are we?" Carter asked.

"Do you smell that?" William asked.

Carter sniffed the air but couldn't pick anything up. "No, what?"

"Nothing, exactly. I don't smell anything at all." He walked over to the sofa and knelt down, sniffing it. "Nothing. I can't smell the leather."

Carter and Jack both did the same thing. Jack then ran into the kitchen and opened the refrigerator, picked up a package of moldy cheese, sniffed it briefly, and then sniffed it again. "I don't smell it," he said to Carter and William, who both followed him in.

Carter ran down the hall then and found what she assumed was Dr. Nathaniel's bedroom and the on-suite bath. She opened up a medicine cabinet and found a half-empty bottle of cologne. Opening it, she sniffed. "Nothing; there's no smell at all," she said, handing the cologne to Jack, who stood closest to her.

"Did the portal take away our sense of smell?" Jack asked.

No one answered. Carter then stomped on the wood floor. "Did you hear that?"

"Hear what?"

She repeated her steps and then took the bottle of cologne from Jack's hand and dropped it on the floor, shattering it.

"No sound," William said.

Carter felt as if she couldn't breathe. "What's happening?" she whispered.

"We seem to be asking that a lot," Jack said.

"We should go find someone so that we can call Chicago," William said.

"We should find Dr. Nathaniel since we're here," Carter said, and then paused. "I can't believe we're back here."

Jack and William nodded in agreement. "Is it me? Or are people doing a lot of disappearing?" Jack asked.

"Well, we just did." William ran his fingers through his hair in frustration.

Jack looked at the books sitting on top of the coffee table, lifting one in his hand and running his fingers unconsciously over the cover. "We should look around and see if we can figure out where he got in his research. Maybe, it will help us figure out where he went."

Carter nodded. "I'll start in the lab." She walked slowly and deliberately down the hall to the lab, and the lack of sounds and smells was disorienting. She opened the silent door and fully expected something to jump out at her. Something was definitely not right, she thought.

Everything looked as she remembered. Vials and tubes of liquids she would never be able to identify sat stagnant in their bottles. She walked around the room looking for anything that might tell her something about the missing Dr. Nathaniel. At the end of the room just under the lone window sat a small workbench with piles of paper.

On top of the bench was a notebook with notes in Dr. Nathaniel's handwriting.

March 12th, 3:02 pm
VI. 1-3 Results 0
VI. 4,5 Results 3
VI. 5-9 Results 3
C.R. — VI. 5,7
W.M. — VI. 4,5
C.F. — VI. 8,9
Tests proved conclusive for C.F. match to W.M. Note: Contact C.R.
with results in a.m.

☆   ☆   ☆

"CARTER."

Carter jumped at the sound of Jack's voice behind her. It sounded as if he were speaking through a tunnel.

"Sorry, didn't mean to startle you. Did you find anything?"

"I think so." She handed Jack the notebook. "You sound strange," she said, looking at his face. "You look sort of strange too, as if there's a film over my eyes."

Jack nodded. "Yeah, we noticed it too. Whatever's happening seems to be getting worse as time goes on." Jack looked back down at the notebook. "March 12? That was what, six days ago?" Carter nodded. "OK, let's take this with us and get out of here."

"You didn't find anything?"

"Nothing out of the ordinary, but William wants to get out of here as quickly as possible, and I agree."

Carter walked out of the room, and Jack followed with his hand on the small of her back. It was a small gesture, but his touch brought comfort to her. She was glad that he was with her and had come through the portal. She'd be terrified otherwise—or more terrified. Her anxiety grew with each passing moment, as did the feeling that something was very wrong.

Don't ignore your instincts. Dr. Nathaniel's parting words echoed in her mind now.

William waited near the front door for Carter and Jack, and he opened the door the moment he saw them. The air outside was just as stale as the air inside the house.

"Why do I get the feeling that we're not going to see anyone?" Jack asked as they stepped out onto the humble porch.

"I share that feeling," William said.

Carter stepped onto the gravel ground and heard no crunch under her feet. No sound of birds sang from the trees. No wind rushed through the trees.

"So strange," she said, and even her voice sounded foreign to her, distant.

"It's as if we're in a vacuum." William looked around at the sky. "There are no animals."

"Maybe we are," Jack said. "In a vacuum."

Carter and William turned to Jack simultaneously, his words resonating. They walked four blocks to the main road, and all shops and streets were devoid of people or animals. They reached a bakery at the corner, and Carter tried the door. It opened.

Carter, Jack, and William walked into the bakery and saw it was vacant. Carter walked behind the counter and picked up one of the pastries from the cabinet. She tried smelling it. "Nothing," she confirmed.

Jack took the pastry from her hand and tasted a bite, then spit it out. "It's like eating cardboard."

William walked to the back room, picked up the phone there, and shook his head when Jack and Carter looked at him questioningly. Carter and Jack followed William into the back room and looked around. It was as if time had frozen. A notebook was sitting on a desk with a half-drawn rough sketch of a cake on it.

"What do we do?" Carter asked.

"We need to figure out how to access that portal again and somehow get back. I have a feeling time is running out here," William said.

"If time even exists," Carter said.

They were stepping back into the main area of the bakery when William held his hand up, stopping Carter and Jack.

Carter looked up to see what William was stopping them for. "Is it getting darker?"

"That's impossible. Isn't it only morning here?" Jack asked.

William shook his head as he stared outside. "It's not getting darker as if it were night. It's as if someone covered us up with a blanket." He was right. When night fell, building and fixtures would cast long night shadows and depth from the darkness. This was like someone lowering the light from all around them. There was no sun setting. The light was simply going out.

There were no shadows—except for one, Carter noticed, across the street under the cover of two buildings. It was a dark, humanoid shadow that Carter hadn't noticed before and would not have noticed under any other circumstances. Shadows didn't belong in this place, just as William, Jack, and Carter didn't. Whatever she was looking at didn't belong here either. And that thing that didn't belong there sought her our as she felt the violating thoughts vibrate through her skin.

"I see it," William said. Carter turned to see him looking in the same general direction. "I can feel your energy more here. I'm not sure if it's because everything else is void."

Carter ran her hands up and down her arms self-soothingly, though deprived of the comforting sensations. She realized that William was correct and she could distinctly feel both his and Jack's energy. Their energies were mirror reflections of each other, filled with apprehension, tension, and fear. Carter reached out her senses farther across the street and stumbled back at the taste of the shadow.

"What's that sound?" Jack asked.

"Sounds like those whispers," William said. "That might be the portal."

"We need to get back." Jack walked forward toward the bakery door. "Now."

"There's another one." Carter pointed to the other side of the building where another shadow lurked. She felt William mentally reach to the shadows and then reflexively recoil when he tasted their energy, just as she had moments before.

"Not good." He ran his fingers through his hair.

The whispers seemed to grow more urgent with each passing moment. "We're trapped." Carter hugged herself tightly as she desperately tried to figure out a way back.

Jack retreated to the room they had emerged from. "Maybe there's a back door? Stay here and keep an eye on those guys."

"That's what you heard on the phone, isn't it?" William asked as he intensely watched the shadows across the street.

Carter nodded in response.

"Was that the first time you heard it? That night?"

"I'm not sure. I don't think so, but I can't remember when or where I heard them before."

Jack returned quickly, calling from the doorway, "There's a window. It's small and up high, and it isn't the type that opens, but I think it'll work. It's our only chance."

Carter remembered being locked in Jibril's basement with Jack and became angry as she recalled that memory. How could she have been so forgiving of him?

The shadow slowly began to seep onto the road toward them.

Again they were in a predicament because of him, and even though it was because of Amelia's death, it was unforgivable.

William pulled Carter toward the back room, where Jack was anxiously waiting. William shut the door behind them as Jack stacked boxes underneath the narrow window. William turned the lock on the door, but of course there was no sound when the lock fell into place. Carter placed her hand on William's arm and pointed to the doorknob, which moved slightly, as if someone were attempting to turn it. Her heart drummed in her chest.

The only sound she could hear were the whispers in the distance, which steadily seemed to grow more anxious with each passing second. Jack wrapped a towel around his hand and punched the glass out of the window, and Carter was thankful, for the first time, that they were void of sounds. He brushed the glass away with the same towel as much as he could and then laid it out on the bottom sill.

"You have to be careful going through the window," he said, and Carter nodded. She saw that William was still watching the doorknob, which seemed to go still.

"William, you go through first and make sure everything is clear, and I'll hoist Carter up behind you."

Carter looked at Jack nervously, not wanting him to be the last out. She realized they didn't have any other choice, though, as she wouldn't be able to pull herself up through the high window herself. From the corner of her eye, she saw movement and looked back toward the door, seeing it vibrate. Something had slammed itself against the door.

"We have to hurry," Jack said to William, who was already in the process of pulling himself up. Carter cringed at the bloodstains left on the towel from William's hands.

Carter turned back to look at the door and saw that the center of it had splintered through, and the doorframe was already starting to give way. They were running out of time. Jack knelt down and hoisted Carter up. She felt the sharp stings as glass scraped her palms and shins. She briefly managed to look over her shoulder before landing softly on the ground as she saw a hand with extremely long, thin, reptile-like fingers grab around the door that now hung half open.

"Jack, they're right behind you!" The sounds of whispers were deafening in her ears, nearly drowning out her voice.

William knelt down before Carter. "Stand on my leg and help pull him through."

Carter quickly stood up on William's knees as she saw Jack's hands pull up on the windowsill. The tall, slender reptilian being was squeezing his narrow body through the half-broken door opening. He, or it, made eye contact with her, and she gasped, distracting Jack. He turned back and cursed under his breath. He half pulled himself up, and Carter found her supernatural strength and practically lifted him up like a feather, pulling him through the window. Jack and Carter crashed to the ground in a pile on top of William.

"Hurry!" William yelled, seeing the long, strange arms come through the window just behind them.

The whispers screamed in her ear as she ran with William and Jack back to Dr. Nathaniel's home. She followed William through the alley and felt Jack on her heels.

The scream barely escaped her lips as a long arm wrapped around her waist, pulling her down to the ground. The reptilelike human lifted her in its arm like a bundled-up sweater, and she thrashed at him, making it more difficult. She felt the cold, rough skin against her arms and felt bile rising in her mouth. *Anunnaki,* she realized—and this was her race gone wrong.

William crashed into the side of the being, throwing him and her down. Carter could see from the corner of her eye that Jack was fighting in a heap with the other being just a few feet from them. The lizard guy punched her hard in the stomach, knocking all the breath out of her lungs, right before William got a hold of his head and turned it. Carter expected to hear a distinctive *snap* but when the creature continued to writhe she realized it was still alive. She looked at it in disgust as it lay on the floor at an awkward, disjointed angle. Purple liquid began to ooze from its nose and ears.

William ran over to help Jack as Carter stayed on the ground on all fours, still gasping for breath. She watched as Jack threw a wicked punch into the lizard man's jaw and saw its jaw pushed to the side. Jack broke the creature's jaw. She watched as the two men she loved beat the creature to death and found herself strangely turned on by the act. What was happening to her?

Jack returned to Carter as William leaned down and checked the creature's pulse.

"Carter?"

"I'm OK. I just had the wind knocked out of me."

"Can you run?"

She nodded as Jack helped her to her feet. Her breath was ragged, and she was sure that the creature had done some damage to her organs. However, right now they needed to get back to Dr. Nathaniel's house. They ran back down the alley, and Jack and William both half carried her. They rounded the corner without incident, and Carter could see Dr. Nathaniel's house in the distance. She felt a renewed sense of energy as they made their last dash for the house, with Jack and William frequently looking behind them for any followers.

"Almost there," Jack said reassuringly to Carter—or to himself; she was not sure.

There was a distinct energy field disruption around Dr. Nathaniel's house similar to the last two portals they had seen in Chicago, but more muted. "It's really there," Carter said excitedly.

"Over there." William nodded to the home across the street. Shadows lurked around the edges of the trees that lined the home. Jack threw Carter over his shoulder in one swoop and ran for the doctor's house as William trailed right behind. "They're coming!" he yelled.

Carter was amazed by Jack's strength as he flew across the yard and up the front steps, crashing through Dr. Nathaniel's front door. Jack sat her down just as William closed and locked the door behind them. Carter saw silhouettes move across the window and screamed when a lizard being threw itself through the window. Whatever it was, it was not immune to the effects of humans as it was covered in slices from the glass. Another lizard being stepped through the glass as Carter, Jack, and William dashed across the living room toward the portal.

Whether it was her mind playing tricks on her or not, Carter wasn't sure. But she felt the grasp of reptilian fingers across her legs just as the three of them jumped through the portal. The sucking sensation seemed escalated now, and she was sure it had to do with the damage done to her insides, but it was over too quickly to hurt. William, Jack, and Carter went through the portal so fast that they slid across the marble floor of the lobby they were in what seemed like just an hour ago.

Carter looked behind her and saw no traces of the portal they just had just gone through or any lizard beings trying to kill her. She collapsed on the floor in relief.

"That was close." Jack lay out on the floor next Carter, breathing heavily.

"We're back in my building," William pointed out.

"Where's your security guard?" Carter asked in fear. "You don't think we are still—"

"No, listen." William stomped his shoes against the marble floor.

"So where is he?" Jack asked again.

Nearly on cue, footsteps sounded down the hall. William ran to the elevators and pressed the button. Fortunately, a car was already in the lobby area, and they managed to get in without detection. They made their way to the top floor, and Carter held her breath. What if the police, or worse, were waiting for them there?

The elevator doors opened without incident, and no one was waiting in the condo. When William let Carter and Jack into the condo, no one was there. All three of them plopped down on the leather sofas.

"Now what?" Carter asked.

CHAPTER 38

"THEY'RE ON THEIR WAY HERE," William said after contacting Stan at the hotel. "They're going to make sure they're not being followed, but that doesn't mean we're safe. We will need to get out of here as soon as we can. We're wanted for murder, and they're going to be looking for us."

Carter was staring at the clock. "Two thirty?"

"We were at Portillo's, came back when we had our run-in with the police, and then what...we weren't gone that long, were we?" Jack asked.

"So there was a time distortion." William stared at the clock along with Jack and Carter. "The question is why."

"How are they going to get up here?" Jack asked.

"I gave them the passcode to the elevator. They'll have to sneak by the guard on duty. It shouldn't be that difficult since he does rounds every fifteen minutes."

"Well, I'm going to take that opportunity to take a hot shower while I still can. Who knows when we'll be settled in again," Carter said longingly.

She walked down the hall and found that all her items were in disarray on the bed—not how she had left them. Must have been the police, she thought. After all, wouldn't they have come back up to the condo to check everything first?

She grabbed some fresh clothes and her toiletries before heading into the on-suite bathroom. She screamed when instead of flipping on the light switch she touched flesh instead. William was behind her in a breath, and Jack wasn't too far behind. Not bad for human speed, she thought. When she switched on the light, she nearly screamed for an entirely different reason.

"Dr. Nathaniel!" Without thinking, Carter leaped into the man's arms.

"I've been looking everywhere for you," the doctor said, exasperated.

"How did you get here?" William asked.

"I think the same way you probably did," he said.

"Why are you hiding in the bathroom?" Jack placed his hand on Carter's shoulder protectively.

"I thought the cops had come back."

"Is that what happened to my stuff? Why it was thrown about?"

Jack frowned at Carter as Dr. Nathaniel nodded.

"No offense, Dr. Nathaniel, but you look as if you haven't slept in weeks, or showered in weeks," Jack said.

"I probably haven't," he agreed. "There's much I need to catch you all up on. But I would really like some food and a shower first, if that'd be all right."

"Of course." William led Dr. Nathaniel from Carter's room, and she heard their muffled conversation in one of the rooms down the hall. She then heard the shower turn on.

Jack stood in the room staring at Carter. "I think I'll just hang out here, if you don't mind—in case anyone else decides to pop up out of nowhere."

"Or you could join me," Carter said.

Jack's eyebrows rose, and his eyes became suddenly hungry. "You don't care that we're in William's condo?"

"Not anymore, I don't. Too much has happened, and I don't know when we'll have time together again." Her body instantly began to heat up as Jack gazed at her like a lion hunting a gazelle. It thrilled her.

Jack locked the bedroom door before stalking Carter into the bathroom. She turned on the shower and spun around to face Jack, who gingerly removed Carter's clothes. "Your injuries," he said, looking down at her hands. "They're gone."

She thought about that for a moment and then remembered when Stan had stuck his finger into the portal. She reminded Jack of that, and he nodded. "So many strange things," he said as he leaned down and kissed her deeply. He kissed her chin, then her throat, the hollow of her neck, and across her collarbone.

He removed his own clothes, letting them drop to the floor, and followed Carter into the already-steaming shower. Standing behind her, he trailed kisses down her neck and across her shoulder, wrapping his arms around her. When she turned to face him, he lifted her against the cool tiled wall of the shower and pressed himself against her. The cool tile, the hot steaming shower, and his tender yet eager kisses sent her emotions and senses into a whirl.

The shower was anything but quick, but Carter didn't care. By the time they emerged, the bedside clock showed the time as 3:30. Even in the cool of the bedroom, her skin was still flush with their heat. He watched her as she dressed, and she was beginning to think they'd never make it back out to the living room to meet everyone.

The pounding on the door said otherwise. "Anytime tonight would be great," Paulo yelled through the door.

"Oops," Jack said.

Carter tied her wet hair into a loose bun and threw her dirty clothes into a plastic bag and into the trash. Jack left her to pack the rest of her things since she knew they wouldn't be staying the night there anymore. As she grabbed her bag and left the room, she looked back one last time. She wondered if her life would always be on the run from now on.

She walked out into the living room and saw that Dr. Nathaniel was drinking a glass of wine with William.

"Where's Rafe and Paulo?"

"They are napping since they're taking the first driving shift tonight," Stan said. "In fact, I should go wake them; we need to get on the road."

"Where are we going?" Carter asked.

"We'll tell you once we're on the road, in case the condo is bugged," Stan said as he walked down the hall to the rooms that Rafe and Paulo slept in.

Jack, Amara, and William stood up and grabbed some of the bags and some boxes of what Carter guessed were supplies. She still held on to her bag, which was now slung over her shoulder. Once Rafe and Paulo emerged, looking fairly groggy, they all filed out of the condo.

They took the stairs down to the parking garage so they could avoid the elevator as well as any cameras. Stan was sure they were detected on some of the cameras, but by the time it would matter, they would be long gone.

"We're not taking the Audi or Cherokee?" Carter looked at the two suburban SUVs, which reminded her of the ones they had used in Bohemian Grove.

"Nope, they'll be looking for those plates." Stan loaded the luggage into the back of the Suburbans. "Carter, William, and Dr. Nathaniel will ride with Rafe. Jack and Amara will ride with me and Paulo."

Jack and William exchanged odd looks. "Dr. Nathaniel has things he needs to share with Carter and William about their bloodline."

"OK, so I'll drive," Jack said. "I don't want to leave Carter alone."

"She won't be alone," William said through clenched teeth.

"No, Jack," Stan said. "You need your rest because you have the next shift anyway. We have a long trip ahead of us. They can catch you up then."

Jack dejectedly walked up to Carter and took her hand, pulling her to him. He lifted her chin with his hand and gave her a deep, too-passionate kiss. Someone cleared his throat, and when Jack pulled away, Carter was turning deep colors of red. He walked away smug and got into the truck.

"Was that necessary?" William asked.

Carter frowned, not knowing what to say.

"OK, are you kids done playing? Can we go now?" Stan asked.

Carter saw Amara giving her a sympathetic look and wished she didn't have to be in a truck with anyone at that moment. Dr. Nathaniel slid into the back seat with Carter, and William took the front passenger seat.

They pulled out of the garage in silence, and it wasn't until they were on the I-94 heading north that Rafe spoke. "We're going to Winnipeg."

"Canada?" Carter asked.

"It's only a stop. Once we get there, we'll switch vehicles and then make the trek into Vancouver."

"My geography isn't that great, but isn't that on the other side of the country?"

"It is."

"How long of a drive are we talking?" Carter asked, suddenly feeling carsick.

"Thirteen hours to Winnipeg and twenty-three hours to Vancouver from there." Rafe seemed to be enjoying torturing Carter far too much.

"Well then, I guess we have some time to talk about what happened."

Dr. Nathaniel agreed. "Why don't you start by telling me what happened to the three of you."

Carter and William took turns explaining everything that had happened to them since they left Peru, and sometime between Chicago and Minneapolis, they all fell asleep.

Carter awoke to the car slowing down and abruptly sat up, alert.

"We're just switching drivers," Rafe said, looking exhausted. They were pulled over in the middle of nowhere, and snow still covered the ground.

"Where are we?"

"About thirty miles outside of Minneapolis."

Dr. Nathaniel and William both awoke at that point and were watching the exchange. Not surprisingly, Carter saw Jack running over to take the driver's seat. He had an energy drink in hand.

"Got any more of those?" William asked, annoyed.

"They're in the back," Rafe said.

Carter reached over the back and found a few energy drinks sitting in an ice cooler and handed an energy drink each to William and Dr. Nathaniel. She also grabbed some bananas and muffins as she looked over to see Stan take the wheel of the other SUV.

"What'd I miss?" Jack asked as he pulled out onto the road.

"Nothing," Dr. Nathaniel said. "They filled me in on what happened, and then we fell asleep."

"Basically what happened with us," Jack said.

"Just after you guys left Peru, Jibril came to me," Dr. Nathaniel said. "He said that you had begun opening portals and didn't even know." Dr. Nathaniel looked to Carter. "Apparently you started having some dreams, and some of them were while you were awake. The Vaticates somehow knew this and were able to monitor you. Each time you had a certain type of dream, there would be energy fluctuations. Each time they became stronger and more detectable. He wasn't supposed to have this information but somehow stole it from his sister without her knowing."

"Do our guys know this?" William asked.

"No, this is the first time I'm telling anyone. That's not the best part, though. He left through a portal, which is how I think he ended up in New Mexico. I guess he didn't think I'd follow him, but I did. Unfortunately, I didn't end up in New Mexico."

"Where'd you end up?" Jack asked.

"The Amazon."

"You're kidding me!" Carter said. "Do you think he did that on purpose?"

Dr. Nathaniel shrugged. "I don't know. I wasn't there long, though. As soon as I saw where I landed, I went right back into the portal and ended up stuck there, in between. I have to tell you, time moves strangely in there. I was there for three months, and when I finally figured out how to get back out, I ended up in William's condo, and it had only been a few weeks."

Carter stared at Dr. Nathaniel, stunned. "You were stuck in a portal for three months?"

"The good news is that you don't need to eat or anything while you're there."

"What's it like?"

"Well, it was Peru, except there was no sound, no smell, no nothing."
William, Carter, and Jack exchanged glances as Dr. Nathaniel explained.
"Just me wandering around the stupid place trying to figure out how to get
back. Fortunately, a portal finally opened up in my home of all places, and
I went through. The interesting thing is, I saw you guys on the way in."

"You're kidding," William said, now fully facing the back seat watching Dr. Nathaniel.

"Here's the thing—and I'm glad it's the three of you in the truck right
now because I was going to skip over this part if Rafe were still here." Carter
stared at Dr. Nathaniel, hanging on every word. "I think the Vaticates *and*
the Anunnaki know about these portals, and I think they're actively using
them."

"What do they want them for?" Carter asked.

"Well, think of how much power it could give them to be anywhere
they needed to be whenever they wanted to be," William said.

Dr. Nathaniel nodded. "These portals also open up a lot more than
just a way to save on frequent flyer miles," he said. "They have opened a
door up to Anunnaki that Enki failed."

"What do you mean?" Carter asked, feeling goose bumps rise on her
flesh.

"Enki was the Anunnaki who manipulated human DNA to advance
them, using his own DNA. The first time he tried, he failed and created
a darker race of Anunnaki. He developed a blend of Anunnaki that were
part human, but the part of humans that contain no conscience"

"How do you know this?" William asked.

"Jibril shared this information with me."

"How does he know?"

"How does he know anything?"

"We saw them, so we know he's telling the truth," Jack said to William.

"You saw them?" Dr. Nathaniel asked, clearly shocked. "And you survived?"

"Well, what do you mean?"

"You two hold a lot more than the key to communicate with the Anunnaki on Nibiru. You hold the power to advance the human race to its final stages and also hold the power to completely annihilate the Anunnaki in the portals, as well as the entire Anunnaki race."

Jack swerved, and it took him a minute to straighten back out. The cell phone in the truck rang, and William answered it.

"Yeah, we're OK. Jack dropped his Red Bull, and it got stuck under the gas pedal," William said into the phone before hanging up.

"It scares me how well you lie," Carter said, and William frowned at her.

"What's Nibiru?" Jack asked.

"The Anunnakis' home planet," William said.

"Well, that's weird," Jack said.

"Maybe we can visit," Carter said jokingly. William looked at her strangely, as if she were serious. "What? I was joking."

William kept looking forward through the windshield, and Carter felt the shift in his thoughts.

"Do you really think we could visit?"

William shrugged, and Jack kept glancing over to him. "I don't know. I mean, if we could go to Peru in half a second, then maybe that's the key."

"Maybe that's why you two are the key," Dr. Nathaniel said.

William nodded. "Yeah, like we can go in the portal and travel to Nibiru?"

"This is crazy; no one's going anywhere. Especially since those crazy lizard guys are in there." Carter saw Jack's hands clench around the steering wheel tightly. "We need to figure out where everyone went first."

"How do you suppose we do that?" William asked Jack, looking at him, irritated.

Just then the cell phone that Stan had supplied them rang. William picked it up.

"Don't tell me that's his dad," Jack said jokingly.

William hung up. "No, not directly."

"What?" Carter shouted unexpectedly, startling Dr. Nathaniel.

"Good lord, child, was that necessary?"

"Apparently Stan just received a call from the Anunnaki center in Anchorage. My father and mother are there, and they're looking for us."

"Well, I'll be a horse's sticky buttocks," Dr. Nathaniel said, grinning from ear to ear.

Carter, William, and Jack all looked back at Dr. Nathaniel and simultaneously burst out into fits of laughter.

"How did they find us?" Carter asked after the laughter died down.

CHAPTER 39

𒌍 𒀸 𒂖𒀸 𒂖𒁁 ⟨𒉌 𒀳 𒁁 𒂖 𒌨 𒂖𒀸 𒀳𒁁 𒂖𒁁

THE REST OF THE TRIP to Vancouver passed by in a haze of uncomfortable backseat sleeping, gas station snacks, and miles and miles of nothing. By the time they got to Vancouver, Carter thought she would lose her mind.

"That," she said, drunken on nothing, "was hell."

William nodded, looking at her through bloodshot eyes.

"Please tell me we get to sleep in a bed tonight," Jack said to Stan as he hopped out of the truck, looking put together.

"Were you just on the same road trip as we were?" Carter asked Stan. "Because you sure don't look like it." She waved her hand up and down in disgust.

Stan chuckled in response. "I'm used to it. My job requires a lot of fieldwork. Anyway, this was nothing."

"You didn't answer my question," Jack said.

"Yes, we will check into a motel for the night, eat a real breakfast, and then we're back on the road again."

Carter wanted to commit violence. She mostly wanted to commit violence against Stan. She assumed either Jack or William would try to calm her energy, but when she focused in on them, she realized they were thinking along the same lines. By the look on Stan's face, he realized that and quickly took off to the Motel 6 lobby.

She worked to stretch out her limbs and get the kinks out of her joints. "I need an aspirin," she said.

"I need clothes," Dr. Nathaniel said. Carter frowned at the doctor, realizing he had been on the run much longer than she had. Besides, was a 150-something-year-old man considered an elder in this world?

"There's a Walmart just down the street. Once you're all checked in, I'll take Dr. Nathaniel down there to pick up some clothes and goods," Paulo said.

Dr. Nathaniel looked relieved, and Carter realized he hadn't complained once the entire trip, when that was all she had done. She nearly forgot how much they were up against and how much she was responsible for. She certainly wasn't acting like it.

"You OK?" William asked, approaching Carter.

"Just tired," she said.

He nodded. She knew he didn't believe her, but he didn't press the issue any further, thankfully.

"We got six rooms," Stan said as he returned from the lobby. "The front desk clerk looked like he struck gold."

There were eight of them; who was rooming with whom? Stan handed a key card to Jack. "You guys are the center room so you'll have one of us on both sides in case you need anything," he said to both Carter and Jack.

"Here's our room key," he said, handing one to Amara. Carter tilted her head at them as Amara blushed. She couldn't help but grin widely at Amara's reaction. It was nice to have someone else blushing for once. Stan handed the rest of the keys out to the group.

"Paulo said he would take me to the store for some clothes," Dr. Nathaniel said.

Stan looked as if he wanted to object.

"I'm going to go too," William said. "I need a drink."

Carter looked at him, concerned, but he ignored her as he followed Dr. Nathaniel and Paulo back to the SUV.

"We're leaving at six a.m.," Stan said.

"Oh come on!" Carter yelled.

"OK, seven thirty. Not a second later."

When Jack and Carter entered the room, she noticed the bedside clock already showing eleven p.m.

"I don't even know what month it is anymore."

Jack walked up to Carter and wrapped her in his arms. "I know, but I have a feeling we'll figure this all out soon and hopefully move on with our lives."

Carter looked up at Jack. "What makes you think that?"

"Just a gut feeling," he said, smiling mischievously. "I can have them too, can't I?"

Carter opened her mouth to answer, but Jack planted a kiss, cutting off her words before she could respond. As soon as his lips brushed hers, her body automatically responded. His kiss was deep and hungry, and she knew if she didn't stop then, she wouldn't be able to.

"Jack, I need a shower."

He growled underneath his breath, sending warm shivers down her body. "So do I."

"Water conservation?"

"You forget that we take a lot longer than if we were actually showering."

Carter blushed as she pulled away and headed into the bathroom to turn the shower on.

"I miss my shower," she said. "It was a really nice shower."

"I have no doubt about that," Jack said as he undressed her. "You will get your home back, I promise."

"You shouldn't make promises you can't keep."

"I don't," he responded and sealed her mouth with another kiss, gently pushing her back into the shower.

Jack soaped up a washcloth and began soaping Carter down. She shut her eyes and enjoyed all the sensations. Jack's sweet side never ceased to awe her. She knew there was still so much to him that she didn't know and hadn't had a chance to learn yet. Their circumstances were far from normal, and she decided that she too would promise to find those moments together with him.

Jack stepped out of the shower first, drying off. Carter ignored that the water had gone cold long ago and instead just enjoyed how it awakened her senses.

"We have yet to try that in an actual bed," Jack said, reminding Carter of their recent shower escapade.

A knock on the door interrupted Carter's response, and she looked at Jack nervously. "Are we expecting anyone?"

"It's Stan!" Stan yelled through the door.

"We need a code word or something," Jack said. "I hope this doesn't take long."

"I bring gifts!" Stan yelled again through the door.

"I don't know if that's your Anunnaki sense of hearing or sense of mind reading, but that can get annoying," Jack said to Carter as he opened the door.

"We don't read minds," Stan reminded him, standing in the doorway. "We read energy. In this case, I read your energy and heard you."

"I would find that more annoying if you weren't standing there with a pizza box," Jack said.

Stan handed the pizza box over to Jack as Carter came out of the bathroom with her pajamas on and hair dripping wet down her back.

"It's not the best meal," Stan said to Carter apologetically. "But I figured it was better than the chips and cookies we have been living on for the last few days."

Jack took a slice of pizza from the box and started eating it before setting the box down.

"Did Dr. Nathaniel and Paulo return yet?" Carter asked, concern etched across her face.

Stan nodded. "They did, about half an hour ago. Everyone is already back in their rooms." Carter breathed a sigh of relief, not realizing how much she always worried about her friends. Stan watched Carter for a moment. "You do know why we have to leave so early, don't you? I'm not trying to purposely upset you."

Carter smiled warmly. "I know. I do. I was just tired and not used to this. Thank you for everything you do, Stan. We all appreciate it even though we, especially I, fail to tell you that."

Stan's shoulders relaxed, as did his face. Carter noticed how much worry and stress he carried with him and felt guilty for not noticing it before.

"Well, I'm going to head out before Jack eats all the pizza and leaves you none."

Carter looked down at Jack sitting on the bed with the pizza box on the bed and three slices already missing.

"I would've probably had eaten more, but the warm-fuzzy stuff you two were doing made me nauseated."

Carter laughed as she turned the knob on both locks of the door. Three pizza slices later, she lay out flat on the bed, and Jack had eaten two more. She was amazed at his ability to constantly eat and not gain an ounce.

Jack sat on the foot of the bed and wiggled her toe, and then kissed her ankle.

"I like this bed thing," he said.

He placed one deliberate kiss after another up her calf, around her knee, and up her thigh, smiling in delight at her gasp of pleasure. Carter didn't think he left a single part of her soul untouched from the inside out. He lifted her up against him as she pushed him down on his back, returning the love. She could never get enough of him, she decided, wanting the night to last forever.

When she lay against him hours later, both covered in sweat and twisted in the sheets, she couldn't help but smile profusely.

"What are you thinking about?" he asked.

"How do you know I was thinking about something?"

"'Cause you're a woman."

Carter burst out laughing. "I'm actually an alien."

"Well, you're a female alien, and I'm sure it's the same whatever planet you're from."

Carter paused, contemplating whether she should say what she was thinking or not.

"Tell me," he said, sensing her hesitation.

"I was thinking about the promise you made earlier."

"And?"

"And I was wondering whether you really can keep it or not."

"Why do you think I couldn't?" Jack adjusted himself so he could see Carter's face.

"I just sort of gave up hope that I'd ever be able to go home. I just assumed that this was my life from now on."

Jack was silent for a long time before speaking again. "Do you want to go home?"

Carter thought about that. She didn't know what it would be like to go home. Everything would be different, and she wasn't sure whether it would even feel like home again. Then she realized what home meant to her. Paulo was still there. Julia was still there. Jack would probably want to go back to Santa Barbara because he still had Mandy. It would take time to readjust, but she imagined she could.

"I do."

"Then that's what we'll do," he promised again.

Carter let those words hang in there as her eyelids grew heavier. She fell asleep against Jack's warm skin and realized that even though he had made the promise to take her home again, even though she wanted nothing more than to go home with Jack, she wasn't sure if she could keep her end of the promise. She had no idea what waited for her with the Anunnaki and knew that she would need to go through the portal with William. Her heart was with Jack, but had the stars decided otherwise for her?

CHAPTER **40**

𒐫 𒐏 𒀭 𒐫 𒀭 𒌝 𒀀 𒁁 𒐫 𒐫 𒀭 𒐫 𒌝 𒐫 𒀭 𒁁 𒀭

"That can't be," Jack said as the alarm blared through their small motel room.

Carter groaned and rolled over, smothering her own pillow over her head.

"I swear we just went to sleep," Jack said.

"Please, no," Carter murmured through the pillow. "What time is it?"

"Seven."

Carter walked to the shower with her eyes closed. When she flipped the light switch on, she felt a strange vibration course through her body. Her eyes flew open, and she screamed. Jack was behind her in a second.

"What? What happened?"

Carter blinked again and again. "I don't know," she said. The pounding on the door nearly caused her to scream again.

"Jack? Carter?" It was Stan on the other side of the door yelling.

Carter backed away from the bathroom while Stan continued to yell through the door, threatening to break it down if someone didn't respond. Jack handed Carter a sheet from the bed. She looked down at her naked body as she wrapped the sheet around herself. Jack slipped on his pants before opening the door. Stan burst in with his gun drawn.

"What happened?" he asked after quickly glancing around the room.

"I saw Jibril's body."

"What? Where?" Stan asked.

Rafe and William appeared in the doorway behind Stan. Carter was sure they looked hung over, and William didn't hide his disgust when he saw Carter wrapped in only a bedsheet.

"In the bathroom—but um, it's…he's gone now."

Stan walked to the bathroom and checked behind the door, and then came back out tucking his gun back into the holster on his hip.

"It was his body, covered in blood, lying in a heap on the floor. As clear as you guys are right now. He was definitely dead."

"What do you think it means?" Rafe asked.

"I don't know." Carter wrapped the sheet around her tighter.

William staggered out of the room, and Rafe and followed him.

"Are you OK?" Stan asked.

Carter nodded. "I'm OK. I'm just going to shower now."

Stan hesitated. "If you need more time—"

She shook her head. "No, I don't need more time. I'm OK."

When Stan left the room, Jack just stood by the door.

"It'll be a quick shower."

Jack watched her sadly as she retreated to the bathroom. She stood there for nearly an entire minute staring at the spot where Jibril had been only moments ago. She knew it meant something; she just didn't know what. She knelt down to the floor and swiped her finger across the cool tile. When she lifted her fingertips, they were dripping with warm, sticky, crimson blood—and then it faded away.

The sound of Jack zipping up his suitcase brought her out of her daze, and she quickly jumped into the shower. When she had finished, Jack took his turn. She finished getting ready and packed the rest of her things up, which wasn't much.

"You OK?" Jack asked as he got dressed. Carter nodded. "We didn't get much sleep last night. Do you think these things happen more when you're tired?"

"It's possible."

He walked over and kissed her softly on the lips. "We should head down. We're already ten minutes late."

Everyone was already at the SUVs when Jack and Carter joined them. She didn't see William and briefly looked around.

"He's in the other SUV already. He's driving first shift," Amara said as she watched Carter.

"I'll take first shift driving," Carter said to Stan.

"I've got gunshot," Amara said.

Carter and Stan, the only ones within listening distance, both burst out laughing. "Shotgun," Stan corrected.

"Hmm, shotgun does not make sense. Gunshot makes more sense because it's faster."

"That it does," Carter agreed as she hopped into the driver seat. "Where to?"

"Breakfast. There's a diner just down the road before the freeway." Stan pointed in the direction for her to head down. When she saw that everyone was in the SUVs, she pulled out onto the road.

The sun cast strong rays over the windshield as they drove north toward Anchorage.

"We're avoiding the main road," Stan said as the road became more desolate. "We'll be taking Cassiar Highway, which is a little bit longer, but it'll keep us away from anyone looking for us."

"You really think the police will be looking for us here?" Carter asked.

"The police aren't our only problem."

Very little conversation took place, and after eight hours of driving, Carter relented the wheel. Not only had she become exhausted, the roads became too treacherous for her to navigate. They pulled over at a local store to stock up on goods.

"Where are we?" Carter asked.

"Prince George. It's our last main stop until we make it to Anchorage," Stan explained. "We're getting new vehicles for the trip."

They picked up coats and blankets and refilled their coolers with food and drink. Carter took in a deep breath of the cold air. She figured by "new vehicles," they would just get new SUVs to remain incognito. When they pulled up to an indiscreet warehouse and saw two military-grade Hummers parked in front, she realized why they needed the vehicles.

When she hopped into the first vehicle, a wave of familiarity hit her. William had ignored her since Minneapolis, but he became suddenly aware of Carter. He walked subconsciously toward her as he sensed her energy, and even Stan raised his head in awareness.

"What am I sensing?" Carter asked, still not able to interpret things as well as Stan or William.

"I didn't think you would still be able to sense his energy here," Stan said. "If I had known, I would—"

"No, that's OK," she said, understanding, as a tear rolled free down her cheek.

"What is it?" Amara asked, concerned.

"It's my father's energy," Carter said.

William stepped toward the hummer and stuck his head in, looking sad. "This was his? When he was in Anchorage?"

Stan nodded in response to William's question.

"We can get different vehicles, Carter. We don't have—"

Carter cut Stan off. "No, this is OK. I don't mind."

Jack looked at Carter with concern etched in his features as she hopped into the passenger seat. "Will you drive?" she asked Jack, and he nodded.

Carter developed a new habit of nail biting over the next four days as they drove the weather-beaten and snow-covered roads to Anchorage. She was convinced they would never make it alive, especially when they drove at night. Dr. Nathaniel distracted her as much as he could with stories of his life and what it was like living through the Great Depression, the Roaring Twenties, and the invention of the telephone. Dr. Nathaniel had become good friends with Alexander Graham Bell and described him as a "man with the curiosity of a child."

"How did you meet him?" Amara asked.

"His father and my father were colleagues. They both were speech teachers," he explained. "I learned a great deal from Alex."

"Alex, hmpf," Jack said.

"Jack, maybe you should let Stan take the wheel again and get some rest," Amara suggested.

Stan nodded. "I think it's time to switch anyway."

"There's less than an hour left. We're fine," Jack said.

Carter rested her head back against the seat and shut her eyes. Her head had started aching recently, and she just wanted out of the truck and onto solid ground.

"You OK?" Stan asked.

She nodded. "Yeah, just a headache."

Stan frowned but didn't say anything. She noticed the strange glance that he exchanged with Dr. Nathaniel, though. By the time they reached Anchorage, Carter had become nauseated from the intensity of her headache.

The phone rang for the first time in hours, and Stan picked it up. Carter didn't know who was on the other line but felt a shift in Stan's energy. He had become worried.

"What is it?" Dr. Nathaniel asked.

"William asked if we had anything for headaches. He has a throbbing migraine."

They all exchanged glances. "Well, we have been on the road *forever*," Carter said, trying to convince herself more than the others.

They found a convenience store that looked as if it hadn't been cleaned in twenty years, but it had a sealed box of Advil. She and William both took four each. By the time they reached the facility in Anchorage, her throbbing headache had turned into just a dull one.

The Anunnaki facility was shocking. Tucked away on the forest side of Campbell Lake sat three separate four-story buildings made of glass and wood. The sharp angles stood in contrast to the organic surroundings of snow-covered mountains and a frozen-over lake.

"Wow," Amara said. "This is not what I am used to."

"Indeed," Dr. Nathaniel said. Amara had seen her first snowfall in Minneapolis, and now she was in a world of mountains, forest, ice, and snow. Even Carter, who had seen the snow at Big Bear Mountain and her family's home in Wisconsin, was in awe of the majestic beauty of Alaska.

"What is that?" Amara asked.

"That, my dear, is a moose," Dr. Nathaniel said, smiling at the large animal.

But it was nothing compared to the complex that they drove up to. "It looks like something out of a real estate magazine," Carter said about the three architectural beauties that stood before them.

"The center building is the main center. The two other buildings are housing for visitors. There are nine homes nestled in the woods away from view that serve as a more permanent residence to those who are studying up here," Stan explained from the back seat.

"Studying?" Carter asked.

"Yes, a lot of the artifacts come through here first before going to Northern California and other locations. They've also taken on studying DNA since Dr. Nathaniel released his study to them last month."

Carter frowned. She didn't know he had done that and suddenly became afraid that they were going to be a part of these studies. Dr. Nathaniel continued staring out the window, ignoring the conversation.

Carter began playing with the hem of her sweater since she had chewed her nails down as far as she could. Jack sat quietly in the driver's seat with his lips pressed in a thin line. She watched him curiously and tried to read his energy unsuccessfully. Somehow, he had figured out how to block her. Now she wondered if he wasn't trying to block her out, but block out Stan instead.

They parked alongside several other hummers and oversize pick-up trucks. Even from the car, Carter felt the energy buzzing from inside—anxious energy. Anxious, she realized, because the keys to their future were coming for a visit, and Carter had no idea what their role would be.

Carter was not surprised to see Harold and Allison Moretti waiting in front for them. She was, however, surprised by the other couple next to them and by the shift in energy from William. She knew, even though he expected his parents, that he was surprised as well. Gregory Moretti was a smaller man, with gray, sad-looking eyes. His skin was pale, and he looked as if he were anything but a powerful individual. How anyone ever thought William was his son was unbeknownst to her.

However, he was the spitting image of his mother, and the love in her eyes for her son made Carter's heart ache. She had never known a mother's love and always imagined her own mom would look at her the same way William's was now looking at him.

"Glad you all made it up here safe," Harold said. Carter frowned at him while Jack and William both made something that sounded like a growl. "I'm sorry, kids, but it was out of my hands."

"What exactly was, Uncle?"

"William, honey, let's go inside, and we'll tell you. Let's not start off on the wrong foot," she said as she pulled her son into a warm embrace. The entire time Gregory Moretti watched them all with curious eyes. "You must be Carter?" Christy Moretti reached her hand out and took Carter's in hers.

"Yes, Mrs. Moretti. Nice to finally meet you." The words felt like a lie.

Christy Moretti introduced herself to everyone as Gregory Moretti and Carter awkwardly stared at each other. He tilted his head, studying her like a specimen.

"Your *son...*" she paused, "is no different from me, Mr. Moretti. So I would appreciate if you would stop considering me the enemy."

A hint of a smile appeared on his lips, though Carter wasn't sure if the humor was on him or her. "You've become very observant, Ms. Robinson."

"And you would know...how?" Jack said, appearing just behind Carter.

Now Mr. Moretti burst out laughing. "Come on, kids, we have much to discuss."

CHAPTER 41

𒂖𒌋 𒆜𒂖𒌋 ⸕𒌋𒌋 𒀹 𒅀𒂖 𒆜 𒌋𒌋⸕ 𒂖𒌋 𒆜 ⸕𒅀𒂖 𒆜𒂖𒌋

THEY SAT AROUND A GLASS table in a room that hung over the lake, making it appear that they were floating right on the water. Carter was distracted by the view, continuously looking over at the white mountains and white-dusted trees. The snow on snow made the lake area look pristine and pure. It made her feel as if she could breathe for the first time. She listened to Gregory and Harold ask questions about the trip and became frustrated that they hadn't brought up Amelia yet. She didn't know where her earlier bravado had come from, but it was gone.

She turned her attention back to the table just in time to see William rubbing his temples. The dull ache at the back of her head was still there, but nothing like before. William seemed to be having a more difficult time getting over his headache, and she wondered if it had anything to do with their connection in DNA.

"Did you kill Amelia?" William asked through gritted teeth. Whether it was from his throbbing head or frustration with his father Carter couldn't tell. But from what she knew of him, she'd guess the latter.

"Honey, you can't talk to your father like that," Christy cut in, appearing nervous.

William eyed his mother daringly, as if to challenge her. Whatever passed between them caused him to relent. "We are on the run because we found Amelia's body in your house, and you were all missing. We're suspects. So I think you'll understand why we may be a tad upset with you."

His mother's face fell. But Gregory's and Harold's remained the same. "Carter," Greg Moretti began, "when you walked through the Sun Gate, you opened up portals for the Anunnaki. Many have been killed because of it." He showed no remorse when speaking, but nearly everyone in the room tensed at his words. Everyone except Carter. Somehow, what he said didn't surprise her, and she thought of him as the type of person who would say things just to get under their skin.

Carter realized he would especially say things to get under her skin. "Why are you so familiar to me?" she asked.

Now it was Greg's turn to tense. He exchanged a brief look with his brother—so brief that she would not have caught it if she weren't playing close attention.

"I don't believe you've ever met my husband."

"I'm not so sure about that," Carter said. "Perhaps I met you through Clifford Hoffman?"

Jack and William both spun their heads at Carter. "Who's Clifford Hoffman?" William asked.

Carter's heart sank in her chest. She had brought up Clifford to throw a wrench in Gregory's scheming but completely forgot what it meant to William.

"Yes, do tell, Carter. Who *is* Clifford Hoffman?" Harold asked, seething.

Carter burned under Harold's and Gregory's stare as her mind reeled.

"You have both keys in the same room?" The woman's voice echoed from around the corner before she appeared standing in the doorway. Her voice reminded Carter of melting butterscotch, mesmerizing in a way.

"Yes, Lala, we do," Christy said.

Carter tensed up at the change of tone in Christy's voice. It was no longer warm and welcoming, and the quick shift startled Carter to the core. A reflection off Lala's neck caught Carter's attention, and she realized it was her necklace—a cross.

Carter's heart began drumming in her chest, and William shifted in his seat as he noticed what Carter was looking at.

"Who are you really?" William asked.

"I'm a Vaticate," she said calmly and with a hint of humor in her voice.

Just then Jack stood up abruptly. What he was planning to do in a room full of people she didn't know—take them all out at once? She knew he felt a threat—because she certainly felt it, and by the look and energy rolling off William, he definitely felt it. They were screwed.

Carter took a deep breath. *Now would be a good time for the whispers to help me,* she thought. Carter shut her eyes and focused—maybe if she called to them, they'd respond with a convenient little portal. She took another breath, steadying herself.

"What are you doing?" Harold asked, standing up now.

She tuned them out. She knew how to do this; she just had to remember how. Another deep breath and her heart pounded loudly in her ears, a reminder of her and her calling. She remembered her comrades: Kalita, drawing light from him in the desert; John, drawing light from him in the jungle.

"What is she doing?" Gregory asked, and in the distance she could feel him stand. Yet it was moot.

She drew in memories of years past, thousands of years past. She felt Dr. Nathaniel's smile widen next to her, and she heard William shut his eyes—heard it in her mind's eye.

"What's going on?" Lala asked, not so smug as before—and it took everything for Carter not to smile at that.

She remembered, and the whispers smiled.

Yes, they said in happy unison. *Welcome back, Carter.* They smiled.

The sounds of drums from a Native American ritual circle sounded in her ears as the memory sprang to life in her mind like a baby's first breath. The soft beats matched the determined and steady beat of her heart, glorious and proud. She knew what she had to do as the lives and minds of all before her in all her lives became as vivid as her own body was in that very moment.

William sat next to her with his eyes closed, and a sadness crept over her skin. With all her memories came the thousands of years that he had been her companion from one life to another on this quest. A silent tear fell from his eyes as the memories invaded him simultaneously. Somehow, for some reason, this was the only lifetime that her heart had even dared go astray, and the reasons were unknown to both of them.

"William." His name escaped her lips desperately as his pain, their pain, struck her like a sword.

Jack stepped closer to Carter. Somehow he knew what was happening with Carter, while most everyone else remained clueless. He always knew what was going on with her. He knew because he loved her and she loved him back. Though now she did not know whether it was enough.

"Will someone tell me what is going on!" Gregory Moretti slammed his fist down on the table, startling Carter and William—thus snapping them out of their...whatever that was.

"Nothing. I just figured something out," Carter said smoothly. "I need to know why there is a Vaticate here."

"Because your stupid portal thing you created sucked up one of our men," Lala hissed, no longer retaining the composure she once held.

Carter felt insulted by the *stupid portal* comment, especially since it had saved them from a mess William's parents had left behind.

"Yes, your portal also killed Amelia," Gregory Moretti said.

"I'm not sure I believe that," Carter said and felt Jack's eyes boring into the side of her skull—all the while memories of her and William in past lives kept popping into her mind like snapping pictures. She wasn't sure whether that was his doing or hers. By the look of William's clenched fists and white knuckles, she would guess it was hers, and it was not helping the situation.

She needed to get away from him, she realized. She needed to gain space and perspective again because when she was around him, she lost all that.

"Believe what you want; it's true," Christy said with her calming, royal demeanor that Carter was fast learning not to trust.

Carter turned to look at Allison, who sat at one end of the table fiddling with her fingers. She was nervous, and Carter could not understand why.

"Did you figure out how to connect to Nibiru?" Gregory asked impatiently.

Carter felt the whispers and drums in the back of her mind, muted for now.

"No."

Gregory narrowed his eyes as he looked at her curiously. He knew she was lying, but she didn't care. The ball was in her court.

"How did the portal kill Amelia?" Dr. Nathaniel asked, breaking the tension—sort of.

"One of those things, lizard things, came through and snuffed the life right out of her, and then it got sucked back in. We followed it through and ended up here. We have been here the whole time," Harold explained.

"And what was she doing in your home?" William asked.

Harold and Gregory froze in place, clearly not wanting to share anything else. William waited patiently and continued eyeing the two men suspiciously.

"We've been working with the Vaticates," Gregory finally said.

"And why is that? Are they not the ones who have been killing off our lines? Specifically killing off my and Carter's line?"

"Excuse me?" Gregory began to sweat.

"How long have you known that I was a link as well? How long have you known, *Greg*?"

"They have known your entire life, William darling. It was planned from the beginning," Christy said callously, smiling.

Carter could see the red tint the edges of William's vision and knew this was not going to end well.

"What do you mean?"

Carter heard William's breath catch as her heart sped up. *Please don't say it,* she thought. *Please don't say what I think you're about to say.* Even Dr. Nathaniel and Amara tensed up, and Jack...well, Jack had been tense the entire time.

"Clifford Hoffman was one of the last two links left, the other being your mother," Gregory said to Carter. "And your mother wasn't exactly forthcoming with what direction she wanted to see the Anunnaki go in. In fact, she was getting too comfortable with Jibril Dekkers."

"What are you saying?" William asked, his voice strained and tense.

Carter felt the whispers strain in the back of her mind, begging to be released.

"Well, we didn't think it was right that the entire fate of our race lay in the hands of a woman who didn't have the balls to make the right decision," Harold said, staring at Carter deliberately. "But Christy here, she had what it took, and she seduced Clifford Hoffman. Once we confirmed that she was pregnant, we made sure that he could no longer be an issue and a threat to us."

"A threat?" Dr. Nathaniel asked. "How on earth was the poor man a threat?"

"Because he knew Christy was pregnant with his child and wouldn't keep it a secret. And we needed to keep you a secret, William. You're far too valuable."

"Valuable?" William hissed. "And what about Ray?"

"Oh no, he's my son." Gregory smiled gallantly.

The next sequence of events happened so fast that Carter wasn't sure whether blinking caused her to miss most of it or it was just that fast, but by the time she realized William had dove across the table, it was too late. No one had time to react. He slammed into Gregory so hard and so fast that they both went flying through the plate glass window and into the frozen water.

Carter heard screaming in the distance and then realized it was her own voice. The sounds of the whispers drowned everything out, as they were no longer in her mind but in the room. Before Carter could figure out how to get down to the lake, Jack had jumped into the water after the two men.

"Will someone please think before they act?" Dr. Nathaniel said frantically.

The rest of the group scrambled out of the room and out of the building. Carter slipped several times down the snowbank, which both helped and hurt in the time it took to get down to the bank. When she reached the shoreline, Jack was dragging Gregory slowly back. They were both already blue around the lips and nose. William was nowhere to be found.

"William!" she screamed as she ran into the freezing water, breaking through the ice.

"Carter, don't!" Dr. Nathaniel yelled after her, but it was too late. The water hit her like a million needles, and she gasped as the shock took her breath away.

She heard Amara yelling at Jack, saying he couldn't go back in the water because he was already a frozen popsicle. If the situation weren't so dire, she'd laugh. The splashing of water behind her said he'd ignored Amara. Whether he was going after Carter or William she wasn't sure, but she didn't want to take a chance. She dove into the frigid temperatures and nearly came up immediately because of the shock of cold. She wasn't sure how she was going to try to find William but knew she'd die trying.

The murky water made it nearly impossible to see anything, and every time she thought she had found William, she realized it was just sand or lake plants. When she came up for air, she realized that William had already been in the water several minutes, and she began to panic.

Carter heard splashing sounds coming from the surface, and when she came up for air, Jack had his arm around William and was already struggling to pull him to shore. She swam up and grabbed William's other arm as they pulled him back. She ignored that his body was limp, ignored that Jack was struggling to stay afloat himself, and just focused on the shore.

The whispers were screaming, and the water began to fizzle around them as the energy shifted. Jack was no longer making progress, and Carter realized he was about to go under. How was she going to hold two full-grown men above water in a frozen lake? She couldn't feel her fingers or toes anymore, and her legs felt as if they weighed a thousand pounds.

They were still about ten feet from the shore, but it might have been twenty. Stan treaded through the water fast, but she didn't think he'd make it in time. She knew she blacked out because the next thing she knew, arms were lifting her and dragging her to shore—dragging her to shore without William or Jack in sight. She tried to say something, but all that came out were jagged coughs.

"Stay with us, Carter!" Stan yelled.

Carter managed to look to her side as Dr. Nathaniel worked on giving CPR to a bare-chested William. Amara, Rafe, and Paulo wrapped blankets around Jack as Stan, Lala, and Allison wrapped blankets around Carter. Carter could hear sirens in the distance and wondered how they managed to get an ambulance up through the snow so fast. She could see Harold and Christy holding Gregory upright in the snow.

An angry bubbling sound came from William just before he coughed up a fountain of water. Dr. Nathaniel tilted him on his side to help him out, but nothing else happened. Carter could hear the sounds of footsteps crunching in the snow from the approaching EMT workers.

"There's a weak pulse, he just coughed up some water, and he was under the water for about twelve minutes. We don't know if he went into the water unconscious," Dr. Nathaniel said urgently to one of the workers. He placed a blanket that looked like foil over William. William's entire face was blue and his lips purple, and his body and face were covered in gashes from the broken glass.

"Is he going to be OK?" Carter asked no one in particular, her voice hoarse and shaky.

There was no reply as they carried William into the ambulance, and she swallowed her fear, refusing to let reality sink in.

"We need to get you into the ambulance as well, miss," one of the older EMTs with graying hair said to Carter. They carried her into one of the three ambulances, and unfortunately she was stuck with Gregory Moretti.

"You've got to be kidding me," she said.

He just looked at Carter and shivered. She sat listlessly and focused on the present. She shivered wildly, trying to gain control of her thoughts as confusion drifted in and out. *Hypothermia sucks,* she thought.

"The other two guys were in more serious condition and needed to go immediately," the EMT in the back said to her as they shut the doors behind them.

"Are they going to be OK?"

"Are they your friends?"

"Yes," she whispered.

The EMT nodded. "I don't know their conditions. As soon as we get you checked out at the hospital, you can go see them."

Her heart swelled, and she shed the tears she had been holding back. How had everything gone so wrong again?

CHAPTER 42

ꔖꔌ ꔌ ꔌꔖꔌ ꔖꔌ ꔌꔌꔌ ꔌꔌ ꔌꔖ ꔖꔌ ꔌꔌꔌ ꔖꔌ ꔌ ꔌꔌꔖ ꔌꔖꔌ

D R. NATHANIEL, AMARA, AND STAN waited in the emergency room with Carter as the nurses brought the discharge paperwork. She paced the room back and forth, counting down the seconds before she could go see William and Jack.

The group asked Dr. Nathaniel endless questions about drowning victims and hypothermia. His responses were minimal, and he continuously tried to change the subject. All the while his expression was grim.

A nurse came in. "I can take you to see Jack," she said.

Carter followed on the nurse's heels to Jack's room just down the hall where Rafe and Paulo were. He smiled at her warmly, and she dove onto his bed into his embrace.

"Thank you," she said.

"Have you seen William?"

She shook her head. "No, they just released me."

"I should be getting out of here soon."

She nodded and nuzzled into him again. "Have any of you seen William yet?"

They all shook their heads, and Dr. Nathaniel resentfully said, "I'll go check on him, Carter."

"I want to come."

"Just wait here for now, and I'll make sure he's OK for visitors."

Jack ran his fingers through her hair soothingly, and she rested her head against the soft and steady drumming of his heart. He instantly made her feel calm. They had been there like that in silence for only a few moments when Dr. Nathaniel came back.

"He had a really close call, but he's going to be OK," he said, visibly relieved. "They're giving him fluids and steadily increasing his temperature. He's also on oxygen as they get his oxygen levels back to normal. He'll be here for a few days under observation because there is risk of side effects from near drowning. But they don't think it'll be an issue."

"Can we see him?" Stan asked.

"Soon. They want to give him another round of fluids before he has any visitors. He's awake, though, and asked about you, Jack."

Every head turned and stared at Jack.

"Me? Why me?"

"Somehow he knows you saved him and was worried."

"Well, ain't that something."

Carter smiled—for the first time in days, she realized. "Where is everyone else?"

"They're at the end of the hall. Gregory Moretti is checking out soon."

"We're not staying at the facility, are we?" Amara asked, and everyone nodded. Carter was relieved they were all on the same page.

"We'll be staying in one of the houses on the property," Stan said. "I don't think we should be near the Morettis right now, but we can't leave until William is OK to travel. I figure that will keep us close enough to keep an eye on everything, at a safe distance."

Just then one of the nurses popped her head around the curtain, smiling. "William can have visitors now, but please, no more than two at a time. We will be moving him to a room tonight, and you will be able to visit again tomorrow."

Carter hopped off the bed and turned to Jack.

"I'm still in lockdown for a little while longer," he said. "Why don't you go with someone else?"

"I'll go," Stan said eagerly.

"Stan, do you think William is safe here? Aren't there a lot of police looking for us?" Carter whispered to Stan as they walked down the hall, so low that no human could hear.

Stan nodded. "Half of Anchorage is Anunnaki, Carter. They don't turn their own in."

"That doesn't really seem to be the case with the Morettis."

Carter frowned as they reached an open room with beeping and breathing machine sounds coming from it. "Stan? Aren't you supposed to be the one to think of this?"

"Carter?" William's voice was barely audible and strained. It sounded as if he had bronchitis.

Stan and Carter stepped into the room, and Carter gasped. It seemed that William was hooked up to every machine possible. He had an oxygen mask, IVs, blood-pressure cuff, and other machines Carter didn't recognize. She watched his heartbeat accelerate a bit when he saw her come in, the beeping sound becoming faster. She blushed.

"How do you feel, kid?" Stan asked as he pulled up a chair next to William. "You gave us a scare there."

"I thought I was a goner," he said.

Carter's eyes welled up with tears as reality sank in about how true that statement really was.

"Jack saved my life," William said as he furrowed his brows.

Stan nodded. "Does that surprise you?"

William let out something that sounded like a half-laugh and half-grunt. "I think it does. I'm not sure I would have done the same thing." He looked up and made eye contact with Carter. "It's true. I don't think I would have. If it had meant having you all to myself, I don't think I would've tried as hard."

"I don't think you give yourself enough credit," she said. She knew he didn't—but she also knew there was nothing she could say to convince him otherwise, at least for now.

A cold child ran down Carter's spine, and she wondered if it was just her nerves or if something else was going on.

"I feel that too," Stan said as William nodded in agreement. Carter wondered how many drugs he was on.

She felt Lala approach and stand in the doorway as if she had seen her with her own eyes. It was nearly shocking how in tune with her energy Carter was. Then she remembered when she had had that feeling before.

Carter turned around slowly, giving herself enough time to regain her composure. "Lala."

"Ms. Robinson," Lala sneered. "I'm so happy to see your crew safe and sound."

Carter gave her a warm smile in return, attempting to guard her energy as William and Stan both were doing. She knew the Anunnaki had primarily been focused on connecting with their ancestors on Nibiru through her and William, their intentions mostly good. Yet she also knew there was no such thing as a perfect race, and she would bet everything that Lala was their hellion.

Lala took a step farther into the room, causing Carter and Stan to reflexively stiffen their stance in alert. Lala looked at Stan for a moment and then to Carter, lingering in what seemed to be a staring battle. Carter knew Lala was deciding something but didn't know what. Whatever it was, she either thought better of it or changed her mind.

"William, darling, hope you feel better soon." She smiled at him, but it didn't reach the rest of her face. She paused one moment longer before finally leaving the room. Carter and Stan both visibly relaxed at her departure.

"I don't know if I should stay here," William said, worry etched across his face.

Carter and Stan looked to each other. "How are you feeling?" Stan asked.

"Alive, which is how I'd like to stay."

"Point taken."

The crackle of a walkie-talkie sounded, and Carter stuck her head out the doorway and peered down the hallway. Three police officers were talking to one of the nurses at the nurse station. The nurse pointed in Carter's direction, and she managed to pull her head back in just before the police officers turned and looked.

Carter cursed. "We have company," she said. She looked at William hooked to all the machines, cursing again.

Stan stuck his head back out into the hallway. "They're still talking to the nurses," he said.

"We don't have much time." Carter walked up to William quickly and looked around the monitors. "I don't know how to disconnect all these."

"I do," Stan said. "We have to work fast, though. The second we start disconnecting these, they'll set off an alarm."

"And then what?"

"Then we run."

Again, Carter cursed and William raised his eyebrows at her while Stan took his place on the other side of the bed. "We have to move fast, Carter." Stan showed her how to disconnect two of the machines while he disconnected the IV.

"Wait, I have an idea," Carter said. "Why don't we cause a distraction?"

"How?" William asked.

Carter thought for a moment and looked around the room. She saw the fire alarm and ran up to it. "This will not only distract them, but it might cover up the sounds of the alarms long enough to buy us more time."

"Too bad we can't set the smoke alarms off and let it rain down in here."

"That might send a signal to the rest to get out of here too. They'll know something is wrong."

Stan pulled a lighter out of his pocket, and Carter looked at him curiously. "Just in case of emergency," he said, shrugging.

Without thinking or waiting, Carter grabbed the lighter from Stan and grabbed William's pillow, lighting it on fire. What she didn't expect was that it would go up in flames so fast. The smoke rose to the sprinkler system quickly but didn't do anything. Stan ran to the fire alarm and set it off at the same time that Carter threw the burning pillow into the sink. Then, ignoring the fire in the room and the alarms, they both worked quickly to disconnect William. She heard yelling down the hall as water began spraying over them. The entire time she expected to hear the police just behind them. Stan pulled the IV out as William pressed against his arm, putting pressure on the blood flow. He helped William out of bed, and Carter gasped softly as William swayed. The explosion behind Carter startled her, and she thought, at first, that the cops had set off the explosion.

"The fire is causing chemicals to explode!" Stan exclaimed.

Stan and William hobbled to the door behind Carter as the room quickly filled with smoke. When Carter stuck her head out the door and didn't come face to face with a cop, she was surprised. Through the smoke-filled hallway, Carter could see chaos around the nurses' station.

She ducked into the hallway as the three of them ran toward the emergency exit.

"Stop! Police!" came the voices that Carter had been expecting. She heard the pounding of footsteps on the linoleum floor growing louder as they moved too slowly toward the exit. Like a bad dream, they could not move fast enough.

"We'll shoot!"

Instead of taking the emergency exit, Carter rounded the corner of the hall, pulling Stan and William with her. She knew if they tried to go through the door, the police would shoot them down. Thankfully, the elevator doors opened up twenty feet down the hall.

Stan, Carter, and William put on a last burst of speed and reached the elevators in a heartbeat. Carter pressed the sixth-floor button. They hopped into the elevator, and Carter began to think the elevator doors were stuck. Stan began a *close* chant as footsteps sounded louder down the hall. Just as shoes squeaked to a halt against the linoleum, the doors mercifully shut. Their relief was minor, as they still needed to escape the hospital. At the very last second, Carter pressed the second-floor button.

The elevator doors opened to a seemingly abandoned hallway with signs above that said Orthopedic Spine Center. They had lucked out that they hadn't ended up on a busier floor. They ran east down the corridor, away from the emergency exit, and William began to slow down even more. Carter risked a glance back at him to see that he had lost more color—unless green was a color.

"Stan, we need to stop," she said as William slumped against the wall.

"I can carry him," Stan said.

William rolled his eyes. "I don't think—"

Voices from the hall interrupted him, and Stan lifted William up over his shoulder without asking. Carter raised her eyebrows at them. She knew the Anunnaki were stronger. She knew it firsthand. Yet seeing them like that was half humorous and half alarming. They ran down one more hall and found another door that led to the stairs.

"The longer we stay in the hospital, the more backup they will call. We need to get out of here."

Carter worried about Jack, hoping they had figured it out and left as well. Their escape would mean nothing if Jack was caught. They made their way down the stairs, Carter in front. As luck would have it, the stairs went directly to the outside. The blistering cold air caught them off guard.

"Geez, it's gotta be below zero," Stan remarked as they looked across the large parking lot behind the hospital.

"Now what?"

"We need to get across the parking lot to that Walmart and call the center, have someone pick us up. We can't get far in this cold, and we can't make William try."

Carter looked at William, worried. She kept reminding herself that if he recovered so well from a gunshot wound, this should be nothing. She kept reminding herself that she hadn't seen him immediately after he was shot, so she didn't get to see how bad he looked—probably worse. Yet her stomach ached with anxiety at seeing him unhealthy and struggling. They were seconds from losing him today, she knew.

Carter felt exposed as they made their way across the parking lot. Fortunately, the highway didn't have too many cars on it. The temperature seemed to drop with each step they took. The sun had just set, casting a strange bluish orange across the sky, and the shadows from the trees seemed to be made of ice, expelling cold fumes against their skin. Her teeth chattered in her mouth, and the cold weather seemed to freeze her muscles—moving was becoming increasingly difficult. It didn't help that she still didn't have her coat on—only a thick sweater that felt paper thin.

William was in a hospital gown and socks. Stan gave him his coat. But Carter was afraid that he was going to get hypothermia all over again. What were they thinking, and how had they become fugitives?

The warm air in the Walmart was such a relief that Carter nearly shed tears of joy. William walked the rest of the way inside the Walmart and sat in the booth at the McDonald's inside.

"Take this," Stan said as he reached into his pocket and handed her eight twenty-dollar bills. "Get some warm clothes for William, a blanket, and a coat for yourself."

Stan walked up to the McDonald's cashier, who didn't seem bothered by the fact that a man in a hospital gown and socks sat in their booth. Carter heard Stan ordering food just before she took off down the aisles looking for warm clothes. She grabbed a black down coat for herself and immediately slipped it on, hugging herself in it a moment before looking for items for William.

Picking up the clothes and checking out took less than ten minutes.

When she got back to the table, William was munching on a fry. She handed him the bag, and he slipped on the sweater and jeans slowly, struggling with getting his boots on. She watched him worriedly, realizing he didn't even bother going to the men's room to get dressed.

"William, should we go back?"

He shook his head. "No, I'm already better. The food helps. The clothes will help too. Thank you."

Stan's cell phone rang as Carter slid in next to William. She could feel the dull electric charge between them, but it felt as if it were on low volume. She tuned into his energy easily now that his guard was down, and she was relieved a bit when she just felt fatigue in it. Otherwise, he felt intact.

"They're just five minutes away," Stan said.

Carter picked up a chicken nugget and popped it into her mouth. "So you think Lulu called the cops?"

William nodded. "I do. She's a Vaticate; why wouldn't she?"

"I don't understand. She knows we didn't kill Amelia."

"Yes, but you forgot what the Vaticates have been trying to do."

"Stop us," Carter said.

Stan and William both nodded. "They're not going to stop, Carter. In fact, they're probably going to do everything in their power to stop you now more than ever. Especially if Jibril knows as much as we think he does," Stan said.

Carter tilted her head as she thought out loud. "They don't want the Anunnaki to come back because it will end faith. Especially now that they realize the Anunnaki may have healing powers and other powers."

"Religion is a very profitable business," William said.

"So we're sitting ducks," Carter said, and William nodded.

Stan shifted in his seat and looked around uneasily, as if the threat was looming nearby. Maybe it was.

CHAPTER 43

𒐋 𒀸 𒆳 𒐋 𒈾 𒈫 𒌋 𒆠 𒄡 𒌋𒈾 𒐋 𒀸 𒋻 𒆳

J ACK WAS SHIVERING IN THE back seat, and Carter watched him
helplessly.

"I'm glad you guys got out," Stan said.

She could hear Jack's teeth chatter. William handed him one of
the blankets that Carter had bought, and Jack just nodded roughly in
response.

"We were too nervous to go into any stores, so we just waited by the
Dumpsters behind the hospital," Dr. Nathaniel said. His nose was bright
red and his lips pale. He shivered slightly. The heater in the car was full
blast, but it didn't seem to be helping them fast enough.

"Where are we going?" Carter asked.

"Kenai, Alaska," Stan said.

Jack finally stopped shivering, and she turned around, smiling at him.
They were all piled into the Hummer, so she sat on his lap.

Stan continued. "Carter, John had a cabin there. No one knew about it except a few people close to him. He had the cabin specifically for times like this, as if he knew something like this would happen."

"How far is it from here?" Amara asked wearily.

"Only three hours."

Everyone visibly relaxed. Carter would be happy if she didn't have to go on another road trip again. She nestled against Jack and eventually fell asleep to the soft rise and fall of his steady breathing. She didn't wake up until they were pulling up to a cabin on the shore.

"Are we here?"

Stan nodded. "We are. Kenai is on a peninsula, and this is the inlet," he said, waving to the shore. "The gulf of Alaska is to the southwest of us."

Carter nodded. The night was pitch black, and there were no lights to be seen anywhere. They were in the middle of nowhere.

"John picked this place specifically because you can easily fly out of the country from here, and as you can see, if anyone approaches, you'll see them coming miles ahead. It's secluded enough to be hidden but open enough to escape."

"Even in death, your father is looking out for you," Amara said quietly.

As Stan pulled onto the gravel drive, everyone stirred awake. They waited in the car while he found the key, let himself in, and turned on all the lights. He was only inside briefly before stepping back to the Hummer.

"We're good; come in."

It was as cold inside the cabin as it was outside. Stan turned on the heaters, and the distinct scent of it wafted through the rooms. Rafe walked over to the fireplace and began putting wood in, setting the fire.

"Did he ever stay here?" she asked.

"We didn't always know where John was, Carter. It was part of who he was—well, all of us, really. We learned to live our lives in secret. But I imagine he did," Paulo said as he watched Rafe throw a match into fireplace. "He brought us up here once, though, after your mother's death. I haven't been back since, but he let any of us use it if we wanted to get away."

"I spent every vacation up here, fishing," Stan said. "Brought Kyra with me once."

Carter thought of the time she met Kyra at Bohemian Grove, and she smiled. William plopped down on the leather sofa facing the fireplace and wrapped the blanket tight around him.

"There are three bedrooms," Stan explained. "There's a fireplace in each one."

"I'm staying here," William said from the sofa, his eyes already becoming heavy.

"There's also a rollaway that I will bring out," Stan said as he walked down one of the halls.

"I'll take the rollaway," Dr. Nathaniel said, rubbing his eyes.

"We'll take the room with two twins," Rafe said to Paulo.

Carter leaned against Jack as Stan brought the rollaway out. Amara and Dr. Nathaniel helped him set it up, and then Stan showed Carter and Jack to one of the rooms. When Carter switched on the light, the energy hit her like a bulldozer. They had gotten John's room, and even Jack realized it.

"Is this going to be OK for you?"

She nodded. The rest of the cabin was sparse, decorated with the bare minimum. His room was different. A hand-stitched quilt covered the queen bed, and Carter ran her fingers over it. It was old, she realized, and she wondered if there was sentimental meaning behind it. In the corner of the room was a simple desk with books and paperwork piled on top. She noticed a stone tablet the size of a postcard in the middle, on top of some papers. When she picked it up, it hummed with energy. Tiny carvings covered the piece, and she recognized the writing.

"Cuneiform," she said.

Jack walked over and took it from Carter's hands. "Where do you think he got this?"

"Maybe Stan knows."

"We should get some rest, Carter. We'll go through this stuff tomorrow."

He gently put the tablet back down on the desk and took her hand, lifting it to his lips and kissing her knuckles. He swooped her up, cradling her, and carried her to the bed. "Stay there," he said. Jack went to the fireplace and lit it. The soft amber glow sensually filled the room.

Slowly and deliberately he undressed her, kissing her warm skin as she trembled beneath him. Their lovemaking that night was tender and delicate, as if they had all the time in the world. And for that night, they did. Nothing would stop them from enjoying each other, from taking their time. Jack and Carter knew all too well that a new day was promised to no one.

CHAPTER 44

𒂍𒌋𒁹𒂍𒌋𒂍𒀀𒌋𒅀𒁹𒌋𒁹𒀀𒅆𒂍𒌋𒅆𒅗

"WE LIVE IN TWO WORLDS," Dr. Nathaniel explained after he handed the tablet back to Stan. "The one you see and the one you don't." He paused, looking out the windows, lost in thought. "The deeper we go into nature, the more powerful it becomes."

"What do you mean, Doctor?" William asked. Carter had felt a breath of relief when she saw William that morning when she woke. His color was back to normal, and his energy was almost back to the way it had been.

"Thought is just another level of nature. Quantum physics teaches us this. We are seeing that thought process is actually energy, so it isn't surprising that you are more connected to the gate to the Anunnaki through your thoughts. They have developed that ability further within your DNA, Carter, as well as yours, William. It's not a matter of figuring out what it is, it's a matter of remembering. This journey you have been on hasn't been to discover that. It's been a way to jog long-rested memories and bring them forth. I think that tablet will be one of the last memory joggers you'll need."

"As soon as we figure out what it says," Jack said.

"That shouldn't be too hard," Rafe said. "John had translated texts here; we just need to find them."

Stan nodded in agreement. "We can start on that right away."

"What should we do?" Carter asked.

"Enjoy the place," he replied. "We already know your mind at rest seems to be the most effective way to remember things and connect."

She nodded. She had been wanting to go exploring since she woke up that morning, and she peeked out the window at the most breathtaking scenery she had ever seen.

The cabin sat just a hundred yards from the gravelly shore backing into the forest that went as far as the eye could see. Water lapped quietly, adding to the peacefulness of the place. They were surrounded by striking and immense mountains covered in snow.

She grabbed her down jacket and slipped on her winter boots and then stepped out onto the shore. She had been out there only a few minutes when she heard the door open and softly shut behind her. Carter listened to the soft crunch of gravel behind her, and the peaceful energy that trailed ahead to her could only belong to one person.

"I think Sergio would love this," Amara said quietly, looking out over the water. "There is so much peace here."

Carter nodded. "I wish he could be here with you."

"I wish John could be here with you too."

"I feel like he is. I mean, he is everywhere here."

The ladies stood there for a while in silence, and then the rest of the group joined them. Rafe came out with a box full of items, and Carter looked at him curiously.

"Bonfire," he said excitedly.

"Really? It's freezing out here," Carter said.

"Hence the fire," Paulo said.

Carter scoffed and then helped pull out the items. "Did you guys find anything out?"

"We did," Stan replied, "which is one of the reasons for the bonfire. We think it'll help uncover some truths."

Stan left for town and returned shortly after with food from a local diner. The conversation was light around the food—almost as if everyone was enjoying peace while they could.

Carter looked around at her friends and realized how close she had become with them in such a short time. A part of her ached, though, because she realized that there was a very big chance that not all of them would come out of this alive. She realized that that someone would very likely be her. She reached her hand out to Jack and grasped it tightly. Did he feel the same way? The night before definitely felt that way.

When they finally gathered around the fire, the frost was thick in the air. It was disconcerting at the same that it was fresh and crisp. It felt as if the fire were fighting and slicing through the icy air.

"The energy you felt in this tablet wasn't just an Anunnaki sensation," Dr. Nathaniel said as he pulled the tablet out. "It is Aswan granite and contains quite a bit of crystals. It's a special combination of stone that causes electromotive flow. The great pyramids are structured similarly."

"What does it do, exactly?" Carter asked.

"It basically makes an electric generator or a resonating chamber in which the sound of certain frequencies can be heard."

"May I see that?" Jack asked as he took the granite piece from Dr. Nathaniel. He flipped it over in his hand. "I feel something, almost like putting your hand over a television that has just been turned off."

"Many believe that in the pyramids, if you lie in the sarcophagus, you will resonate with the gods—essentially, communicate with them," Dr. Nathaniel continued. "It never occurred to me to connect the two until Stan brought me this piece this morning. I would bet anything that your DNA is structured to pick up on this resonance specifically and communicate with the gods that way."

"The Anunnaki, you mean," Stan corrected.

Dr. Nathaniel waved him off, and Jack chuckled.

"Is that why you had certain pharaohs who communicated with the gods frequently? Were they part of my same line?"

"I'm not sure," Dr. Nathaniel said. "But I imagine so. I'm also sure history's messengers of gods were also a part of your line."

"What? Like Joan of Arc?" Jack asked, bewildered.

"The very," Dr. Nathaniel said.

Jack grunted as he threw a pebble into the fire, causing a small spark.

"It makes sense," Amara said. "The messenger of God."

Carter nodded. It did make sense, but it was still strange to be connected to such major individuals in history.

"Any idea what it says on the tablet?" Rafe asked.

"None," Dr. Nathaniel said. "But this looks like a piece of a larger artifact. It might not be anything."

"Wait a minute," Carter said after thinking momentarily. "Do I need to go to the pyramids now?"

The sounds of the water lapping against the shore and the cracking of the fire were all that could be heard. Carter's mouth turned upside down.

"Great," was all she said. She let out a big sigh as frosty air billowed from her mouth. "When do we leave?"

"In a couple of days," Stan said.

"So that's why we're really out here, then," she said. Another thought hit her. "Are we all going?"

"No, Amara and Paulo will stay here."

Carter nodded. This was the trip that could change everything, the one they had been waiting for. A chill ran up her spine as she looked around at the snow-covered mountains and calm water. The fire crackled and burned in stark contrast to the whites and blues that made up the environment.

"There's one other thing," Stan continued.

Jack and William lifted their heads in interest.

"This cabin was left to you in John's will."

"What? When did he have time to put a will together?"

"While we were in Peru."

Carter tilted her head. "You don't think he…" She couldn't finish her sentence.

Stan shook his head. "I don't think so, Carter. He knew his job was dangerous, and I think he had been wanting to do that since you came back into his life."

Her eyes welled up with tears as Jack placed a supportive hand on her back. She looked over her shoulder at the cabin on the shore, and when she looked back to Jack, he smiled warmly at her. Could they live here? After everything that had happened in the last ten months, it seemed more than inviting.

"Carter, the winter here is more than harsh. We always used the cabin during the spring and summer months. It's May, and it still drops below zero. In December and January, it can get twenty below zero, and it only stays light for a few hours a day."

Jack grunted as his eyebrows shot up comically.

"Well, good thing I still have my home in Santa Barbara, I think."

Stan chuckled. "I can't believe we haven't told you about your home all this time." Carter felt her breath catch. "Your home is perfectly fine. After the last time with the break-in, our crew went in and cleaned everything up and changed the locks. We have random patrols set up to check the home out to make sure everything is OK and have set up an alarm system. When you're ready to go back, you can choose to keep the alarm if you like, but it'll be there for you regardless—just the way you like it."

Carter wiped away the tears that freely flowed now. An electric charge formed at the tips of her fingers, and she looked at her hand curiously. She looked, and everyone seemed faded around the fire. Stan stood abruptly as William looked anxiously from face to face. It wasn't just she who felt the change in the atmosphere.

"*Escaaaaaaape,*" the whispers spoke.

William shot his head up. "I heard that."

"Heard what?" Rafe and Amara asked simultaneously.

"*Escaaaape nowwwww.*"

William stood up now, looking around. "Carter, are those the voices you hear?"

Carter nodded.

Whispering chatter sounded in the distance now.

"The portal," Dr. Nathaniel said.

"Someone found us?" Paulo asked, disbelieving.

The air fizzled over the fire as frigid air whipped around everyone, making the already-freezing temperatures colder.

Jibril stepped through the portal, and the image was so shocking that Carter didn't even notice him cradling a body until he dropped Harold Moretti onto the sand roughly. She didn't know whether she saw the reflection of the fire in his eyes or if the fire was lit from within. Dark shadows cast under his eyes and his cheeks were hollow.

"Turns out I can't travel through this thing without one of you guys," Jibril said, his voice loud and booming in the silent Arctic air.

William lowered his eyes to see his uncle. "Is he dead?" William asked with an icy, level tone.

"Shouldn't be," Jibril said as he stepped forward. He looked briefly to Carter, a fleeting moment that was barely noticeable. Just then, quicker than a blink of an eye, he wrapped his fingers firmly around William's wrist, smiling sardonically.

In that moment the portal fizzled around them both, swallowing them quickly, faster than it took Carter to take a single breath. When the portal vanished, the stillness of the air became deafening. In that beat, three things happened: Harold Moretti died, Carter fell to her knees in recognized failure, and a phone rang from inside the cabin. Only thing was, they didn't own a phone.

CHAPTER 45

ᚺᛁᚲ ᚲᛁᚺᚲ ᚹᛁᚺ ᚱᛁᚱᛁ ᚾ ᛁᚾ ᚺᚲ ᚲᛁᛁᚱ ᚹᛁᚺᚲ ᚱᛁᚾ ᚲᚹᛁ

STAN WAS THE FIRST TO make it inside the cabin. The phone incessantly rang as if urging him to pick up. When he did, he could hear only a crackling sound from the other side, and underneath that layer, a sound that even Stan couldn't hear. Startling, dark whispers warning them.

The next few hours passed in a whirl, and Carter had all but forgotten about that phone call. But it nagged in her mind, a tickling memory far in the back reaches of her thoughts. The only problem was that she wouldn't bring that memory forth until it was too late.

Somehow, from their remote corner of the world, Stan and his team managed to get everything in order for their trip to Egypt, in two hours. Carter was in a daze. Not only was she going to be visiting the great pyramids of Egypt, but she would be going inside one of the hidden tombs. She only hoped they would get there in time to bring William back.

"So how exactly are we getting inside anyway?" Carter asked.

"We have a team there waiting for us. They are part of the American consulate in Egypt and are pulling in some favors from the local government," Stan said as he printed off boarding passes.

Carter noticed that only Jack and she got tickets.

"Wait, is it just us?" Jack asked.

"The three of us, yes." Stan waved his boarding pass in his hand. "The rest will stay here and try to figure out what's going on with the center in Anchorage and the Morettis."

Carter looked down at the flight information and frowned. "Travel time is forty-four hours?" She hoped that was a typo.

"It's the best we could do on such short notice, and most flights land in Chicago, which we want to avoid right now for obvious reasons. Jack, are you OK?"

Everyone in the room turned to look at Jack, who looked a little green. He swallowed hard as he pocketed his boarding pass. Carter frowned as she watched him. She thought about telling him to stay behind but knew he wouldn't.

Carter threw the few belongings she had in her bag as they headed to a waiting helicopter that would take them to Anchorage. Before they left, Dr. Nathaniel gave Carter a warm embrace, tears in his eyes.

"You come back soon, you hear?"

Carter nodded, slightly taken aback by his display of emotion. When she turned to say good-bye to Amara and the rest of her friends, she saw they all had the same grim looks on their faces.

At a loss for words, she smiled warmly at them, making a point not to say good-bye.

Jack held Carter's hand as they dashed under the rotating blades of the helicopter, slicing freezing air against their faces. The last time she had ridden a helicopter was leaving Bohemian Grove, just after the loss of Carl. She thought of her friend and that night in Bohemian Grove, and it seemed like another lifetime instead of ten months.

Their forty-four-hour trip turned into a fifty-two-hour trip as their flights to both Boston and London were considerably delayed. Fortunately, during their stop in London, Stan reserved a hotel room so that the three of them could shower, take a short nap, and eat a real meal.

On the return trip to the airport, they stopped at a department store and picked up more appropriate clothes for their trip in Egypt.

When she emerged from the dressing room with her black cargo pants and black ribbed tank, she saw Jack eyeing her hungrily.

"I kind of feel like Lara Croft in these." She smoothed her hands over her pant legs self-consciously.

Jack raised an eyebrow at her.

"What?" she asked.

A smile played at the corner of his mouth, and his eyes sparkled in delight.

"Oh my god, you are such a guy!" Carter said half jokingly.

"Excuse me, Stan," Jack said as he swooped Carter off her feet and threw her over his shoulder.

"Jack! What are you doing?"

He pushed the door of the store open, stepped out onto the sidewalk under the chilly London rain, and finally put Carter upright on her feet.

"It's raining, Jack."

He lowered his head and hovered just inches above her face. The darkness that hooded his eyes stopped her short in her tracks, making her forget whatever she was going to say next.

"I thought women liked to be kissed in the rain?" he said in a low, gravelly voice.

She laughed nervously. "I'm not your typical woman."

"No, you definitely are not," he said breathlessly, watching her, searching her eyes. She didn't know what it was, but worry was etched in the creases of his skin.

"Carter, I don't want you to leave me."

She half pulled away from him in surprise, but his arm was wrapped around her waist tightly.

"That's not what I mean. I meant I don't want you to go after William."

Carter's heart sped up. "Jack, you know that I—"

"No, hear me out. I know how you feel about him; I know that you…" his voice hitched, and he took a shaky breath. "I know you care about him." Carter opened her mouth to interrupt him, but he just placed his hand over her mouth, and she raised her eyebrows at him. She shivered slightly but didn't think it was from the rain.

Jack removed his hand gently, watching the rain leave trails of water over her skin and eyelashes.

"If you go after him, there's a chance you won't come back. I could stand your choosing someone else over me. It would break me, but it would be better, better than not having you here or knowing what happened. Not knowing what happened would drive me mad, drive Stan and your dad mad." He stopped abruptly at his own words. "You still have Paulo and Julia. These guys here, they know what this life brings. They put their lives at risk for a mission. But our family at home doesn't get it—and I can't go back there and tell them that I lost you. I won't."

Salty tears mixed with the rain that now fell softly around them, and the world became silent. Carter could no longer hear the traffic on the road or the chaos of the city. She closed her eyes and could only hear the frantic drumming of Jack's heartbeat.

"But you've already made up your mind," he said as he pulled away from her. She leaned in to him automatically, wanting his warmth back.

"Jack, what kind of person would I be if I didn't go after him? We already know I'm the only one who can."

He nodded solemnly, looking down at the ground.

She pressed both her palms to the side of his face, forcing him to look at her again. "I will return."

Jack sighed deeply and pressed his lips together. "Carter, you don't know—"

"Yes. I. Do." She looked at him intently. "I know, Jack. Otherwise, what is all this? What has all of this been for? I still feel him, Jack. I know that bothers you, but I do. I'm connected to him somehow, and I know he's still alive, and he's stuck. He's a friend, and this is what friends do, isn't it? You saved him once."

Jack looked defeated, and Carter wouldn't feel bad about it. "Jack, please."

She wasn't sure what exactly she was asking for, but she needed him to bend a little. She ran her hand from his face through his hair and rested it on the back of his neck.

"I love you. You know that, right?" Jack said, his eyes burning.

She took a deep breath. "It never mattered whether you did or not because you always had my heart regardless."

He pressed his lips against hers, hard, as tears and rain ran down their faces. She wrapped her arms around his neck, pulling him down closer to her as her heart drummed loudly in her chest, proclaiming its own love.

"I love you Jack," she whispered between kisses.

"And I love both you guys, but we're going to miss our flight." Stan stood under the awning of the store with bags in his hands and a sloppy grin on his face.

All three laughed as Stan hailed a cab to head back to the airport. In fifty-two hours they had gone through three continents and three vastly different climate changes. Alaska was freezing, a landscape of pure-white serenity; London was cold, green, and rainy; and Egypt was hot, brown, and dry.

She was surprised by the modern airport. What she had been expecting, she wasn't sure. Yet this was certainly not it.

"Jack, are you OK?"

"I'm fine, just tired."

Carter watched him worriedly. His skin was pale, and he dragged when he walked. She didn't realize how much better she and Stan had held up with the traveling simply because of their alien blood until that moment. She thought about asking to send him to their hotel but knew he would refuse.

Their team waited for them as they walked toward the baggage claim area. Carter had already removed her sweaters and was still hot in her camisole. They were enduring a near-one-hundred-degree temperature change from Alaska, making the heat in Cairo seem especially sweltering.

"Ms. Robinson? It's a pleasure to meet you. I'm Paulo Sarayan." The handsome older man shook Carter's hand and looked at her with kind and wise eyes. She immediately trusted him. "I would ask how your trip was, but a long trip like that could not have been fun."

She smiled back. Carter could hear a slight accent but couldn't place it. Jack, Stan, and Carter were introduced to the rest of their team. Marie De Marcus was a tall, slender woman who could have easily have passed for a supermodel. Her pulled-back hair, plain clothing, serious expression, and lack of makeup showed that she wanted to be anything but a model. Logan Reed reminded Carter of Stan. They were almost the exact same height and had similar sharp features, fair skin, and light eyes. They could almost pass for brothers.

Marie wasted no time in directing them through the airport to their waiting car. Stan's attempts at small talk failed miserably when she shut down any conversation he brought up by just staring at him with daggers in her eyes. Carter got the distinct impression that they were all an inconvenience to her.

Phillip chuckled softly when Jack started asking her about Egypt and her response was to hand him her iPhone, telling him use Google. That was the last attempt at conversation with Marie.

"Are you sure you don't want to rest first?" Phillip asked as they got into the van.

"How long a trip is it to the pyramids?" Jack asked.

"Just about fifteen minutes," Logan said.

Jack and Carter both breathed a sigh of relief. Even though their trip seemed endless, it was strange to Carter that she was only minutes away from seeing the Great Pyramid of Giza. It was just on the other side of the Nile River, which they were now crossing.

If this river could tell a story, she thought, *what stories could it tell?*

Logan magically maneuvered the crowded streets of Cairo while continuously honking the horn and parting the crowds.

Carter half-listened to Stan explain to the others what had happened in Alaska when Jibril picked up William. She was more interested in Marie, who seemed to increasingly become uncomfortable the more they discussed their situation. Marie must have sensed Carter watching her because she suddenly turned and glared. Carter spent the rest of the short trip gazing at the passing landscape and watching the pyramids magically rise out of the sand.

By the time they had reached the pyramids, it seemed as if they had been transported in time back to when pharaohs roamed the land. For centuries humans had been mystified by the pyramids and their reason for existence. It seemed strange that the answers had been right under their noses the entire time.

"So who's an alien here?" Jack asked out of the blue.

Phillip smiled warmly when he said, "Just me and Logan."

"So you're human like me, huh?" Jack asked Marie, who stiffened in response.

"Are we riding camels?" Carter asked as they pulled up to the parking area.

Stan nodded. "Kyra should be waiting for us when we get there."

Carter was anxious and excited to see Kyra, whom she hadn't seen since that fateful night in Bohemian Grove. Stan had explained on their flight that Kyra had been teaching English at the American University in Cairo for the last six months.

Carter pulled Stan to the side as the workers began helping everyone mount the camels.

"What's Marie's deal? Are you sure she wants to help us?"

Stan sighed heavily and looked for a long moment into Carter's eyes. He wanted to say something, she knew. She reached out, trying to sense his energy, but he blocked her.

"What? What aren't you telling me?"

He pressed his lips together into a thin line and shook his head just before he walked away toward the group. Carter saw Jack watching her across the distance. She shrugged at him, and he just looked confused.

When they were all riding the camels, he hung back from the group, so she did as well.

"What was that all about?" he asked.

"I don't know," she said. "He's holding something back. I asked him what was with Marie."

"You think she's a problem?"

She shrugged again. "Well, I definitely don't think she wants to help us."

"Maybe she doesn't like the Anunnaki?"

Carter thought about that. "No, I don't think that's it. Stan seems to know why she's acting this way, and I don't think he would let her help if that's what it was."

They rode the rest of the short distance in silence, both deep in thought. All was forgotten when Carter saw Kyra waiting for them. She ran into her friend's arms, genuinely excited to see her.

"You're skin and bones," Kyra said.

Carter looked down at herself and the pants that were two sizes smaller than she used to wear. "It's been a long year."

Kyra smiled sympathetically. "Well, hopefully we'll figure this all out soon and get some answers, and then you can go back to your normal life."

Carter huffed under her breath. She knew Kyra was just trying to make her feel better. She knew too well they'd never have a normal life. If she didn't connect with the Anunnaki soon, the Vaticates would find a way to get rid of her and William. They left her without a choice.

"So this is the famous Carter?" The man approached Kyra and Carter, extending his hand. Carter took it and grimaced at his too-firm handshake.

Kyra introduced them. "This is Omar. He is an archaeologist on site here and will be helping us with the translations on the tomb, hopefully leading us to the correct sarcophagus."

Carter nodded at him, uncomfortable with the way he watched her, as if she were his next meal. Over his shoulder she saw Marie talking to another woman casually. They clearly knew each other.

Carter sighed heavily. She was uncomfortable with the team they had together and wasn't sure whether she should do something about it. She turned to look at Stan, who was also watching the two women curiously. She realized then how much she trusted Stan, and if he put the team together, they would be OK. Besides, she would conduct her job alone regardless. They just needed to figure out what tomb to find, and the rest was up to her, wasn't it?

Marie walked back with the woman, and Carter noticed that she was about their age. She smiled warmly at Carter and seemed genuinely happy to meet her.

"I'm Femi," she said.

"Femi is an Egyptologist and will be able to translate hieroglyphics for us once we're inside the pyramid," Phillip said.

"When will that be?" Stan asked.

"Now," Omar said abruptly.

Kyra looped her arm into the crook of Carter's elbow. "Beautiful, isn't it?"

Carter turned to see Kyra looking up at the pyramid before them, and she nodded. Beautiful didn't seem like an appropriate word. But when she tried to think of a better word, she couldn't. It was majestic, beautiful, powerful, and so many other words in one.

She looked and saw the peak still covered in limestone, and she got a sense of déjà vu. She squinted against the sun and became dizzy at the sight of the pyramid.

"You OK, Carter?"

Kyra was watching her, concerned. Stan stood on the other side watching her, and Carter never even noticed his approach.

"Yeah, just hot."

Kyra smiled. "Especially after Alaska."

She looked back at Stan, and he frowned at her. She knew he didn't believe her, but he didn't risk asking in front of his sister.

"This is Khufu," Kyra said. "The largest of the three here. Most people know it as the Great Pyramid of Giza—named after the Pharaoh Khufu. What you see here is the core, and the casing stone has been mostly removed."

"By who?" Carter asked.

Kyra shrugged. "It was used to help build some of the homes here in Cairo. But that didn't happen until recent centuries. The outer casing was intact until then—and would still be today, most likely, if not for that. Just shows how incredible the architecture was." Kyra laughed suddenly. "That alone should show these humans they had some help, shouldn't it? I can't wait until we connect with the Anunnaki on Nibiru, Carter. I can only imagine all that they can show us and hope they'll finish what they started."

A shiver ran up Carter's back, even though the sun was beating down on them.

Carter listened to Omar and Femi speak in Arabic and desperately wished she could understand them. She slowed down to where Phillip was behind them.

"Phillip, do you speak Arabic?"

"No, I speak Armenian, French, and Farsi." He laughed. "I should learn Arabic, though, considering where I work."

Carter smiled at him. "So you're Armenian?"

He nodded. "I am. I was born in Iran and grew up there until the revolution, and I then moved to Paris, where I was until two years ago. Then I came here on duty."

They continued their small talk as they reached the entrance of the pyramid, and Carter stopped just before stepping into the chamber. She looked up at the pyramid and again had a sense of déjà vu. She wondered whether it was from only seeing the pyramid in thousands of photos and stories or if there was something more to it.

"Look familiar?" Stan asked, startling her.

"Yes, how did you know?"

"I could tell by the confused look on your face and the energy you're sending off."

"What does it mean?"

"It's possible you've already been here, in your other lifetime."

That idea had already briefly crossed her mind, but it seemed too unreal to be a possibility.

The stones were massive. She had always known they were massive—who didn't? But it was something else to see it in person. The magnitude of what stood before her was mesmerizing. She reached out and touched the cold stone, running her fingers over it. The human side of her was in awe.

"I've seen these pyramids hundreds of times." Kyra spoke softly in the entrance of the chamber, her voice carrying in the enclosed room. "And they never cease to amaze me."

Jack smiled at Carter and took her hand in his, squeezing softly. She took a deep breath. "Here we go," she said as they stepped inside the chamber.

They traveled a short way on a downward slope in the drafty passageway before they reached another passageway that ascended. Omar led the team, taking the ascending passageway. Everyone remained silent as they traveled down the claustrophobic and dusty path.

Just when Carter didn't think she could take any more and it felt as if the walls were caving in, they stepped into a larger passageway where the ceiling opened up to nearly twenty feet above them. Though the sidewalls still seemed to be closing in on them, the height gave her some reprieve.

"This is the Grand Gallery," Omar said from the front.

"Not very grand," Jack said from behind Carter, and she and Stan chuckled in agreement. Carter thought she heard Omar grunt and mumble something about stupid Americans under his breath.

"And this is the King's Chamber," Kyra said excitedly.

"There's not anything here," Carter said, defeated.

"Not anymore there isn't," Phillip acknowledged. "Most of the items here have been either stolen or taken back to museums."

"So what are we looking for?" Jack said as he peered into the empty sarcophagus.

Phillip and Omar both looked up at the same time and the rest of the team followed their direction.

"There's nothing there," Carter said.

"Oh, but there is," Omar said.

CHAPTER 46

𒀭𒀸𒂖𒀭𒈨�ᚾ𒌋𒂖𒌍𒀭𒀸𒌐𒌋𒂖

"THE KING HAD A LOT of secrets," Phillip said excitedly.

"And how exactly do we get up there?" Jack asked as he looked around the room.

Carter yawned as the humidity of the chambers and the long journey began to catch up. She caught Stan rubbing his eyes at the same time.

"Do you still feel him?" Stan asked and saw Marie turn sharply in their direction as she narrowed her eyes at them.

Carter shut her eyes a moment to feel William's energy. "I do, but it's faded a little."

"What does that mean?" Marie hissed. "Is he not dying?"

"I don't know."

"What do you mean, you don't know? What's wrong with you?" Marie spoke through clenched teeth, and Carter noticed her hands were balled into fists on her side.

"Marie, please." Phillip rested his hand on her shoulder to calm her down. Carter's heartbeat sped up, and she saw that Stan and Jack shared a look of concern.

Carter narrowed her eyes at the tall woman, who avoided eye contact. She was beginning to have second thoughts about this mission.

Omar pointed to the ventilation system in the corner, which looked as if it had been recently installed. It stood on cinderblocks. "We can move these over and use this to hoist ourselves up."

"What about the ventilation system?" Kyra asked.

"We'll have to do without."

Carter raised her eyebrows.

"Just be glad it's only spring," Phillip joked.

"Aren't these tombs booby-trapped?" Jack asked as he and Stan helped Omar move the ventilation system.

"Not anymore," Kyra explained. "Between tomb robbers, archaeologists, and everyone else who's been through here, there's virtually nothing left."

Liarssssssssss, said the whispers.

Stan's and Kyra's heads popped up as if they had heard that. Carter looked at them curiously and then noticed everyone else was continuing with stacking cinderblocks or watching the process, but they were the only three who had heard the whispers.

Jack stood up and wiped the dirt off his hands onto his pant legs and caught the trio watching one another trepidly. He raised his eyebrows at them, and Carter subtly shook her head.

"OK, we're good to go," Omar said.

Carter's heart rate sped up.

"Are you OK?" Phillip asked. "It's only one level up; we'll be OK." He misread her apprehension.

"We're OK," Stan said. "I'll go first."

Kyra and Carter looked at him worriedly, and Carter followed close behind, not giving anyone else an opportunity to go ahead.

Stan helped pull her up into the room above, and Carter was surprised to see how big it was—nearly the same size as the King's Chamber below. She gasped when she saw the sealed sarcophagus in the middle of the room and felt the electrical buzz from it. It was ordinary looking—not elaborate, but she knew this was what they were looking for. The walls of the eight-by-ten room were covered in hieroglyphics, but what she found most peculiar, and something she had become increasingly familiar with, was that the sarcophagus was not covered in hieroglyphics, but cuneiform.

They would need a cuneiform translator, not a hieroglyphics translator.

"Cuneiform?" Kyra asked as she peered over Carter's shoulder.

"You don't happen to understand it, do you?"

"I do, actually."

Carter raised her eyebrows at her friend. "Well, that's nice and lucky."

"I have a feeling luck has nothing to do with it," Stan said morosely.

Cuneiform was one step above looking like chicken scratches and one of the earliest forms of writing, older than hieroglyphics. Cuneiform was so old that it had become extinct before the pyramids ever existed. What it was doing in an ancient pyramid on a sarcophagus was baffling.

"Who did this belong to?" Stan asked his sister.

She shrugged and turned to Phillip, who was the last to climb into the room. He wiped the sweat off his eyebrows with his handkerchief, and Carter could see him struggling to catch his breath. She hoped he would be OK in the heat and humidity.

"No one knows," he stated.

The air became increasingly denser, and breathing was becoming a task. Carter wondered how long this would take.

"So what do we do now?" she asked.

"Well, Dr. Nathaniel said that your energy will resonate inside the sarcophagus chamber," Stan said.

"She's going to go inside the sarcophagus?" Jack asked, his eyes narrowing.

"Well, there's got to be more to it than just sitting inside the sarcophagus," Marie said sadistically.

"There is." Kyra ran her fingers over the writing on the side of the sarcophagus as she sat, crouched down. She had her flashlight in her mouth, pointing at the engravings as she used both fingers to wipe over the dusty letters. "I'm not quite sure I understand what this is really saying, but it doesn't sound good."

"What does it say?" Omar ran to hunch over Kyra.

There was a sudden shift in the energy in the room that sent a chill up Carter's spine. She turned to Stan, who shared the same worried expression. Femi watched them both, and Carter didn't miss it. She didn't trust the woman.

Kyra pointed to what seemed like the first part of a paragraph. "This symbolizes female, and this," she pointed to the next set of symbols, "represents male. It's almost like the Adam and Eve story."

"That is something we already knew about," Stan said.

Carter struggled to take a deep breath as her anxiety rose. She felt as if she were drowning and fighting for air. She looked around and noticed that the others seemed to be uncomfortable, but not to the extent that she was. She tried to focus on what Kyra was saying and ignore her sudden bout of claustrophobia.

"Well, it continues—this is a symbol for travel and rebirth."

Stan nodded, and Carter wished she would translate faster so they could get on with it.

"But this symbolizes death."

"I don't understand," Jack said. "Whose death?"

Kyra swallowed heavily. "I don't know, Jack." she spoke barely over a whisper.

"It looks as if it's over the female sign, but that doesn't mean anything, right?" Jack spoke quickly and urgently. "I mean, this is something that has happened, right?"

"No," Kyra said sternly. "No, it's a prophecy."

Carter walked over to a wall and slid down to her butt, sticking her head between her legs. Her head began throbbing, and she could barely hear anyone over the pounding between her ears.

"It's a prophecy that we're ending right now."

His voice was unmistakable. She heard it in her waking nightmares, and it haunted her in her dreams. Carter didn't bother lifting her head from her knees because she knew it was pointless.

The scuffling of feet and shouting was enough to confirm her fears. What she didn't expect was to look up and see who was standing with Jibril.

Carter saw Omar and Femi flanking Jibril with guns drawn.

"Funny, Marie, I expected you to be standing with Jibril," Carter said with a strained voice as she struggled to get to her feet.

Marie practically hissed at Carter. "You don't know anything, Miss High and Mighty!"

Jibril raised his eyebrows at the girls and quirked a smile.

"Are you OK?" Stan asked Carter, who was the only one standing close enough to her to notice anything. She just nodded.

"What's going on here?" Phillip asked as he glared at Omar and Femi.

And then Carter saw who stepped out from behind Jibril, and her heart sank. She blinked several times as she stared at her best friend, who looked nothing like how she remembered. Carter was sure it was a mistake. But by the way Julia glared at her, she knew it wasn't. She had been betrayed to the deepest levels.

Julia's arms wrapped into the crook of Jibril's elbow, and it was clear they were close—very close. Jack cursed, and Stan scooted in closer to Carter. He didn't know what was going on, but he knew enough to realize there was more danger here than they ever imagined.

"How?" Carter choked out the word and saw the corner of Julia's mouth turn up in a wicked grin.

Jibril looked down at Julia and smiled affectionately. Yet Carter could see the smile didn't reach his eyes.

"How long?" Jack asked. At a glance Carter saw Jack's jaw clench and the vein in his neck throb. It wasn't just her, she realized, that this affected. Julia was best friends with Jack's sister, Mandy. This hit him in more ways than one.

Julia looked to Jack, and for a fleeting moment Carter could see apprehension flash across her features. But just as quickly as that apprehension appeared, it was gone, replaced with a vicious-looking Julia—one Carter didn't recognize and had never seen before.

"Longer than you are thinking," Jibril said.

Carter saw Marie shift toward the wall from the corner of her eye. Marie was up to something; Carter just had no idea what it was or whose side she was playing on. She still didn't trust Marie. But as of right now, they had bigger problems to deal with.

"How long?" Jack said through gritted teeth.

Stan and Kyra watched the exchange curiously. Carter could sense the confusion in their energy. Heck, she could sense the confusion in everyone's energy, including her own.

"Since you two were in college together," Jibril said in a coy tone.

Carter stumbled, and Stan moved in just in time to brace her by the elbow. She realized it showed her weakness, but she didn't care. Up until that moment, nothing had stunned or hurt her as much as this betrayal.

"I don't understand," Carter said. "Why?"

"Why?" Julia hissed. "It's what your kind did to my family."

Dark spots formed on the edge of Carter's vision. "My kind?" she whispered, barely audible.

"Yes, your kind. The Anunnaki."

"Your parents were killed in a car accident…" As the words came out of Carter's mouth, she suddenly figured it out. Jack looked to her with his brows furrowed. "But it was a fire," Carter said more to herself.

"No, it wasn't." Julia took a step toward Carter, and everyone became tenser. Stan reciprocated by taking a matching step in front of Carter, partially blocking her from Jibril and Julia.

"Enough chitchat," Jibril said, chuckling. "We've got some things to take care of."

Marie took another step toward Jibril, and Carter watched her from the corner of her eye. *What is she doing?*

Jibril raised a gun and pointed it toward Carter, and Stan took a step in front of her, completely standing between her and Jibril. Carter's breath hitched in her throat.

"He's a liar," Carter said with bravado. "Your stupid little boy there," Carter pointed to Jibril as she stepped around Stan, simultaneously placing a hand on his arm to keep him from interfering, "is a liar."

"No, he showed me the pictures."

"No, the story he told you is the story I was fed about my own mother!" Carter took every breath, every ounce of her energy, and screamed the last three words. She was sick of the games, sick of the conspiracies, and sick of the cat and mouse. Her friend was in dire need of help and was closer to losing his life every second they waited. Her voice boomed through the small room and clearly startled every person. All eyes were on her.

"He's lying to you. He lies to everyone. He killed my father, he killed Carl, he's killed many others, and he does it over the sob story of his son."

Jibril growled at Carter, completely animalistic. She didn't care anymore. She narrowed her eyes at him and then continued speaking to Julia. "The story isn't yours. Your parents died in the fire just as the police told you." For the first time, Carter caught a glimpse of the old Julia she knew, but it was too late. "You bought his story, hook, line, and sinker. And you lied. This entire time I thought you cared."

Marie was nearly completely behind Jibril now, and no one noticed except Carter because everyone was riveted on the exchange between her, Jibril, and Julia. Carter reached out her energy to Marie and couldn't sense anything sinister, yet she still couldn't figure out what Marie was doing.

Carter jumped when Jibril began applauding loudly. "That was quite the speech, my young alien friend." Then Jibril turned to Jack. "Hi, honey."

Phillip grabbed Jack's shoulder as he lunged, stopping him just in time.

"You always had quite the temper," Jibril said, gleaming.

In the blink of an eye, Jibril threw Marie against the wall and held her up by her neck. Marie's feet dangled in the air and her face quickly turned red and then purple.

"Buongiorno, Senora De Marcus," Jibril said in a smooth Italian accent. "Do your friends here know what you're doing helping them?"

Carter could barely hear what Jibril was saying as Stan, Phillip, and Jack all were yelling at him to let her go. Carter was more interested in hearing answers. Without realizing it, she took a step toward them, and Jibril took the hand that wasn't holding Marie up and pointed the gun toward Carter again.

"How poetic would it be," Jibril said jubilantly, "if you both died simultaneously—and William wasn't here to rescue the two loves of his life. Oh, that's right," Jibril laughed boisterously. "William's—not—here."

It was the last stab to the heart. Carter looked to Marie. It all suddenly made sense, and she kicked herself for not seeing it before. "Jibril," Carter said calmly, barely above a whisper. Somehow he heard. "One of the happiest moments of my life was seeing your sister *dead*. The only thing that will make me happier is seeing *you* dead."

She knew she should've expected the gun to go off. Yet it still surprised her. The pain was instant. She didn't expect that. For some reason, she always remembered people in the movies not realizing they were shot. Yet she knew right away.

The room broke away in chaos. Jack tried to run to Carter, but there were too many people between them. She stumbled into the sarcophagus, banging her knees against the stone. She barely felt it.

Kyra and Phillip both pulled on Carter as she heard the struggle in the background. Carter wasn't sure who was getting the upper hand, but she knew she couldn't look or it'd make her falter.

"Carter, what are you doing?" Kyra yelled as Carter crawled into the sarcophagus.

"Please, Phillip, Kyra—close the lid." She managed to get out as she clutched her shoulder.

"No, Carter, you're injured! We need to get you out of here."

Carter could hear Jack yelling for her to stop. "Please," she begged. "I'm running out of time. You need to do this. *Please!*"

Kyra briefly looked to Phillip, who nodded at her, and they slid the lid closed. The darkness wrapped her up like a package, and like that, Carter was gone.

EPILOGUE

𒂼 𒀭 𒂼 𒂼 𒐖 𒀹 𒀭 𒑊 𒌈 𒂼 𒐖 𒌋 𒐏 𒂼 𒐖 𒀹 𒑊𒌈 𒀭𒐖

J ACK THREW HIMSELF AGAINST THE sarcophagus using every ounce of his strength to push the lid off. Surprisingly, Jibril helped him. Jack knew it was about severing the connection with the Anunnaki forever. It was too late.

The cover slid off, and a streak of blood stained the inside wall where Carter had been, the only trace that she had even been there.

"This is your fault!" Jack yelled as he threw himself against the stone sarcophagus so hard his head jolted against the corner, knocking him instantly unconscious for an instant.

Jack wasn't sorry.

He stared at the empty tomb and felt his rage build inside him. She had left him, he realized, for William. Even after he had begged her not to. The ultimatum had not made a difference.

"Jack," Stan said softly, standing beside him.

"Are you OK?" Marie asked, concerned.

Jack turned and glared at her. "Who are you?" he hissed.

She recoiled in fear at his tone. "I…William and I."

It dawned on Jack then. "You're in love with William."

She responded by blushing a deep scarlet red.

"Yes, and I want to get him back, and you want to get Carter back, don't you?" She whispered trepidatiously.

He nodded and knew then what their next step was.

END

Character List—Sun Gate

Carter Robinson

Peter Robinson

John Smith**

Jack Freeman

Clifford Hoffman*

Peru

Sergio Perez**

Amara Perez

Dr. Edward Nathaniel

The Morettis

William Moretti*

Ray Moretti

Harold Moretti**/Allison Moretti

Gregory Moretti/Kristy Moretti

Yolanda Vermeer **(Housemaid)*

Protection Detail

Stan Kirkpatrick

Rafe Wallace

Paulo St. Montgomery

The Zuni

Makalita

Owana

The Vaticates

Jibril Dekkers

Amelia Dekkers**

Luis Sulu

Lala Bell

Protection Detail—Egypt

Phillip Sarayan

Marie De Marcus

Kyra Kirkpatrick

Logan Reed

Femi Chalthoum

Omar Mubarek**

Misc

Detective Samuel Flores

M.E. Dr. Asha Bankowski

NIBIRU

𒀭 𒁹 𒍑 𒂔 ⸢𒅆𒊑⸣ 𒐊 𒁺 ⸢𒀸⸣ 𒀭 𒁹 ⸢𒐊𒊑⸣ 𒍑

WILLIAM IS GONE, TAKEN BY the portal. There's only one person who can find him, only one person who can go after him—if he is even alive. Traveling to Nibiru is no easy feat, which is why everyone is urging Carter not to go after him—not until they know what to expect. Yet time is running out, and she doesn't have a choice.

What is waiting on the other side of the passage, and what will meeting their Anunnaki ancestors finally be like? Is Nibiru even friendly anymore, or is it run by the Anunnaki who haunts Carter's nightmares? No one has any idea what the giant planet is like, and there is only way to find out. If Carter and William survive, will they finally be able to bridge the gap between humanity and its future?

And after all that, Jack gives Carter an ultimatum—stay behind with him, or he won't be there for her when she comes back.

ACKNOWLEDGEMENTS

𒐊𒐊 𒐊𒐊 𒐊𒐊 𒐊𒐊 𒐊𒐊 𒐊𒐊 𒐊𒐊 𒐊𒐊 𒐊𒐊 𒐊𒐊

MY FIRST THANKS GOES TO those who believed in me enough to support the Sun Gate Kickstarter project; Vernon Lucas, William Gunderson, Elize Marx, Jerry Charette, Cherie King, Anthony Reed, Brenda Gorski, Markus Ruediger, Nichole Kempton, Steven Mentzel! Without you, I'm not sure this project would have happened! Thank you to my loyal readers who are always sharing and posting on my fan page and blog. You keep me going! A super duper special thanks to my bff and best beta reader ever, Jules Uhlman. (b d) You really are the sister I've never had and the bestest friend a girl could ever ask for. Much love to Nichole Kempton and the Kempton family. It's nice to have people around that are like family to me and I know I can always count on. I love you guys! To the guys at Create Space for giving authors around the world another choice. Another thank you to Cherie King who has fast become such an awesome friend and supporter. To my dad who got really into Bohemian Grove and has kept asking me for Sun Gate. Best feeling in the world! To

Markus, my editor and friend at United Networker magazine. Thank you for giving me another opportunity to expand my writing career and supporting my books! To Jason Vollario, the most awesome graphic designer EVER. He not only created the covers for all my books and put together such a kick ass book trailer, he was just as passionate about my vision as I was. To Patty Hulstrand, editor at WOD magazine, thank you for the numerous opportunities, radio interview, and helping get my foot in the door at all the cons. That has been, by far, my favorite experience as an author! To the Wolf Pack, thank you for supporting my writing career and being the most awesome Empower Network team ever! AWOOOO!!! To Melissa and Matt, love you guys! I'm so glad you both came into my life. To every sci-fi fanatic out there – you guys rock! Kindred spirits, baby – kindred spirits! The music that got me through: Birdie, Lana Del Rey, and Ben Howard. Saving the best for last – the two most important guys in my life, ever. My hubby and son – you are my breath, my life, my world, and you make me the happiest woman in the world!